THE COLDEST THUG EVER

A Thug's Rise - The Prequel

QUAN MILLZ

CHAPTER ONE

Black... I'm so black.
Sometimes, I wished I wasn't so damn dark.
Why did I need to be born so damn black?
Why couldn't God bless me with light yellow skin like everyone else I knew?
Everyone pretty much in my family had glowing tan skin. But not me...
I was black as fuck.
I must've been cursed or something.
I really hated my skin color.
But I also despised my nappy ass hair. My hair was so damn beady. Everyone else in my family had good hair. Straight jet-black hair ran down Mama's back. She always told me she got her good hair from the white and Cherokee in her. And even Tay'Quan – I envied his naturally curly hair. That punk ass nigga was lucky as fuck. Everyone said he looked like he was Dominican or Cuban.
Ughhh! And my nose, too. I hate my nose...
The sight of my big ass, bell pepper-shaped nose irritated

the fuck out of me. My shit was so big and hideous sitting in the middle of my black, chubby ass face.

Mama would always tell me if I ever got rich enough, I could go to a plastic surgeon somewhere in California and get nose surgery. And to be honest, I might just get it done, too. But I wouldn't get my shit to be too small like Michael Jackson's nose. That weird ass lookin' nigga didn't even have a nose anymore. His shit looked like just a thin piece of paper in the middle of his face with two holes on the side. I just wanted my nose small enough to look normal. Normal like everyone else's...

But see, out of all the things I disliked about my body, I really hated my skin color the most. And I hated it 'cause everyone kept calling me all types of names for being so black. Especially that nigga, Tyrone, at my school. He was the main one that had a range of names for my complexion.

Oil field. Midnight. Tar baby. Dark ass nigga. Black ass nigga. Dirty ass nigga. Ashy ass nigga. Burnt ass nigga. Dirty ass Haitian. The list could go one...

Just last week, Tyrone embarrassed the fuck out of me by asking me in front of my class if Shabba Ranks was my dad.

Kids at my school calling me all types of names used to drive me so mad, but I grew numb to their name-calling, truth be told. However, when Mama would call me those names, the hurt was brutally deep. She always made it a point to call me black. Said she didn't even know how I came out so black 'cause no one in her family or my dad's family was black like me.

So, once and for all, I decided to end her constantly shaming me for my skin tone. It was time to bleach my skin...

I didn't want Mama knowing what I was up to inside the bathroom. So, I quietly stood in the spotty bathroom mirror and carefully stared hard my black ass face. A great debate took place in my head as to whether or not I should start with my face.

Maybe start with my arms?

Starting with my arms made the most sense. I'd know in a few seconds if the bleach would burn my skin. See, if I started with my face, the bleach might get into my eyes and I'd go blind. Then, I'd be black and blind. So, nah, fuck that. I'd just start with my arms first. And if bleaching my arms turned out to be a success, then I'd proceed with bleaching my legs. If the bleaching seemed to be working miracles with no issues, then I'd proceed to my face.

But I still needed to be careful...

Lord knows I do not wanna go blind. I couldn't afford to be black and see black.

A tad nervous about what I was about to do, I took a deep breath. *Relax, Dru. You gotta do this.* I exhaled and turned my attention toward the small bottle of Clorox bleach sitting on the edge of bathroom countertop.

I had warm water running from the bathroom sink's faucet. For the bleach to really work, I assumed you had to use it with piping hot water. Something told me hot water would make the black peel off faster. However, it was probably wise to start first using warm water 'cause I definitely didn't wanna burn myself.

Taking another deep, cautious breath, I reached my black ass, ashy hand out to grab the bottle of Clorox.

BOOM! BOOM! BOOM!

"DRU! WHAT THE FUCK IS TAKING YOU SO LONG, BOY?!? HURRY YO BLACK ASS UP! SHIT!"

Mama's yell suddenly made me snap my head to my side. I tossed my fearful, widened eyes toward the bathroom door thinking she was about to burst through the bathroom door.

"I'm about to get in the shower now! I was just brushing

my teeth!" I lied, giving her some believable reason it was taking me so long to get ready.

"HURRY THE FUCK UP, GODDAMNIT! I SAID WE NEEDED TO BE READY BY TEN! I'MMA FUCK YOU UP REAL GOOD WHEN YOU GET OUT THAT BATHROOM!"

"Sorry, Mama!" I screeched, quickly grabbing the Clorox bottle and throwing it back into the cabinet underneath the sink. "I'mma be done in like five minutes!" I said back to her, quickly dashing over to the shower. I turned on the water, running it super-hot. Taking the hottest showers was necessary since Mama said my skin was probably just dirty.

With a good four minutes to wash up, I hopped in the shower and let the billions of hot water beads quickly burn the dirt off my skin. I reached for my bar of soap then quickly lathered my entire body.

"FINE! HURRY YO FAT, BLACK ASS UP! SHIT! I SWEAR I CAN'T WITH YOU TODAY! ALREADY GETTIN' ON MY MOTHAFUCKIN' NERVES! I GOT OTHER SHIT TO DO TODAY! YOU GOT FIVE MINUTES, NIGGA!" Mama screamed. I could hear her footsteps thump back down the apartment hallway.

Our crackhead neighbor, Willie, would usually wake me up every morning with his whistling. His crackhead ass started his begging and hustling at the crack of dawn. But today, Willie wasn't the one who woke me up — it was Mama cussing me out at seven am, telling me I needed to have my fat, black ass up so we could head down to South Dade County ASAP.

Mama told me today was gonna be the last day I was gonna be able to see my biological father. I asked her why, but she told me that my fat, black ass didn't need to ask a million fucking questions. *'Just do as I fucking say!'* was her simple morning instruction and I obeyed...

However, when I got into the bathroom and began gawking at myself in the mirror, I wondered if Mama would treat me differently if I wasn't so black. She probably would. I knew she would. So, that was why I thought maybe I should start bleaching myself this Saturday morning.

See, I figured if I bleached myself for a few weeks, Mama would start to treat me better. She'd call me handsome and fine like she often called my brother, Tay'Quan. She'd show me off to her friends and people around the neighborhood like she showed off Tay'Quan. She'd buy me better clothes and I'd get some good, brand new shoes like Tay'Quan. If I was Tay'Quan's color and also possessed his slim size, things would probably be a lot better for me. Shit, now that I think about it, I could probably get me a girlfriend, too. Just like Tay'Quan...

Mama often told me girls didn't like fat, black ass niggas like me. She said bitches desired a pretty, in-shape nigga with good hair, light skin, green eyes, a big dick, and money. *"Yo fat ass ain't got none of that,"* she'd often tell me. Mama said my hair was too nappy. Said I looked like a nasty ass Haitian that just got off a boat straight from Port-Au-Prince. Mama even said my eyes were ugly. Said my dick was little 'cause I was fat and had a belly. *"But you is smart. Book smart. Not street smart though. But yo ass stay in them books,"* was the only compliment Mama would ever give me from time to time. Other than that, she said, hopefully, one day I'd grow out of being so black and fat and then I'd get all the pussy in the world. Just like Tay'Quan...

Still in the shower, I counted in my head exactly how many minutes I had left before I needed to hop out. Two minutes remained. So, I quickly rinsed myself off, turned the water off, and dashed out of the shower. I grabbed my towel and dried myself off, rubbing the remaining dirt I had on my skin. I wiped my face hard and then looked in the mirror. The hot shower made the entire bathroom steamy and the mirror was covered in fog. I wiped down the mirror and then caught a glimpse of myself.

I was still the same color.

Black.

Goddamnit!

"Finally! God-fucking-damnit! What fuck was takin' yo ugly, black ass so long in there?!? What the fuck was you doing?!?" Mama yelled when I sauntered into the living room dressed and ready to go.

Sitting back on the main couch in the den, Mama was smoking a Newport. BET was blasting on the television.

"Sorry, Mama," I apologized, strolling over to the other couch where Tay'Quan was sitting. He was staring at the television watching one of 2Pac's music videos. I scanned Tay'Quan, noticing he had on entirely new clothes. His punk ass was dressed in FUBU from head to toe. Fresh Nikes Air Jordans were on his feet. Mama must've just bought those for him 'cause I saw a tag hanging from his pants. She didn't buy me shit though, of course. I had on a faded navy blue Polo and some jean shorts. My old-ass Reeboks squeezed my feet.

Before I could take a seat, Mama yelled, "NO! Don't sit yo fat ass down!" Her yellow, slender face was twisted with anger. "We 'bout to go! Fuck you gon' sit down for?!?"

"Okay...," I replied and just stood off to the side of the couch. Mama quickly smoked down the rest of her cigarette.

"Tay'Quan, you ready?" Mama asked, blowing smoke from her nostrils like a dragon.

"Yeah. But I'm hungry, Mama," he said.

"Okay, well, we'll stop by Burger King on our way. Hopefully, they still serving breakfast. Whatchu want?" Mama asked.

"Some french toast sticks and a sausage croissant," Tay'Quan mumbled.

"I'm hungry too," I said.

Mama tossed me a nasty look. "Boy! No! You better go in there and eat an apple. Fat ass know you don't need no damn Burger King!"

"But why Tay'Quan get to eat it?" I snapped back.

"'Cuz! He skinny! You fat! He need to gain a lil weight! You, on the other hand, need to lose some of that nasty fat! You don't need to eat not a single damn slice of bread! We already went over this a thousand times! The damn doctor already said you gon' get the sugar! You want diabetes? You wanna get your leg cut off? That's what happens when you get diabetes, you know?"

"That's not fair though," I replied back to her, pissed as fuck. I was tired of Mama treating me differently.

"I don't care what the fuck is fair! You already know your fat ass doesn't need it! Now shut the fuck up, go get you an apple if you really hungry and walk over to the door. I really don't wanna hear another mothafuckin' word from you. You already on my shit list for taking so goddamn long in the bathroom. UGHHH! I swear you just like your damn daddy! Both you dumb niggas just think you can get your way. Not today! I'm so glad this is our last time running down to that damn prison, too!"

Swiftly rising from the couch, Mama slammed the cigarette into the ashtray sitting on top of the den's coffee table. She glanced over at Tay'Quan saying, "Get up, boy. My nerves are already bad. I need a stiff drink after dealing with y'all. Shit!"

I was so pissed. So pissed I wanted to fight Tay'Quan. I'd punch him in his shit just for being a mama's boy. My face twisting with slight anger, I strolled over to the front door and waited for Mama and Tay'Quan. Mama walked over, noticing the anger written all over my face.

"Boy! Fix your face! You already black, fat, and hard in the face! You don't need to make yourself look uglier! Gon' embarrass me! Boy, you got another thing coming, I swear! I'mma make you go stay with your grandma! I know she'll get yo ass right!"

Not responding, I kept my head low, turning my attention away from her. Tears of anger almost rushed out of my eyes; however, I had to suck that shit up. I always had to unless I wanted to get my ass beat.

Mama grabbed her keys and purse off the dining room table. Then, she marched back over to me and Tay'Quan. "Boy, your clothes already wrinkled," she said to Tay'Quan, running her hands through his outfit. She quickly picked off lint and pulled out small wrinkles in his shirt.

Once she got done, we headed out into the blazing sun. It was hot as usual. Shit, Miami was always hot. The sun was blinding. We trekked downstairs into the parking lot then made our way over to Mama's Pontiac. Tay'Quan got in the front, I got in the back.

Before Mama chucked up the engine, she looked back at me and said, "You better make the best of this visit, too, Dru 'cause like I said, this will be the LAST time you see your father. You understand me?"

"Yes, ma'am," I mumbled, my eyes staring out the tinted window, taking in the open blue skies.

"And when we get back, you need to clean up your room, the bathroom, and the kitchen. I got company coming over tonight."

"Yes ma'am," I replied.

"And take another bath. Why you look so extra dark? I thought I told you to stop spending so much time out in the sun. I really hate the fact that school got y'all out there always in the sun, too. Ain't no need to be out in the hot like that. Shit, this Miami. People can die from heat strokes. Die from dehydration," she complained, starting up the car's engine then slowly backing out of the parking spot.

"Mama, what's dehydration?" Tay'Quan asked.

"How you not know what dehydration means?" I asked, sounding kind of annoyed. How did he not know what that meant? He was in seventh grade. I knew what dehydration meant when I was in seventh grade. I learned that last year. He should've known that.

"Boy! He asked me, not you! Just sit back and hush your mouth! You think just because you get all As and whatnot you know everything fucking thing? Well, you don't! And dehydration is a big word!" Mama spat. "It means when you don't have enough water. When you thirsty. Your body needs water. That's what dehydration means..."

Sometimes, I prayed I could get away to get away from Mama. Like, far far away. I hated her. And I knew this bitch hated me. And she hated me more than I probably hated her. I really wish I had another mother. Someone who loved me. Someone who didn't make fun of me. Someone who wasn't so cold to me.

CHAPTER TWO

Tay'Quan's spoiled, punk ass, as usual, got his way. Before we hopped on the expressway to head down to South Dade, Mama stopped by Burger King and got Tay'Quan whatever he wanted to eat. Greedy little nigga got two orders of french toast sticks, a large order of tater tots, a sausage and egg croissant and a bottle of Tropicana orange juice.

And, of course, as usual, I didn't get anything. Mama didn't budge...

I just sat quietly in the backseat of the car, letting my stomach growl with hunger pain. Guess Mama was right though – I didn't need no damn Burger King. With so much fat on my body, maybe I could just survive off it. My science teacher, Ms. Reid, told me that it takes weeks for your body to starve to death. So long as I drank enough water, she said I could go weeks, sometimes months, without food. Maybe that's what I should do, too. If I bleached my skin and starved myself, then I knew I'd look better than Tay'Quan. I'd get way more attention than him.

Every couple of months or so, Mama would take us all the

way down to South Dade to go visit my father. He wasn't Tay'Quan's dad though. His father was locked up too, but he was serving time at a prison up in North Florida. My father was locked up at the prison down near Metro Zoo.

I didn't know why my father was locked up though. He had been in prison as long as I'd been alive. I used to ask Mama from time to time why he was locked up, but she wouldn't tell me. She said I wasn't old enough to know yet. She said if I knew what he did, it would change my outlook on everything. She said it would make me a different person and that I would become mean and angry.

Mama really treated me like I was super-stupid. She obviously didn't think I was old enough to understand that people make bad decisions, like committing crimes. Obviously, dad committed some crime. And whatever he did had to be bad because it seemed like he wasn't getting out any time soon, especially now that Mama told me this would be the last time I'd see him.

Was he on death row? Did he kill somebody? I really didn't know. I just wish there was a way for me to find out. Maybe I could go to the library and ask someone to get on the computer and help me look. Mr. Davis, my math teacher, told me you could look up anything on the computer. He probably could help me look up what my dad did.

I remember one time I tried to ask my grandma what my dad did to end up in prison and she, too, told me I was too young to understand. Told me to stay out of grown folks' business and just focus on being a kid. That was a bullshit excuse, of course. I'm thirteen-years-old about to go to high school. How long did they think they could keep what my dad did a secret? These damn adults, I swear…Why try to hide the world from us kids? Like, don't they understand that eventually we'll find out all the truth they keep trying to hide from us?

Since we stayed all the way up in Opa Locka, it usually took us about a good hour or so to get from our apartment all the way down to Southwest Dade County. Mama said eventually once she saved up enough money, she was gonna move down this way 'cause the houses were bigger and better. She also told me the schools were better, too. However, I liked my school a lot and I really didn't want to leave. She told me that South Dade county was more diverse and she didn't want me to be around so many niggas. She wasn't lying though 'cause Opa Locka had tons of niggas. But shoot, there were plenty of niggas who lived down in South Dade, too. I think Mama was just thirsty to move down here 'cause her boyfriend, Michael, lived down that way over in Cutler Ridge. He stayed in some nice townhouse not too far away from Cutler Ridge Mall.

We hopped off the turnpike and headed west on 152nd street. Still gazing out the back passenger window, it was just so crazy to me how this area was so different from the rest of Miami. To me, it was kind of country. Well, not country, 'cause I'd been to North Carolina before to visit my auntie. That was country. But this part of Dade County was still so empty. There was just so much more open land. Then again, Hurricane Andrew did come through a few years ago and fuck this area up really bad. When we got off the turnpike, it was still blowing my mind how a lot of houses were still not fixed yet. Like, why did it need to take so long to get them fixed? Mama did tell me a lot of people left Miami after Hurricane Andrew though. Maybe that was why the area still seemed so empty. There were a few shopping centers here and there, but it wasn't as jam-packed as North Dade. As we got closer to the prison, we passed a large row of two-story townhouses currently under construction. See, those houses were nice as hell. Much nicer compared to the old ass houses up in Opa Locka and Liberty City.

We got to the entrance gate of the prison. We pulled up to the security booth and Mama flashed the Hispanic-looking guard her visitor's pass. The tall metal opening of the gate pulled apart and Mama slowly drove through, making her way into the parking lot.

We parked and got out of the car. Soon as I stepped foot outside, the blazing sun cooked my skin. I could already feel myself getting darker by the second. Shit! We had to rush inside quick, so I wouldn't get any darker. God knows Mama was gonna say something about my skin suddenly getting darker, too. But luckily, she was in a rush to get in and out. We dashed through the parking lot toward the entrance of the visitor's center so the sun didn't have opportunity to blacken me that much.

The three of us walked inside and hopped in a quickly moving line of other visitors. We checked in and went through metal detectors. I was used to this entire routine by now. It was just weird how this was going to be the last time coming here though. At least, I think it would be... Maybe if I did something crazy, I'd end up here, too. Then again, I wasn't gonna do no stupid shit like that. I was too smart to get caught doing anything stupid. Shoot, if I was gonna be a criminal, I was gonna be a smart criminal. That was why I hated why Mama always called me stupid like my dad. I wasn't stupid like him. I wouldn't be either...

Once we checked in and were given visitor IDs, we were escorted into another room, which was the actual visitation area. Seemed like there were more visitors here than usual. Damn, the prisons were filling up fast! There were so many Black people, too. Mainly women with their kids. There were a few people here and there who looked old enough to be grandmas and grandfathers. However, most of the women in here looked just like they were around Mama's age.

Mama, Tay'Quan and I sat at a round red table, anxiously

waiting for my dad to walk in. "So, if this is the last time I'm gonna see him, can you at least tell me what he did?" I asked Mama.

Suddenly getting annoyed with me, her eyes almost popped out of their sockets. "You know what! Since you wanna know so bad, let ya daddy tell you!" she snapped back.

"Okay. Well, I will," I said back to her, somewhat rolling my eyes.

Without hesitation, Mama punched me in the shoulder, damn near knocking me out of my chair. "Boy, don't get fucking smart with me!"

"I ain't say anything though. I just said I'll ask him," I responded, concealing my anger. All morning she'd been taunting me. But now, with this hard ass punch she just gave me, her ignorant ass was pushing me to really go the fuck off on her. However, she'd fuck me up if I went at it with her. So, I had to get myself together.

"No! It's not what you said, it's *how* you said it. You've been getting real snippy lately! Don't make me take my belt off on you up in here. I'll embarrass you in front of all these folks," Mama angrily stated.

"Yes, ma'am," I replied politely so she would shut the fuck up and leave me alone. I learned that sometimes it was just best to just give in to whatever she said so that way I wouldn't further piss her off.

"Good. I'm glad you'll ask your rotten ass father about why the fuck he's up in here. Then you can leave me the hell alone asking me all these damn questions," she huffed. Rapidly tapping her heel against the dirty white tile floor, she held her arms by her elbows, scanning the other visitors. Light chit chat filled the room. "I'mma be so glad this my last time coming up in here, too. Shit is depressing. Y'all really don't need to be seeing this bullshit. It's so many niggas getting locked up left and right. It's a damn shame," she groaned. Even with all the make-up on her face, she couldn't conceal her disgust and contempt for being here. She just kept gazing around, furiously shaking her head as if she wasn't used to coming here.

I looked at Mama, wondering why in the hell she even came here dressed the way she was. She swore she hated my father's guts but spent all Friday afternoon getting this crazy looking new blonde weave stitched into her head. Big gold earrings hung from her ears. Her face was covered in layers of make-up. As far as her outfit, she had on an all-leather bodysuit with matching stilettos. You would've thought she was going out to the club. However, her crazy ass wasn't. She was dressed up to see my father. Honestly, I think she still had a thing for him and just didn't want to admit to it. I mean, she was dating Michael and I'd never seen her get this dressed up for him. But any and every time we came to visit my dad here, she was dressed like she was about to go hang out on South Beach with them hoe ass friends of hers.

Some moments later, a door off to the side of the visitor's room opened and then a flood of prisoners entered the room. My empty, growling stomach boiled with instant anxiety as I eagerly awaited Dad to enter the room. A good thirty seconds later, he stumbled in. Once he saw us sitting at our table in the center of the room, his face lit up with a gigantic smile.

Mama and dad were damn near the same complexion – both light-skinned. Dad was a tad lighter than Mama though. He could pass for being Cuban or Puerto Rican. Shit, he could've been Hispanic though. I never knew because he never told me about his parents or where he came from. All I knew was that he and Mama grew up together over in Liberty City. And there weren't a lot of Hispanics over that way, so I just assumed dad got his extreme light-skin from possibly being half-white or somethin' like that. Dad even had jet-black wavy hair that he always managed to keep in a fade.

That was always strange to me 'cause I didn't even know they had barbers like that in prison. Even his full-beard that wrapped his entire face was taped up real nice. Dressed in his brown prison jumpsuit, he got closer and his smile seemed to get bigger, exposing his gold grill. Mama, Tay'Quan and I stood up.

"Sup, y'all!" he announced with his muscular arms open wide, ready to give us a hug.

"Hey, baby," Mama purred. Irritation she had in her tone moments ago was now missing.

They leaned into each other and planted kisses all over each other's neck and face. I stood there, motionless with confusion. Mama was definitely playing the part. She was acting like she was still in love with this nigga, however, I knew she was clearly fucking someone else. I just wondered if Dad knew she was fucking someone else though. I mean, he had to have known 'cause Tay'Quan was born when Dad was already locked up.

Once they got done smooching and shit, they pulled apart from one another. Dad then threw his gaze at me, scanning me up and down. An enormous smirk came across his chiseled face. "Give me a hug, boy! You gettin' taller and bigger! You been hittin' them weights?"

Before I could answer, Mama smacked her teeth and playfully rolled her eyes. "Hah! Now you know his fat ass ain't been hittin' no damn weights! Only thing he been hittin' is them damn Debbie cakes and potato chips. Need to put him on a diet," she snickered.

Smacking his teeth back at Mama, Dad said, "Woman, leave him alone. That's just baby fat. He'll grow out of it soon. I was his size when I was his age. And you know it, too..."

"Yeah, but you weren't *that* big. You were a lil chubby. But Dru...His ass is just fat. The doctor said he damn near need to be on insulin if he don't stop eatin'," Mama replied, annoyance returning to her tone.

Dad and I hugged each other real hard. He then looked over at Tay'Quan. "Give me a hug, Tay!"

Standing off to the side, Tay quietly nodded no. His lips tight and his eyes widened, he acted like he was staring at a ghost or some shit. He never liked coming here and I never knew why Mama dragged him here.

"Boy, he still scared of me, I see," Dad said then looked back down at me. "Anyways, let's sit down and talk."

We all pulled out our seats from the table and sat back down. Dad sat next to me, playfully punching me in my shoulder. "This boy gonna be built once puberty really kick in," he said.

"Yeah, yeah, yeah," uttered Mama, rolling her eyes to the room's flickering ceiling lights.

"So, how you doin' in school? You gettin' good grades or what?" Dad asked me.

"Yeah. Straight As," I replied with a slight smile.

"Boy, you lyin'! I don't believe it! Let me see!" Dad screeched through a wide grin.

Since I knew he'd ask about my grades, I kept my last report card folded up in my pocket. I quickly stood up, pulled it out, unfolded it and then handed it to him. Staring at him as he scanned it, I sat back down, waiting to see his next reaction.

"Damn! You weren't lying! Boyyyy! You smart as hell!" His wide-open gaze skimmed me up and down and then he glanced at Mama. "Damn, buy this boy some new clothes! You don't see these grades?!?"

"I see 'em. But good grades don't deserve new clothes. He needs to be getting good grades any damn way."

Dad then threw his gaze at Tay'Quan. "But what about Tay'Quan? He look dressed to the nines."

Suddenly twisting her yellow face with anger, Mama replied, "Well, that's because his *daddy* still found a way to send me some money so that way *his son* can still rock the best threads. Can't say the same about other fathers..."

Dad raised a brow. "Oh, so you just gonna rub that in my face?"

"Yeah...," Mama replied.

"Well, look, it is what it is. But that still doesn't mean you can't at least give my son some better looking clothes. Got him out here looking damn near homeless. But from the looks of it, seems like you got the cash to get yourself some new shit. Hair and nails all did up."

"Nigga, whatever. Look... the reason why we came here is because this is going to be our last visit."

Dad's face instantly screwed with shock. "Fuck you talkin' 'bout?"

"Yeah, this is going to be our *last* visit here...," said Mama as she rummaged her purse, quickly pulling out a folded-up thick envelope. She slid it across the table along with an ink pen.

I had no idea what was going on. I didn't even have any idea what was in that envelope.

"What's that?" Dad asked.

"Divorce papers... I'm ready to move on. I can't keep doing this with you. I'm ready to move on with my life."

Dad looked over at Tay saying, "Well, you already did. You obviously moved on and got with someone else."

"Look, I don't have time for all that, Andrew. The reality is you're gonna be in here for the rest of your life. I ain't trying to be like the rest of these stupid bitches, coming up here every weekend trying to be some wifey to an incarcerated nigga," Mama said.

Dad's mouth damn near dropped to the table. "Woooow! It's like that?!?"

"Yeah... it's like that. Sorry, but I gotta do me."

"Obviously..." Dad shook his head while scanning the divorce papers in his hands. Turning his attention back to Mama, he said, "You know I told you I've been working on my appeal. I told you it takes time."

Mama smacked her teeth and rolled her eyes. "Andrew, you've been saying that shit now for years. When in the fuck is that gonna really happen? Next year? Five years from now? A decade? You got slapped with eighty fucking years in prison. Shit, by the time you get out I'mma be fucking dead. Look, just sign the damn papers."

"So, you not even gonna bring my son up here to visit me?" Dad asked as he slowly rubbed his beard.

"He can come visit you when he has the means to do so on his own. But until then, I ain't wasting my time no more. And don't even bother calling because I'm not paying for any more of those expensive ass collect charges. BellSouth damn near charged me $400 last month fucking around with you."

"WOOOW! I should've seen this coming," Dad roared, shaking his head out of utter disbelief.

"Yeah...Your ass should have nigga," Mama grumbled, throwing her right hand into her purse. She yanked out a pack of her Newports and a lighter.

Although my stomach ached with hunger pains, the anxiety of hearing the thick tension between Mama and Dad was killing my appetite. Then, nausea gripped me, making me want to damn near throw up. I couldn't believe she was doing this to him. I mean, I didn't even realize they were even married. However, I really couldn't believe Mama wasn't going to take me here to visit my dad anymore simply 'cause she was ready to move on with her life. This was exactly why I despised this bitch with all of my soul. Dad skimmed the divorce papers one more time. His entire demeanor quickly changed into anger. He grabbed the ink pen off the table and signed the papers and then lightly threw the papers back in Mama's direction. "You satisfied now? So, what's his name? He got money? Big dick? Cars? All the things you need to feel content in life?"

"That's none of your business..."

"Any nigga around my son is my business... believe that!"

"Or what the fuck you're gonna do?!?" Mama yelled. Suddenly, the chatter inside the visitor's area got quiet. The eyes of everyone in the room were now on us. One of the prison guards who stood off in the corner gawked in our direction. Seemed like he was seconds away from rushing over here to figure out why Mama was getting so loud.

Dad didn't say anything though. He just lowered and shook his head. "Whatever, man. Well, let me have these remaining minutes with my *son*. Alone..."

"Fine. Come on, Tay! Let ya brother have his quality time with his *dad*," Mama grumbled, quickly standing up as she grabbed Tay'Quan's hand and yanked him out of his seat. Mama threw me a nasty look, noticing I was crying. "Wipe ya damn face and stop making me look stupid in here," she said to me.

"Man, leave him alone," Dad shot back with irritation.

"I'll be out front smoking me a fuckin' cigarette," Mama spat, smacking her snaggled teeth. "Come on, Tay." She and Tay'Quan strolled out of the room.

Dad tugged his chair up and leaned into me. He then dug his hand under my chair and pulled me closer. "Come on, son. Don't cry. It's gonna be alright."

My head tilted low to my chest, heavy tears escaped the corners of my strained eyes.

"Come on, Junior. Don't cry... you 'bout to make me cry," he mumbled. His deep voice now cracked with deep hurt. My head raised a bit. I noticed his eyes were watery. "It's gonna be alright... I promise. I'm gonna get out of here and we won't have to do this," he cried.

"Dad..."

Now was the time to ask since this was gonna be my last time seeing him or even hearing from him. "How come you're in here? What did you do?"

Dad wiped his face and cleared his nose. "I made some stupid decisions in life," he said.

"Like what?"

"I sold drugs. Lots of them," he confessed.

"So, that's the reason why you gotta be in here for the rest of your life?"

"Unfortunately. Yeah...and you can thank Bill Clinton. That no-good, lyin' ass cracka got all the brothas locked up over some BS. Took everything away from us, too."

I didn't know why he was blaming President Clinton for being in jail. "Can you still send me letters?" I asked.

"I'mma try. But knowing your mama, she may throw the letters away. But I'mma figure out a way to stay in contact. Don't you worry about that," he said.

"Okay..."

"Listen... Look at me. We don't have that much time left but promise me you don't do the same stupid things I did. Don't mess with those streets. They ain't no good. Shit, they might seem tempting, but trust me on this; them streets ain't nothin' but Satan's playground."

"Yeah... I know."

"But do you *know*?"

I froze, not knowing what he meant. "I think I know," I answered.

"Well, this is pure wisdom I'm giving you. You're gonna have a lot of niggas out there trying to convince you it ain't nothing but fast, easy money to be made out them streets. Never trust niggas like that. They may seem like they're your friends, but niggas like that always end up being your number one enemies. Just do yourself and stay in school. Go to college. Find you a nice woman and get married. Don't even have kids before you get married either. What do you wanna be when you get older?"

"A doctor..."

Dad smiled. "Good... hell, we need more black doctors," Dad said, sniffling. "Doctors make good money, too. Even if you don't wanna be a doctor, you can be anything you wanna be so long as you put your mind to it and be disciplined. Discipline is the key. A lot of niggas lack discipline. You master discipline, you master the world. You'll even master the universe." He then pulled out a black handkerchief from his pocket and wiped my face. "Don't be afraid to cry sometimes, too. Not enough brothas cry. You can't always keep that rage and anger pinned up in you."

"Okay."

"And don't let your mama trample over you. You gotta be a man now. Stand up for yourself. You're the oldest in the house. If any nigga try you or your brother, you need to fuck them up. Don't let no man try to disrespect you or your mother. You understand me?"

"Yeah... I understand completely."

"And you might hate her mothafuckin' guts, 'cause I know you do, I see it all over your face, but still treat your mother right. Respect her. Try to love her, even when she doesn't love you... okay? She might be hard on you now but she'll eventually come around. She's just going through some things. That's all..."

"Okay..." was all I could say to that last statement.

"And one more thing...," Dad said.

"What's that?"

"I love you. I'll always love you. You my first born. My only child. I know you may not hear that a lot. May not hear it all. But I love you. Always know that. If we never talk to each other or see each other again, just know I love you. Okay?"

"Okay... I love you, too...," I managed to mutter, fighting back tears. However, the tears fought me back, flooding my face.

Not noticing earlier, but that same big ass Arnold Schwarzenegger-like prison guard had quietly walked his terrifying ass over to us and stood a foot away from Dad and I. "Okay. Visitation is over. Time to go," he said, his hands gripped to his wide waist.

"Damn...," Dad moaned, wiping my tear-damp face again with the handkerchief. Balling the handkerchief up, he then grabbed my hand and opened it. He placed the balled-up handkerchief in my palm then closed it saying, "Here, take this. Anytime you find yourself in a crazy situation, I want you to think about everything I just told you. Okay?"

Nodding my head yes, I simply said, "Okay..."

Dad stood up, staring at the guard with his hands stretched out. The guard then proceeded to slap cuffs on his wrists. The two of them turned around and began to walk off.

I stood up and watched Dad slowly move away from me. Every step he took was like a tear at my soul. Dad and I didn't have a real relationship, but that didn't stop me from feeling like I was being robbed. Someone so important to me was being unnecessarily taken away from me.

"DAD!"

My squeal made both Dad and the prison guard escorting him turn around. I took off running toward him. Once I got close to him, he opened his arms then hugged me tightly.

"Please, don't go!" I cried. "Please try to get out!"

His wrists now bound with cuffs and chains, Dad couldn't quite open his arms all the way but he managed to open them enough to hug me. "I'mma try! I promise I'mma do everything I can. Now go back to your mama."

"Okay," I replied as I glanced up at him, hoping this wasn't the last time I'd see him.

"Alright, we really have to go back now," the guard said. "I'm sorry, kiddo…"

Dad grabbed me, held me tightly and planted a kiss on my forehead. "I love you, boy. We're gonna be together again. Watch and see…"

CHAPTER THREE

What I didn't understand was how Dad said he was working on trying to get out. He mentioned something about an appeal. I didn't know what that meant. So, I was gonna ask Mama. I didn't care if I was gonna get on her nerves. I just simply wanted to know what that word meant. We were cruising on I-95 headed back home. Traffic was somewhat light, although earlier we hit a jam when we passed Downtown.

"Mama, can I ask you a question?" I asked, staring at the rearview mirror to see if she'd look back at me.

And she did—

Her eyes reeked anger. "What's up?" Mama replied; however, it seemed like her tone didn't match the annoyance in her gaze. Shit, I guess now that she had those divorce papers signed and sealed, the bitch was a happy, free spirit.

"What's an appeal?" I asked, hoping she'd explain Dad's situation to me.

"It's when you try to get your court case overturned," Mama said, tossing her eyes back onto the road.

"So, like if you are found guilty and you want to be found innocent? How does that even work?" I asked again.

"Well, you gotta see another judge. You gotta get another lawyer to help you out," she explained.

I had another question on the tip of my tongue, but I was somewhat afraid to ask. But fuck it. I wanted to know what was really going on. "How come you ain't help Dad out?"

"I did!" Mama snapped back with her face scrunched up. Now I was beginning to get on her nerves, I could tell. Whatever.

"Goddamnit, Dru! All of these goddamn questions! C'mon now! Give me a break!" Mama shouted back to me, punching the steering wheel.

"I just wanna know why Dad is still locked up. I mean, why can't we just find a different lawyer for him?!" I couldn't stop the questions.

"DRU! How much do you think fuckin' attorneys costs?!?" Mama said, smacking her teeth.

Silent, I shrugged my shoulders.

"Exactly! You don't know! That shit is expensive. Lawyers are expensive. Shit, you can't just hire any ole attorney to work on no damn court case!" Mama shouted, her eyes darting back and forth between the road and the rearview mirror.

"Why not get Johnnie Cochran?!?"

"UGHHHH! Boy, shut the hell up! Johnnie Cochran is more expensive than these damn white folks around here! How much you think OJ paid him? Twenty-fuckin'-dollars?!?" Mama snapped, slapping the steering wheel.

"No..." I replied.

"Well, okay then!" Mama moaned. "Now, leave me the hell alone! Ya daddy ain't gettin' out of fuckin' prison. I don't know what bullshit he put into your ears, but he ain't getting out of his prison. His stupid ass should've never been selling all them drugs in the first place! Thought he was all big, bad and untouchable! Welp! Good riddance! Now, I'm fucking free!"

I had one more question for Mama and I knew I was really pushing it with this one. But I just had to ask. "But don't you love him?"

"DRU! I swear to God if you ask me one mo' mothafuckin' question, I'm gonna pull over the side of the road and slap the SHIT out of you!"

Not giving her any eye contact, I just smacked my teeth, continuing to stare out of the passenger window.

"OKAY! KEEP IT UP! WATCH AND SEE WHEN WE GET HOME! YOU KEEP PLAYIN' FUCKIN' GAMES WITH ME! WATCH AND SEE!" shouted Mama.

Obviously, she couldn't answer my question. The truth was out the bag. She didn't love Dad. Honestly, her ass just probably got with him for his money. And that fact alone would explain why he said what he said back at the prison. The new nigga she was messing with probably gave her all the material things she wanted and that was the only thing keeping her trifling ass happy. Well, Dad did mention Mama needed a nigga with a big dick, too. And based on how often I heard Mama have sex, she probably only dated dudes who she felt like could fuck her right and good. Gosh, I swear she was such a hoe, too. Aside from Michael, Mama was messing with some other dude named Randy. He'd come around once in a while. But truth be told, Michael and Randy were cool dudes. I just didn't know why Mama couldn't choose any of those guys and just settle down.

Love...

That was such an interesting word to me.

I mean, I knew what love meant. But I wondered what Mama's definition of love was. Now that she was pissed as fuck, I definitely wasn't going to ask her. But obviously, Dad loved Mama more than she loved him. Hell, seemed like he loved me more than she probably loved me. I should've asked Dad the definition of love before we left the prison. Maybe the next time I talk to him on the phone, I'd ask him.

Some thirty minutes later, we were now back in Opa Locka, pulling up to the entrance of the apartment complex. Mama turned into the parking lot and strolled straight down to her same spot that was close to our unit upstairs.

The three of us got out of the car and made our way upstairs. Once inside, Mama threw her purse and keys onto the dining room table and then went into the kitchen, quickly searching for something in one of the cabinets.

"Tay'Quan, go to your room and lock the door. Dru, go to the bathroom, take off all your clothes and wait for me there."

Confused, I stood in the middle of the den wondering why she wanted me to go to the bathroom and get naked. "I know you told me to take a shower earlier, Mama. I know. I'mma do it."

"DRU, I SAID GO TO THE MOTHAFUCKIN' BATHROOM RIGHT NOW AND DO AS I SAY!"

I jumped out of fear and, for a second, I couldn't move. She sounded so angry that I now knew she was gonna do something to me. She was gonna beat me. I knew it.

"Mama, what did I do?!?" I cried, my body beginning to tremble. I kept my eyes glued to her as she pulled down a bottle of vegetable oil from one of the kitchen cabinets and then made her way over into the living room.

Not saying a word, Tay'Quan dashed out of the living room and went to his bedroom and slammed the door shut.

Mama walked up to me, got close into my face and then pointing at me, she said, "If yo black, fat, ugly ass don't get in that mothafuckin' bathroom right now, I swear I will kick you out of my house. You will be living on the goddamn streets! NOW GO!"

Heavy tears falling out of my eyes, I did as she said and then trekked down the hallway and into the bathroom. I was getting so nervous anticipating what she was about to do to me. All I simply did was ask questions and now she was going to beat me for just trying to help my dad out.

I should just run. Run as fast as I could out of the apartment and get help elsewhere. I should probably try to ask one of our neighbors if I could call 9-1-1, so I could report abuse. But something told me if I did that, Mama would figure out a way how to lie and the police would never believe me.

Now in the bathroom, I slowly took off all of my clothes and threw them into a pile in the corner. I now stood in the chilly bathroom, my entire body shivering. I clasped my chest, a tad embarrassed knowing that I had titties.

So many thoughts swam through my head as to what Mama was about to do to me. Suddenly, the bathroom door exploded open. My watery eyes quickly landed on a bottle of vegetable oil in one hand and a brown extension cord in the other. "GET IN THE TUB!"

Crying uncontrollably, I held my hands out, trying my best to persuade my mother from hitting me with cord. "Mama, no! Please! I swear I won't ask any more questions! I PROMISE!" I begged.

"TOO LATE! NOW, STAND YO FAT, UGLY, BLACK ASS IN THE TUB!" she screamed, her vicious eyes skimming me up and down. "LOOK AT YOU! SO NASTY! ALL OF THAT! I know you been hiding candy in your room! Running up the doctor's bills, too! With yo fat, nasty ass! You gon' learn today! And all that bullshit ya stupid ass daddy put into your head is about to be gone! NOW, GET IN THE MOTHAFUCKIN' TUB!"

"Mommy! Please!"

"DON'T CALL ME MOMMY, NIGGA! STOP ACTING LIKE A BITCH AND GET IN THAT GODDAMN TUB! NOW!"

Doing as she said, I slowly got into the tub. She then opened up the bottle of vegetable oil and doused my entire body with it. I was now completely covered in cooking oil.

"Mommy! Please!" I continued, begging as my sobs filled the entire apartment.

Mama wrapped the bottom end of the cord in her hand a couple of times and had the other end dangling to the floor. I held my hands out, trying to stop her. She yanked her hand back and, without hesitation, she cracked the makeshift whip onto me.

"AHHHHHHHHH!"

"SHUT THE FUCK UP! I'M SICK OF YO SHIT!"

She cracked the whip on me so many times, to the point where the pain almost made me black out. I was screaming to the top of my lungs But at this point, I had no idea why. It wasn't like anyone was going to hear me. She didn't relent. She just kept whipping me, over and over again. The oil made the stinging from the whip even worse. It was almost as if it the whipping had shot up steroids.

"YOU GON' LOSE THAT GODDAMN WEIGHT, TOO! AIN'T NO SON OF MINE FINNE BE FAT!"

At every word she pronounced, she gave me a lashing.

"THE NEXT TIME SOME SLICK SHIT COME OUT YO MOUTH, I MIGHT JUST KILL YOU! DO YOU UNDERSTAND ME?"

"Ye-yes, mm-mm-mmma'am," I stuttered as I leaned against the wall and slowly slid down until my ass touched the bottom of the cold tub. Huddling in the corner of the tub, I held myself as comfortably as I could. My entire body was cloaked with stinging pain 'cause bleeding welts that looked like tiny garden snakes ran across my legs, stomach and arms.

"You gon' do everything I mothafuckin' say from here on out! I don't want no more lip from you! Do you understand me, nigga?!?"

"Yes, ma'am..."

Mama threw the extension cord off to the side. Leaning into the tub, she growled into my ear, "And if you tell anyone what I did to you... if you as much as tell anyone at that school or anyone else around here, I will send your fat ass off to go live somewhere else. I will put your fat ass in a foster home. And if you think I'm bad, wait until you get inside of a foster home. They will fuck you up even more. You will get your ass beat every minute. Do you fucking understand me, nigga?"

"Yes, ma'am," I cried with a stutter. I wiped my face free of tears.

"Yeah, wipe your fuckin' face. Ugly ass. Gosh, I wish sometimes you weren't my child. Can't believe I gave birth to something as fat and ugly as you. Get your fat ass up, take a shower and go straight to your room. I'll call you out when I'm ready." She stood there, analyzing me for a second before she spun around and headed out the bathroom door, slamming it so hard that the entire walls in the bathroom shook.

"Tay'Quan, you hungry, baby?" I could hear her say as she knocked on Tay'Quan's bedroom door.

"Yeah."

"What you want? You can have anything you want since you been on your best behavior. Unlike your fat ass, no-good ass brother. Fat ass don't need to eat anything anyways..."

"Pizza. Can I have pizza?"

"Of course you can..."

I swear to God, I was gonna kill her. Kill her and Tay. She was Satan.

Slowly standing up, I had to be careful 'cause the oil made the entire floor of the tub slippery. Pressing against the walls,

I leaned toward the shower valve, running the water this time cold. Cold water was what I needed right now to get the pain to go away. Cold water would numb away everything. For a moment, I thought maybe I should just kill myself. Maybe I should just go into the cabinet and drink the bleach. But no. I couldn't do that. I was too afraid to die. And I was too afraid to my break my Dad's heart. If I killed myself, I just knew he'd kill himself, too. He said he loved me and that was the only thing keeping me alive right now. *He said he loved me.* That was the first time I'd ever heard someone say they loved me.

CHAPTER FOUR

After Mama beat me, she made me clean up the den, kitchen and my room. Mama said she had company coming over later tonight and didn't want her house to look a fucking mess. Once I got done with my chores, she told me I had to go straight to my room and stay in there for the rest of the night.

Mama said if I didn't make a single sound, she'd think about letting me come out into the living room to watch some TV and have something to eat. Her words exactly were, 'If you act right, I might, just *might*, let yo ugly, fat, black ass out to have something to eat and watch a lil TV.' Fuck you, bitch. I didn't want to go out there any damn way. I wasn't even hungry anymore either. I'd rather just starve myself at this point. And I didn't want to eat whatever nasty ass food she was gonna try to give me since she said I had to be on a diet. Tay'Quan could eat pizza, but Mama was gonna make eat some nasty ass frozen, fat-free dinner that tasted like dried-up leaves.

Besides, how could I even have an appetite after what she did to me? Often when she was mad with me, Mama would just slap me or punch me, however, she never whipped me like this before. Just thinking about what happened was making me nervous all over again. So nervous I became nauseous thinking about it. I wanted to cry all over again...

Now I was sitting in my bed, my science book open in my lap, my sore thighs aching.

Most of the times when Mama would cuss me out or beat me and then send me to my room, I often would drown myself in my textbooks just to distract myself. Get my mind off her bullshit. Often, reading was like an escape for me. However, tonight, I couldn't seem to escape. I was enslaved to the nonstop pain from the brutal whooping Mama put on me. The physical agony gripping my body was so distracting, my mind couldn't even focus on the words in front of me. Although I was reading, I didn't understand not a damn thing. Everything was just a blur at this moment.

But I had to read though. I had to escape.

I had to force myself to get my mind away from thinking about what Mama did to me. And I also needed to finish all this homework I had next to me in my book bag.

Glancing up to my bedroom ceiling, I prayed to God, hoping Mama would never beat me like that again. And I wasn't just praying for my protection. I was praying for her protection as well. 'Cause I swear to God the next time she tried to whip me like that again, I'd fuck her up. I would kill her. I just wish I was in school right now. Seemed like I was happier when I was in school, especially in Ms. Reid's class. Even though a lot of my classmates made fun of me from time to time for my size and skin color, school was still so much better than living here with Mama. I really hated that bitch. I swear, one day I was gonna kill her. It was just a matter of time. Yeah, I knew Dad said treat Mama with respect. But why in the fuck should I treat her with respect when she wasn't giving me any? That shit just wasn't fair. Not fair at all. That was not how the world should work. Besides, I was just a kid.

I still didn't understand why Mama just had so much resentment for me. Then again, the more I thought about it, the more I realized something in me probably reminded her that I was a spitting image of Dad in some way. That was probably why she hated me. 'Cause she obviously hated him, too. She probably low-key envied me 'cause, truth be told, Mama was a dumb ass bitch. She didn't even graduate from high school. I knew my dad had his associate's from Miami-Dade Community College, so he obviously graduated from high school. Yeah, my dad may have fucked up and landed in prison for selling drugs, but he still had to be smart to make money.

However, Mama didn't have no type of education 'cause she was obviously just lazy and stupid. All she knew how to do was cuss people out and fuck. I was obviously smarter than she was, too. So, yeah, I think I'm gonna have to kill that bitch real soon. Like, I really mean that. I didn't care about going to jail either. I would go in the kitchen, grab the biggest knife I could get my hands on and slice her fucking throat. And when the cops come, I'd just say I was defending myself. They'd see all of my bruises and welts and believe me. And if anyone doubted what I did was self-defense, then all they had to do was just look at my report cards. They'd see all the straight As and know I wasn't a bad kid. They'd know I wasn't a monster. It was my mama who was the monster. It was that stupid, evil bitch who was the crazy one. Not me. Then, the cops would set me free…

As I sat in my bed continuing to read my science book, every other minute or so I'd grab my side or my leg, trying to my best to massage the throbbing pain away. The welts Mama put on me were now big, swelling bruises. Well, at least they felt like they were bruises. I was too black to see I was bruised. Damn, maybe the cops wouldn't believe me then, since they wouldn't be able to see the bruises either...

Some moments later, I heard Tay'Quan bust out in a roaring laugh from the den. As usual, his stupid, skinny, punk ass was allowed to do whatever the fuck he wanted to do. Crazy how he could laugh and giggle all he wanted and Mama wouldn't say shit to him. But when I'd laugh or giggle, she'd call me all types of names and whatnot. She'd say stuff like, 'STOP GIGGLING LIKE THAT! YOU SOUND LIKE A FUCKIN' STUPID ASS FAGGOT. AIN'T NO SON OF MINE NO DAMN HOMOSEXUAL. AIN'T NO SON OF MINE GON' BE SOME PUNK ASS NIGGA GETTIN' DICK IN HIS ASS! DO YOU SUCK DICK? DO YOU LIKE MEN? YOU NOT A FAGGOT, IS YOU?'

I'd tell her no. *'No, Mama. I ain't a faggot...'*

'THAT'S WHAT I THOUGHT THEN! AND YOU TOO BLACK, FAT AND UGLY TO BE A FAGGOT ANY DAMN WAY. FAGGOTS ARE SKINNY AND MOST OF THEM LOOK GOOD. YOU TOO BLACK AND UGLY TO BE A FAGGOT. I KNOW A LOT OF FAGS AND NONE OF THEM LOOK LIKE YOU!'

But let Tay'Quan laugh and giggle like the little bitch he was, she'd say he was *cute*. He had a nice smile. He was fine. Attractive. Handsome. All the ladies were gonna marry him. He was gonna be a model. Bleh. Bleh. Bleh. I just kept hearing him laugh and giggle while he was out in the den, probably playing his Sega Genesis. I hated that little nigga so much that I just might kill him, too.

Fury boiled deep within me. "Man, fuck this shit," I groaned to myself, slamming my science book closed. Tossing it off to the side, I was now more than ready to storm out there and kill them both. It was time to free myself. No one should have to live like this. I didn't deserve this shit at all. Hell, maybe if I got locked up, I could be with my dad.

It was so fucked up, too, 'cause Mama put me on punishment for an entire month and a half. She said I needed to be grounded because: (1) I was fucking around in the bathroom this morning, taking so long to get ready. And (2) I didn't know how to control my mouth and I asked way too many inappropriate questions. Questions only adults should ask. It was crazy 'cause little did she know, I was just trying to bleach my skin and get lighter so she could finally stop treating me so differently. Stop bothering and making fun of me. Deep down, I really wanted lighter skin, so she could say she loved me. Loved me like she like loved Tay'Quan. Bleaching my skin would make her proud of me. She'd like that more than my As on my report card.

As far as me asking questions though, I only asked questions 'cause I simply wanted to know why things had to be the way they were. Why was Dad locked up? Why did we need to live in this part of Opa Locka in this shitty ass apartment? Why couldn't we just stay with grandma over in Carol City? She had a bigger house. And why couldn't she get a job like everyone else?

Calm down, Dru. Calm down.

I closed my eyes, took a deep breath and exhaled. I couldn't even muster up the strength to even get up.

So, glancing back over at my science book, I grabbed it and opened it back up to the last page I was reading. I just needed to stop thinking about everything that happened earlier and just finish up all of my homework.

Right now, the best thing I could do, honestly, was just focus on school and continue to get all straight As. I really needed to focus on all of this crazy homework Ms. Reid gave our class. Seemed like I had to read almost a hundred pages about the human body. I had to memorize a million muscles for this big test we had coming up on Monday. Since it was almost the end of the school year, Ms. Reid said if I did good on this test, she'd recommend me to take advanced biology in high school. She said if I truly wanted to be a doctor, which I did, I needed to take as many advanced and honors classes in high school.

So, this was my goal – study and read as much as I could and do good in high school. Then, I'd be able to go to college and become a doctor. That would allow me to make a lot of money and get away from here. And not only that, but I now knew that since Mama wasn't going to help Dad with his appeal, I could use the millions I'd make from being a doctor to hire Johnnie Cochran to be his lawyer.

I didn't know exactly what time it was but at least a good six or seven hours passed. Felt like it was close to eleven pm at night. Usually, Mama would've spent her weekends over Michael's place or some other nigga she was messing around with. Felicia, one of our neighbors, would watch Tay'Quan and I while Mama was gone. But tonight, Mama said she had company coming over. From the sound of it though, Mama was having a party out in the living room.

Bass from some Uncle Luke shook the walls throughout the entire apartment. I didn't know exactly how many people were out in the den. Sounded like it was like ten or fifteen people. Among the rumbling bass-heavy music, I could hear Mama laughing and screaming. Sounded like they were out there playing Spades or shooting dice.

My mouth dry and sticky, I really needed to get something to drink. I still wasn't hungry. However, at this point, I just wanted some water. I also wanted some ice, too, for my arms and leg. Those welts were still stinging.

I pretty much finished most of my reading assignments about a good hour ago. After I got done, I read a few of my comic books until I got bored. I would've gone straight to bed, but I was thirsty.

Mama didn't even bother to come check up on me. I knew she was lying, too, when she said she would let me out to get something to eat and watch some TV. Lying ass bitch. She told so many lies; she couldn't even tell the truth if her own life depended on it.

A part of me wanted to just get up, run to the kitchen and get some water and ice. But I knew Mama would fuck me up even more if I did that. I was just gonna have to settle for possibly going out into the hallway and to the bathroom to drink from the faucet. Faucet water was nasty as shit. Tasted like it was all types of chemicals up in that water, but I had no other choice at this point.

Cautiously standing up, I strolled over to my bedroom door, gluing my ear to it to see if I could hear exactly where Mama was at. I couldn't exactly make out her voice since it was so many other people laughing, talking and screaming. Everyone was probably drunk as hell, I bet.

Fuck it. Slowly opening the door, I peeped my head out into the dimly-lit hallway to see if anyone was hanging out there. Clear. Everyone was probably in the den. Perfect.

I stepped out into the hallway, taking gentle steps toward the bathroom. I noticed the bathroom door was slightly creaked open. I peeped inside and noticed someone was in there. It was Mama and some other nigga. She had her head leaned down to the countertop. A rolled-up dollar bill lodged in her right nostril. She swiftly ran her nose across a mirror sitting on top of the countertop. My eyes popped open in surprise. This evil bitch was snorting cocaine. Just like how I seen people do in the movies. She suddenly shot up, grabbing her nose and sniffing uncontrollably.

"FUCK!" she grunted. "Damn, baby! This shit is strong."

I couldn't quite make out who the dude was, but he was

some light-skin nigga with a bald head and a chin-strap beard I never seen before. He hugged her from behind as he grinded up on her. "I told you I had that good shit," he said as he planted kisses all up and down her neck.

"Hell yeah! Fuck! I wanna fuck now!" she roared.

"Oh yeah?" the guy said as he quickly unbuckled his pants and slightly tugged his jeans down. Mama wasn't dressed in her leather bodysuit no more. She was in a blouse and some jeans. Following suit, she quickly unbuckled her pants and pulled them down. Not wanting to see anymore, I dashed back to my room and quietly closed the door. Guess I was just gonna have to suffer from both the stinging and dehydration for the rest of the night.

CHAPTER FIVE

It must've been six in the morning...
How'd I know?
Crackhead Willie was outside my bedroom window whistling some Marvin Gaye song. Sounded like Sexual Healing. Man, that seemed to be one of his favorite songs. That was one of Mama's favorite songs, too.

I swear to God that dude Willie was consistent with waking me every morning. Crackhead Willie had been waking me up now for years. But why I didn't hear him whistling this past weekend? Shit, his ass probably got arrested or somethin', I bet. I was gonna ask him where he was at this past weekend if I had the chance to run into him this morning.

But just to make sure Willie's whistling woke me up at six am, I glanced over at my alarm clock. Six am on the dot splashed in blinking, bright red neon digits on the clock.

My room was extra-muggy, so I bet today was gonna be a hot ass day. Miami was always hot, but I had a feeling today was gonna be super-hot. Shit actually made me a bit annoyed 'cause on days like this, I always sweated out my school uniform.

I was usually tired on Monday mornings, but today, I was ready to get up and go straight to school. I hopped out of my bed and dashed into the bathroom. Mama was still asleep. She usually didn't wake up until seven anyways to take Tay'Quan to his school. He and I didn't go to the same school. His dad didn't want him going to public school so, apparently, he was paying to have Tay'Quan go to some private Christian academy up in Broward. Mama didn't take me to school though. My school wasn't that far away from our apartment, so I walked there every day.

With about a good hour to get ready, this morning I decided I was gonna try to bleach myself again. Once inside the bathroom, I ran over to the shower and turned the water on, running it too hot as usual. I then dashed over to the door and locked it. Obviously, I didn't want Mama to come in and see what I was doing. I opened up the sink cabinet and pulled out the bottle of Clorox. But as I pulled it out, I saw a mirror, a small bag of cocaine and a razor blade hiding behind it. I guess Mama forgot to bring it back to her room.

Shaking my head out of shame, there was a part of me pretending I didn't see it. I slammed the cabinet door then proceeded to take off my pajamas, getting completely naked.

The vapor from the hot water began to fill the bathroom, making the medicine cabinet's mirror become slightly foggy. I could still see myself though. I grabbed a towel and wiped it down, so I could now see my entire body.

Once I screwed the cap off the bottle of bleach, I reached over and grabbed a washcloth sitting on top of the toilet lid. Bleach fumes could kill you, so I held my breath as I poured some of the bleach onto the washcloth. Not too much though. Didn't know if this would actually work. Staring at my welt-covered arms, I began to rub the bleach slowly up and down my arms. "Ouch!" I bit my lip, trying my best to fight off the burning sensation coming from rubbing the bleach over my welt-covered arms. Slowly getting used to the pain, I slightly rubbed my arms harder and harder until the stinging managed to subside.

But the bleach wasn't working though. My arms still looked black as hell. What the fuck?!? Then, again, maybe I was being impatient. So, I continued onto the next arm, rubbing them gently with the washcloth, hoping the bleach would slowly lighten my skin.

That wasn't that bad after all. So, I grabbed the bottle of Clorox and poured some more bleach onto the washcloth, then began to rub my chest and stomach. But damn, how was I gonna bleach my back? *Fuck!*

Three loud pounds boomed from the bathroom door, taking me by surprise. "DRU! HURRY UP! I LEFT SOMETHING IN THERE!" Mama screamed, her voice hoarse. Shooting my widened eyes to the door, I got stiff for a second. I didn't know what to do next. *Damn*. Mama was probably looking for her little coke stash, I bet.

"Okay! I'll be done in a few minutes, Mama," I said to her.

"Okay, well, hurry up! I'll be waiting!"

I could hear her footsteps march away and I quickly jumped in the shower. Once I got done showering and brushing my teeth, I rushed back into my bedroom to get ready. My school uniform was already ironed and laid out on the bed, so I quickly threw it on. My shoes and socks were on next. Then, I grabbed my bookbag and headed out the door and into the kitchen to grab something to eat.

I opened the fridge then leaned down, scanning to see what I could grab to eat for breakfast. A big box of plain Cheerios was right in the center of the fridge. A carton of half-filled whole milk sat off to the side. Mama instructed me to eat Cheerios or an apple every morning from here on out since she said I had to lose weight. Truth be told, I wasn't hungry. Starvation was gonna be my breakfast. I closed the fridge door and was immediately surprised to see Mama standing next to me, her arms folded, her right foot tapping against the kitchen floor.

"Did you go through my stuff, boy?"

I stood up, my fearful eyes popping out of my head. I didn't know what to say. But I really didn't go through her "stuff". I mean, I saw it, but I didn't mess with it.

"No, ma'am..."

"You not lying to me, are you?"

"No, ma'am..."

Mama's eyes morphed into slits as she skimmed up and down with her crazed eyes. Without hesitation, she yanked me into her face and said, "You better not be fucking lying to me. I swear to God."

"I'm not lying, Mama... I swear I'm not," I squealed like a toddler, almost wanting to cry again.

"And what in the fuck were you doing with that bleach?!?"

Silent, I couldn't confess to her I was trying to lighten my skin. Lighten my skin for her.

"ANSWER ME! What in the hell were you doing with that bleach?!?"

"I... I umm... I was just cleaning the bathroom... There was still some oil on the tub floor from Saturday. I almost slipped," I lied.

She let go of me and then pushed me off to the side. "Hurry yo ass up and take yo black, fat ass to school."

"I will," I replied, swiftly dashing toward the front door and heading out.

The fifth period bell was about to ring. Quiet as usual, I was sitting in my seat in Ms. Reid's science class. Tyrone Jackson, my number one bully, strolled inside the classroom. With five minutes to spare before the final bell rang, Ms. Reid told me she had to go use the bathroom. There were only about six students in the class of twenty so far. Everyone else usually trickled in at the last minute.

Loud and cracking jokes as usual, Tyrone looked straight at me saying, "Boy, you blacker than ever. Look like a mothafuckin' Exxon oil spill!"

Latisha and Tatiana, two girls who were sitting in front of me, erupted in crazy laughter.

I hated Tyrone. Like, I really hated this nigga's guts. Aside from killing Mama and Ty'Quan, Tyrone was someone who I wanted to murder so badly. This nigga always bullied me. And he'd been doing so since we had our first class together in the sixth grade. Every day I had to deal with his shit. The non-stop name calling. The punches. The slaps. The kicks in my ass. The grabbing of my chest. Tyrone also loved tripping me in the hallway or in the cafeteria. It was always something... and I just took it. I didn't know why.

I didn't say anything to him as he coolly walked past me. Ms. Reid sat him behind me. That was the only thing I hated about her, too. She knew Tyrone was always fucking with me. So, why would she sit him behind me?

There were times where I used to try to fight him off or go back and forth with him, but I learned sometimes the best thing to do was just to ignore him. If I gave him the attention he craved, his taunts got worse. And that was exactly what I was doing now – ignoring his stupid ass.

Tyrone thought he was better than everyone else because his mama was mixed. His mama was Cuban. Dude walked around the halls of the school like a king just 'cause he had all the girls over him all the fucking time. Yeah, that might've made him the shit, but he was stupid as hell. Honestly, I couldn't lie – deep down, there was a part of me that wished I was like Tyrone. If I could just have what he had but also keep my intelligence and good grades, I knew I'd be better than him. Shit, I'd be better than all of these guys that went to my school. I definitely envied his caramel skin complexion. I envied his weight, too. Tyrone was the quarterback for the varsity football team, so he was definitely in tip-top shape.

Ms. Reid still wasn't back yet, so now I had to spend the next few minutes hoping Tyrone wouldn't keep fucking with me. But my hopes were squandered when I felt a balled-up piece of paper hit the back of my neck. "Fat, black ass nigga. You need to have Coach Martin run yo fat ass around the track. You look like Fat Albert covered in tar. Black, fat ass nigga! Boy, I'm glad I ain't that black!"

"HAHAHAHAH!" a few other students roared.

"Man, leave him alone, Tyrone. You always startin' some shit with him," Aniyah, one the other girls sitting next to him, said.

"Bitch, mind your own damn business!"

"Who you callin' a bitch?!?" she spat back

"Bitch, I'm callin' you a bitch!" Tyrone howled.

"Ya bean-eatin' mammy's a bitch!"

"Bitch, ya mama's a crackhead!"

"Yeah, my mama might be a crackhead but at least she still takes care of me. Yo mama abandoned you 'cause she didn't want yo black nigga ass. You know them Cubans racist as fuck!"

"BITCH! Fuck you! I'll knock yo skinny ass out!" Tyrone screeched. Damn, the way he sounded I knew that dig obviously got under his skin.

"Nigga, I'll fuck you up and you know that with yo pussy

ass! That's why you lost that football game, with yo non-throwin' ass!" Aniyah shot back. "Weak ass arm!"

"OOOOOOOH SHIT!!!" the entire class erupted.

Ms. Reid exploded through the classroom door. "HEY! CUT THAT OUT!" she yelled, rushing over to Tyrone and Aniyah as they continued to go at it.

"Ms. Reid, Tyrone called me a bitch!" Aniyah cried. Looking over my shoulder, I stared at her brown, skinny self. Aniyah was so slender, you would've thought she was smoking crack her damn self. But her size didn't stop her from fighting girls AND guys. She definitely had some hands on her.

Ms. Reid bumbled her chubby behind over to Tyrone and Aniyah. "Tyrone! What in the hell did I say the last time you called someone out of their name?"

Tyrone smacked his braces-covered teeth. "Okay, Ms. Reid. I'm sorry…"

"Oh, no! Don't apologize to me! Apologize to Aniyah! Look at her and apologize."

I turned back around in my seat to see if Tyrone would apologize. Tyrone suddenly shot me this angry look. "Why you lookin' at me?!?" I turned back around in my seat.

"TYRONE! Apologize to her!" yelled Ms. Reid.

Although I couldn't see, all I heard Tyrone mumble was, "I'm sorry…"

"Good!" Ms. Reid exclaimed, a big ass smile stretched across her brown face.

The fifth period bell rang and Ms. Reid swiftly made her way over to the classroom chalkboard. "I hope y'all studied! We are going right into the exam!" she announced.

"AHHHH!" groaned the entire class.

"No! No! No! I don't give a damn!" Ms. Reid screamed back to the class. "Y'all had plenty of time to prepare!"

Hopefully all the studying I did this past weekend paid off. I think it did. Well, I knew it did. I loved science class, but I couldn't say the same for everyone else.

I quickly finished my test within thirty minutes and was the first to turn it in. While everyone else seemed to have their heads still buried in the test, I happily spent the rest of the class reading over my notes for Algebra.

Some time passed.

I glanced up at the clock and saw we had about five minutes remaining until the bell would ring. I tried to devour as much as I could from my notes because I had a test in my algebra class, too. Once the bell rang, everyone scrambled to get to their next class. Before I could make it out the door, I heard Ms. Reid calling my name. "Andrew, don't leave yet. I wanna talk to you."

"Yes, ma'am," I replied. I walked over to her desk.

I'd known Ms. Reid now for over two years. Although there were times I thought she could be very hard on all of us, I think she was only that way because she really wanted to see us succeed. I didn't know exactly how old she was, but I believed she was in her early or late-twenties. She was slightly chubby and had mocha brown skin. Her hair was extra-wavy though. Not like the typical nigga. She probably got her good hair because she was probably either Jamaican or Trinidadian. A lot of Caribbean niggas seemed to have good hair. I never asked Ms. Reid where she was from though...

"Have a seat next to me," she instructed.

"Yes, ma'am," I replied politely, taking a seat next to her without hesitation. Ms. Reid pulled out my exam and showed me the grade I got.

"I don't know how you manage to do it all the time but you scored a perfect grade on the exam," Ms. Reid said, smiling. "You know... there are times I wanna believe you're cheating, but I know you're not. What high school are you going to again?" she asked.

"Turner Tech," I told her.

"Oh, hell no!" Ms. Reid exclaimed, her face twisted with disgust. "I really think you need to go to MAST Academy. Have you heard of them?"

I'd never heard of MAST Academy. "No, ma'am. Where is that school?" I asked.

"Well, they are a very good science and math high school on Virginia Key. North of Key Biscayne and Crandon Park," Ms. Reid explained as she threw my exam back onto a pile of papers in front of her.

"I don't even know where that's even at," I replied, shrugging my shoulders. Like, I really didn't know the locations of any of those places she just mentioned. Sounded like they were close to Miami Beach.

Ms. Reid stared at me and lifted an eyebrow. "You never been to Virginia Key or Key Biscayne?" she asked.

"No, ma'am," I replied, a bit embarrassed. Damn, I really probably looked stupid as hell to her.

"Wow! Dru, aren't you from Miami?"

Feeling somewhat ashamed, I replied, "Yes."

"And your mother never took you there?"

Shaking my head no, I replied, "No, ma'am."

"Hrrrm. Okay. Well, I think I'm going to talk to Dr. Simpson and see if we can put in a last-minute recommendation to see if we could get you in there. It makes no sense at all for you to go over to that raggedy Turner Tech. I might give your mother a call too," she explained.

"Yes, ma'am," I replied.

"Well, go on to your sixth period. I don't wanna hold you up," Ms. Reid said.

"Yes, ma'am. See you later, Ms. Reid," I said and dashed

out of the classroom. I quickly made my way down the hall to Mr. Davis' classroom.

Mama never really cooked for us. I couldn't even remember the last time she even scrambled some eggs. For dinner, she'd usually order takeout from her usual neighborhood spots like Lem's BBQ on 135th Street or Gloria's Soul Food on 32nd Avenue. Mama loved to eat. Just like Tay'Quan. And that was exactly what those two were doing while I was in the kitchen cleaning up.

"I love they rib tips. I love they fries, too," Mama mumbled, smacking her teeth as she chewed on a piece of meat. Her entire mouth covered in BBQ sauce, she always looked a mess anytime she ate BBQ. With the aroma of food running in the air, I kind of became hungry but I fought it off. I was still gonna starve myself for the most part until I lost this weight.

"Dru, bring me some grape soda and napkins," Mama mumbled with food rolling in her mouth.

"Yes, ma'am," I replied as I quickly dashed over to the fridge and pulled out the bottle of Chek grape soda. I grabbed some paper towel sheets off the roll next to the toaster oven and strolled over to the dining room table. I sat the bottle of soda and napkins on the table next to Mama and made my way back to finish washing the dishes.

"Boy! How in the hell am I supposed to drink soda with no glass??!?"

"Sorry, Mama," I apologized. I grabbed a glass from the cabinet above me and brought it over to her.

"Boy! Put some ice in there! Damn!"

"Sorry, Mama." I grabbed the glass and then dashed back over to the fridge. I opened up the freezer and scooped up a few cubes of ice into the glass and brought it back over to Mama.

Grabbing the glass out of my hand, she looked at me with disgust, rolling her eyes to the ceiling. "You don't mothafuckin' listen. Stupid ass."

Not saying anything back to her, I just strolled back into the kitchen. I didn't have that many dishes left to wash and I wanted to get back to my room to study for my history test that was tomorrow.

All of a sudden, I heard some knocks at the apartment front door.

Both Mama and Tay'Quan stopped eating. All of us looked at the door. "Who is that?!?" Mama asked. "Go check, Dru."

"Yes, ma'am," I said as I dried off my hands with a dishrag and walked over to the door. Looking out the door's peephole, my gaze exploded with surprise when I saw it was Ms. Reid standing at the door.

I stepped back and then looked at Mama. "It's my science teacher, Ms. Reid."

Mama screwed her face up. "Why in the hell is she at my damn door?!?"

Shrugging my shoulders, I said, "I don't know."

"Boy! Did you get in trouble at school?!? Don't fucking lie to me!" she growled through a whisper.

"No, I swear I didn't!"

Mama grabbed one of the paper towel sheets next to her and quickly wiped her face and hands. Looking at her, I had no idea why she was dressed up. She was wearing some shiny red bodysuit and stilettos, once again looking like she was about to go out to the club. She walked over to the door, shoving me out the way. She leaned down and looked out the peephole. "Yes. Who is it?"

"Mrs. Geter... I'm Ms. Reid. I'm Andrew's science teacher.

I wanted to talk to you for a moment. I know this is last minute but this is very important..." Ms. Reid said.

"About what?"

"About his future... can we talk?"

Mama looked at me, skimming up and down with her hazel eyes turning to lethal slits. Taking a deep breath, she burped and then opened the door. A fake ass smile came across her face. "Hey, how are you doing? We were just finishing up our dinner."

"Oh, I'm so sorry about that! I really am! I would've called, but I thought it would've just been best to swing by."

"Oh, okay. Well, come on in. Don't mind my house. It's a bit dirty right now. You know these boys don't like to clean up behind themselves." She grinned. "Have a seat over in the living room. You can see our dining room is a mess. We just got done eating some BBQ."

"Smells good." Ms. Reid smiled as she trailed Mama into the den. She took a seat on one of the couches. Mama took a seat in another. I was still standing near the kitchen. Ms. Reid looked over at me, saying, "Hey, Andrew! Come over here and let's talk..."

Motionless and in utter disbelief, I was so shocked that Ms. Reid would show up to our apartment unannounced. I knew Mama was fuming on the inside. This was the first time one of my teachers had ever done a home visit. I never would've even imagined Ms. Reid even coming here because she acted kind of boujee. From her weird facial expression, it looked like she felt uncomfortable being deep in the hood like this. Our apartment complex was right in the heart of Opa Locka, too. Ms. Reid told us she lived over in Pembroke Pines, which was a nice, fancy area about twenty minutes away from here.

"Yes, ma'am," I responded as I jetted into the living room.

"Ooooooh, you in trouble!" Tay'Quan snickered.

"No, he's not in trouble. Actually, I have some good news," said Ms. Reid. She yanked out a manila folder from her big black purse and then pulled out a piece of paper. "I spoke with Andrew earlier about his awesome grades. He's a very gifted child. I understand he's going to Turner Tech, correct?"

"Yes, he is," Mama said.

"Well, I think Turner Tech is a wonderful school, don't get me wrong. But Andrew, he is exceptionally bright and I think he needs to go to a better school. I spoke to our principal, Dr. Simpson, about seeing if we could get Andrew to take the test to get into MAST Academy. However, it turns out because Andrew has gotten nearly all A's in his entire academic career at Westview, we could actually bypass the test and get him in ASAP. They have limited enrollment and Wednesday is the last day to get him a spot. I am so happy we were able to pull this off!" Ms. Reid exclaimed.

"MAST Academy? What and where is that?"

"You've never heard of MAST Academy either?" Ms. Reid asked.

"No. No, I haven't. Sounds far as hell, to be honest with you."

"Well, MAST Academy is quite some distance away from here. It's all the way out in Virginia Key."

"Virginia Key! Oh, hell no! Ain't no other schools like that around here? And what is such the big difference between MAST Academy and Turner Tech? I mean, Andrew is smart But damn, he's that smart?!?"

Ms. Reid paused for a moment. "Well, Mrs. Geter-,"

"That's Ms. Greene. I just divorced his daddy," Mama said.

"Sorry, Ms. Greene. But MAST Academy is not only one of the best science and technology magnet programs in Miami but in all of Florida. Actually, in the nation. Andrew has a strong affinity for the sciences. He is a scientist or a doctor in the making. They offer dual-enrollment classes where Andrew would be able to take courses at Miami-Dade and FIU. This would be an incredible opportunity for him. Not too many of our people get into institutions like this," Ms. Reid explained.

Mama looked a tad perplexed. "Hrrrrm. Well, I don't know... what did you say your name again was?"

"Ms. Reid... I'm his science teacher... I thought you would've known that."

"Yeah, well, I don't, Ms. Reid. I'm a busy, working single mother trying to raise two kids myself. My ex-husband is incarcerated, so life ain't easy. MAST Academy sounds good and all, but it just sounds like it's a bit out of our league and too far to get to every day. Besides, Andrew is smart but he needs to be thinking about more realistic jobs. All of that medicine and science stuff is for white folks."

"Excuse me? What are you talking about, Ms. Greene?"

"What I'm saying is I appreciate you coming over here thinking you know best for my son, but he's going to Turner Tech. It's right around the corner. They got good programs, too. Besides, he needs to be close enough to watch after his brother. How would I even arrange for transportation and whatnot?"

"I'm sure we could figure something out, Ms. Greene. I just don't think it's wise to squander such a once-in-a-lifetime opportunity. The registration deadline is literally in a few days and we don't have much time to think this through. I, along with Mr. Simpson, can definitely—"

Suddenly interrupting Ms. Reid, Mama threw her hand up in her face saying, "Stop! Stop! Stop! Stop right there! I don't need any of y'all help and, truth be told, I find it quite offensive that you would come over to my house all unannounced while me and family are in the middle of eating dinner. Like I said, I know what's best for my son. You don't. And we ain't some charity case either. I may not live in some fancy part of Miami and I may not drive a nice car, but I'm not a stupid woman. I have education, too. I know what's best for my family. What you talkin' about is just out there and just unrealistic. Yeah, Andrew may be smart and whatnot, but he ain't that smart to think he finna become some nuclear scientist or somethin' like that. The boy can't even talk to people right from time to time."

"Wow..." Pursing her lips, Ms. Reid glanced over at me then threw her gaze back onto Mama. "I think you need to do your research, Ms. Greene. But if that's how you feel, then fine." She stood up, grabbing her purse and clutching it tightly to her side. "I'll see you tomorrow in class, Andrew," said Ms. Reid.

Although I was burning with anger, I couldn't let Mama think I was mad. So, I looked at Ms. Reid with a fake grin and said, "Yes, ma'am."

Why was Mama robbing me like this? Granted, I didn't know much about this school. But from the sound of it, it just seemed like a good opportunity. Mama was only doing this to punish me. I should've said something. I should say something right now and stand up for myself. I should tell Ms. Reid right now that my mama was a stupid, crazy bitch. She'd believe it, too. But I knew if I dared to open my mouth and said some reckless, Mama would try to kill me. I'd try to kill her, too. But Mama had more strength than me at the moment. I was still reeling in pain from the whooping she put on me over the weekend.

Ms. Reid extended her hand to shake Mama's but Mama just looked the other way. Ms. Reid slowly pulled her hand back and walked toward the front door. She looked at me saying, "Have a good night, Andrew. I'll see you tomorrow."

"Good night, Ms. Reid," I said back to her as I watched her exit the apartment.

I sat back on the couch, my arms folded. I should kill this bitch right now. Like, I really should.

As Mama sat next to me, completely silent, she glanced over at me and said, "Get your big ass up and go finish cleaning my kitchen and go to bed when you done."

"Yes, ma'am." I got up and walked over into the kitchen. With a few glasses left to wash, I slowly took my time thinking if I should just grab one of these knives and go kill her right now. I should. I should kill her. My blood boiling with rage, I had to do this now to escape. Not wanting her to hear me, I slowly opened the drawer where the knives and forks were at. My eyes landed on the sharpest steak knife.

CHAPTER SIX

P*ow!* "STUPID, BLACK ASS... FUCK WRONG WITH YOU!"
I suddenly blacked out...

"**L**ADIES AND GENTLEMEN! Please rise! We are now about to give our highest honors to a student who has survived many challenges to be here today. A wise man once said that the only constant in life is the gift of learning from our adversity. However, while many shun their trials and tribulations, not taking heed to such wisdom, a few will. And those few will learn how to use their darkest moments to mold themselves into greatness. Today, we would like to honor someone who has survived his darkest tribulations, learning much from them to arrive at his moment of greatness today. His name is Mr. Andrew Geter! Our Valedictorian of the class of 2004!"

Millions of eyes from the audience were now laser-focused onto me. I burned with nervousness. But this was my moment. A moment I'd been waiting for forever…

"Mr. Geter," the President of Harvard University grinned, turned his attention to me. He reached his right hand out, welcoming me to walk across the stage to receive my diploma.

But before I got up from my seat on the stage and began to walk, I took a quick glance at the nearly packed auditorium. A sea of mostly white faces filled the room. But as I scanned the center of the room, I saw my entire family waving at me. Seemed like they were the only black face there. Mama kept waving at me and then blew kisses at me. "I love you, baby! I'm so proud of you!" I could see and even hear her telling me.

"I love you, baby!"

See, I knew deep down Mama did love me. Those words made a tear trickle from the corner of my eye. I knew she always did. I just had to prove myself to her.

Trepidation cooked my insides; millions of butterflies invaded my stomach.

But I had to be confident. This was my time…

Dad told me to keep my head up and walk straight as I walked up to receive my degree. He wrote to me, telling me he was proud of all of my accomplishments. He said in his last letter to me, "Son, when you walk across that stage, keep your head high to the sky. Be a proud black man. Be the representation of the millions of people who paid a heavy price to be where you're at today. Be the man millions will look up to one day. When you walk, let those white folks know despite your background, you made it. You did it. I love you, son. We'll see each other soon…"

So, with those words etched in my conscience and heart, I stiffened myself up and then began to proudly walk across the stage to receive that piece of paper. That paper was a sign of all the sacrifices I made over the years. All the hours of studying I put in. All the nights I spent crying, hoping my professors wouldn't fail me. I arrived at my moment; it was my time to shine.

I strolled up to the George H.W. Bush-lookin' President with my hand extended to shake his. "We are all proud of you, son," he uttered and then handed me my diploma. My eyes glued to the diploma, I realized I received the keys to heaven. My heaven. This was my key to do all the things I ever wanted to do.

"Thank you, Mr. President."

He smiled once again saying, "Congratulations, son. You've accomplished something that no one else has been able to do. You're the first Black man to graduate from Harvard with honors."

Now armed with my degree, I looked back into the crowd, my eyes now attached to Mama. And there she was, now the only person standing up, the bluest tears falling down her cheeks. "I'm so proud of you, baby. I love you so much."

"I love you, too, Mama…"

Once the graduation ceremony was over, I met up with my family near the entrance of the auditorium. Mama, Tay'Quan, Granny, and a few other relatives were standing there, anxiously awaiting my arrival.

"Mama!" I exclaimed, rushing over to her.

"YOU DID IT, ANDREW! YOU DID IT!" everyone screamed out, their joy beaming from their faces.

With her arms wide open, Mama beckoned me to fly into the biggest hug she'd ever given me in my life.

"I'm so proud of you, son! My firstborn! My future doctor! You're so fine, too! I can't wait until you have some grandbabies!" she bawled.

"I love you, too, Mama. I'm glad I made you so proud.

That's all I ever wanted to do. To make you proud and make you happy."

"I know, son. I love you so much. I've always loved you."

"I know, Mama. I know you've always loved me. And I love you, too. I've always loved you."

She then looked at me in my watery eyes saying, "Turn around. I have a surprise for you."

"What's that?" I asked, slowly turning around in my brown leather Stacy Adams.

It was Dad.

Was I dreaming? I quickly flashed my eyes closed then opened them, my gaze zeroing in on Dad once again. It was him and he stood there with his arms wide open.

"My firstborn. Come give me a hug, man!"

My already watery eyes shuddered with disbelief. "Dad?!?"

"Yes... it's me, son. Come on over here, man!"

Suddenly screaming to the top of my lungs, more tears gushed out of my eyes. I lost control of myself. "Daddy!!!"

I ran up to him, touching him just to see if it was really him. "When did you get out of prison?!? You won your appeal?!?"

"Yeah, I did! I'm free now. I ain't never going back. And I won just in time to see you walk across that stage. Damn, I'm so proud of you, son. I love you so much!"

"I love you, too! I missed you so much!"

"Can you believe Mama finally told me she—,"

CHAPTER SEVEN

SPLASH!
"GET THE FUCK UP!"

My hazy eyes flickered open. Gasping, I damn near drowned in a rush of cold water flooding my face.

"I SAID WAKE THE FUCK UP! GET UP!" Mama hovered over me, a red bucket swinging in her hand. A cigarette dangling from her lips, smoking pouring from her nostrils. She tossed the bucket off to the side.

Everything was blurry. Well, except that dream. It seemed so clear. Like I was actually there. Mama must've knocked me over the head really hard with something and I passed out, going straight into another world. A world that obviously wasn't real.

But now, I returned to consciousness, now back to my real life, my real nightmare. It was so crazy 'cause I swear I was about to murder her. But she was two steps ahead of me. Damn. Did she know what I was about to do or something? I didn't even see her as she snuck up behind me and slammed either a pot or pan across my head.

Still laid out, I used my still fuzzy vision to scan around me.

What did she use to hit me? I noticed shards of glass splattered all over the kitchen floor. Remnants of what was the lamp from the den rested near my side. Mama obviously used it to bust me across my head.

The side of my temple throbbing with a horrible headache, I began to cry, rubbing the left side of my head. The area above my left temple was wet, raw and tender. That had to be blood I was feeling on my fingers. Then, again, it could've been water. But once I pulled my hand in front of my face, I saw my fingertips painted in fresh blood.

"I ain't even hit you that fuckin' hard! NOW, GET THE FUCK UP!" Mama growled, still hovering over me. Groaning in pain, I tried my best to lift myself off the floor, but I was too weak and nauseous. The entire room was spinning.

"I SAID GET THE FUCK UP, DRU!" Mama's scream cracked my ringing ears. "Gon have the mothafuckin' audacity to bring that fat, Jamaican bitch up to my house and try to question my parenting! Who the fuck she think she is?!? Oprah?!? And you knew that bitch was coming over to my mothafuckin' house?!?! Why the fuck you ain't tell me?!?"

I glanced up at Mama. "I didn't know she was gonna come here..."

Rapidly tapping her foot against the floor, she kept shaking her head as she puffed on her cigarette. "My house a goddamn mess and now you just embarrassed the fuck out of me! Now that bitch gon' think I got rats and roaches foolin' with y'all! Bitch talkin' about you smart in science and math. Yeah the fuck right! Nigga, you don't know shit! I don't know who the fuck you foolin' at the school, but you're dumb as shit! You will never be shit. And nobody will ever want a fat, black, dumb ass nigga to be their doctor. You can't even run a fucking mile, so how the fuck you gonna be a doctor?!? I wouldn't want yo ugly, fat ass to be my doctor! I know that for sure! What the fuck kind of health advice can you give someone?! Boy, get your fat, dumb, black ass up off that mothafuckin' floor before I really give you somethin' to cry about! I can't believe you had the nerve to sit up there and lie to me! You knew that bitch was coming over here! You knew it! You fucking with me! You fucking with me really good! I should make you sleep outside!"

"Mama, I ain't know she was gonna come over here," I mumbled, a mix of snot and tears painted my face. Somehow, I managed to muster up enough strength to stand up. However, I had to grip the handle of the stove to keep myself balanced, so I wouldn't fall back down.

"I'm bleeding, Mama. I don't feel good." I was trying so hard not to collapse back onto the floor.

Mama lunged at me then grabbed me by my shirt collar. She spun me around, twisting and turning my head, analyzing it I guess to see exactly how bad she hit me.

"He's bleedin' really bad, Mama," I heard Tay'Quan say.

"Boy, mind yo own mothafuckin' business. In fact, go to yo room and be in there for the rest of the night!"

"But I ain't do nothin!" he shouted back.

"BOY! Who the fuck you think you raisin' your voice at! Go in the room and play on yo Sega Genesis!"

"Okay," he mumbled, sprinting off to his bedroom.

Mama spun me around again and then leaned into my face. "Stop all that crying. I said I ain't hit you that hard. You must've hit yo head on the handle of the stove."

Sniffling, I wiped my face, attempting to control my heavy, rapid breathing.

"You need stitches. I'mma take you to the hospital. But if you ever in yo mothafuckin' life have a teacher come over to my place unannounced, I promise you it'll be yo last mothafuckin' day standing. You understand me?"

Tears and more snot trekking down my face, all I could say was, "Yes, ma'am."

"Now, take yo ass into the bathroom and go get some of that blood off you before we leave! And hurry up!" Mama shoved me out of the kitchen and trekked into the den, still puffing away on her half-smoked Newport. "I need me a blunt and a stiff drink. Damn kids gon' drive me fucking crazy, I swear!"

Wobbling down the dark hallway, I was almost one-hundred percent certain I was gonna blackout again. Before I reached the bathroom, Tay'Quan slowly opened his bedroom door and peeked his head out.

Holding the side of my head, I slowly turned my attention to him, not saying a word. I almost had enough strength to suddenly punch him in his fucking yellow face. Bitch ass nigga.

"You alright?" he asked in a whisper, I guess so Mama wouldn't hear him. He didn't want to get knocked across the head either. But I knew Mama wouldn't put her hands on him. She never did. She might scream and cuss at him from time to time, but she never hit him. Never...

"Yeah," I angrily replied.

"Okay," he replied, then closed his door. "It's gonna be alright. Just be strong, okay?"

"Okay..." I got inside the bathroom and closed the door. I stood in the mirror and turned my head to the left to see whatever gash Mama gave me. The wound was so deep, you could see white meat. I grabbed a fresh blue washcloth hanging from the towel rack. I began lightly tapping the side of my head. The gash was stinging really bad. Worse than the welts she gifted me just a few days ago.

Rather than murder her, I just needed to go ahead and kill myself. That was the only logical thing to do at this point. There was just gonna be no way to escape from her because it seemed like she was able to read my mind. I threw the washcloth off near the sink faucet. I leaned down and opened the sink cabinet, ready to grab the bottle of Clorox. But then I noticed the Clorox and even Mama's cocaine was missing. The entire cabinet was empty. Damn. Drinking bleach would've been the easiest way to peace out, I assumed. But it seemed like Mama knew I was gonna try to kill myself by drinking the bleach. So, maybe she was right – maybe I wasn't that smart after all. Maybe she really did *know* more than me.

I slammed the cabinet shut then grabbed the washcloth to wipe off blood still oozing from the gash. Most of the blood had dried up but the wound was white and open. Cool air from the AC vent inside the bathroom whisked against the gash, making it sting even more. Fuck it. I just had to go the hospital and get my head stitched up. But all I knew was the first thing I was gonna do when I went to school in the morning was tell Ms. Reid what happened. I knew then she'd tell Dr. Simpson and then they would get Mama arrested for doing this to me.

After waiting for about five hours in the ER waiting area, we were now inside of a chilly hospital room. Sitting upright on a bed, some older white nurse was running a thread and needle in my numb head.

Once the nurse bandaged up my head, she patted me on my back saying, "Alright! I'm all done. You needed a total of eight stitches!"

Mama was sitting over in the corner of the hospital room watching a rerun of Martin on TV. She hadn't even been paying attention to the nurse stitching up my head.

The nurse glanced over at Mama and said, "Ma'am, I'm

done now... I'm gonna have the doctor come in and speak with you all for a moment."

Mama threw her gaze toward us. "Oh, okay," she mumbled and shot her eyes back toward the television.

Some moments later, a tall, dark-skinned slender dude who looked around Mama's age entered into the room. Armed with a clipboard in hand, he quickly shut the door. He was about my complexion. Damn near darker it seemed... I wonder if he was Haitian or Jamaican. Those Caribbean people tended to be darker than regular niggas. Mama always said that, too. And she wasn't lying 'cause I knew a few people at my school who were Haitian like Pierre. That nigga was dark as hell. He never really got picked on though 'cause he was big as fuck and he would often fuck people if they made fun of him.

"Hey guys. How y'all folks doing this evening?" the man said, smiling.

Mama looked at him, a flat, unamused facial expression came across her face. "Hi."

"I'm Dr. Basquiat. I'm the attending emergency room physician..."

Basquiat. That was definitely a Haitian ass last name.

"Hey there," Mama replied nonchalantly.

"I assume you're his mother?" the doctor inquired, skimming me up and down with his beady eyes. He then walked over to me as I sat on the room bed. His slatted eyes were glued to my head. Seemed like he had a million questions running through his mind.

"Yes...yes, I am," Mama replied.

"Cool. Well, I just have a few questions before we discharge him," Dr. Basquiat explained as he pulled out a pen from his right shirt pocket and pulled the clipboard up to his face. "Andrew... that's your name?" Dr. Basquiat asked, looking at me.

"Yes, sir," I replied.

"Cool. Andrew, tell me, how did you get that gash on your head? Were you fighting?"

"Umm, he already told y'all he fell down the stairs at our apartment complex," Mama interjected as she stood up and walked over to us.

"Hrrrm, well, I only asked because the nurse also noticed some slight bruises on his back and stomach when she was taking his vitals. And the nurse also told me there were tiny pieces of glass in his head. Is everything okay at home?"

Mama's face suddenly twisted with astonishment at the doctor's question. "Excuse me?

"Yes... is everything okay?" the doctor asked again. "We are mandated child abuse reporters. I need to know if anything is going on..."

"WOOOW! Really?!? Let me ask you a question, Dr. *BAS-SQWEET* or however you pronounce your last name."

"It's *Basquiat*. Bah-skee-ahh. That is how you pronounce it."

Mama continued, "Okay, well, thank you for the proper pronunciation, Mr. *BASQUIAT*."

"That's Dr. Basquiat."

Mama smacked her teeth and grabbed her waist as she scanned Dr. Basquiat up and down saying, "Okay, whatever, dude. Dr. Basquiat. I don't care, whatever you wanna call yourself. How dare you come in here and the first thing you insist is that I had been hitting or abusing my son?" she asked with fake outrage. She continued, "That is racist. So, just because a white woman doubts his story, all of a sudden, I'm the one who had to hit him? You know, I should sue this place. That is racism. I feel like I'm being discriminated against!"

"Please, Mrs. Geter, please calm down. I was just-,"

"That's Ms. Greene!" Mama interrupted. "Look, dude, can

we just please get the discharge papers so we can leave? I have to be up at work at seven am in the morning. This is just absolutely ridiculous. I bet you if I was one of those white Russian Jewish bitches that live up in Aventura or some lil spicy Spanish Cuban bitch, you wouldn't ask me these crazy ass questions. How dare you?!? And you supposed to be a black man at that, already assuming the worst in your people?!? I'm a good mother! I take good care of BOTH of my children. I may not be the richest woman in the world and I may not have all of that fancy-schmancy education you got, DOCTOR, but I sure know one thing! I know how to raise my kids and keep them out of trouble. Andrew is a straight A student who goes to a good middle school. All of his teachers know that! He never gives me any issues. None of my kids do. They never even give me a reason to raise my voice at them, let alone hit them. So, please, if you don't mind, I would like those discharge papers so we can leave already." Mama then looked up at the clock in the room. "It's 11:48. It's already a shame we had to wait hours just to even see you! And this is the bullshit you wanna do before we get ready to head out?!? Man, fuck you and just give me those papers. Fucking asshole. Gon' come up in here and ask me if everything is okay. You got some mothafuckin' nerve, you know that!"

Motionless, Dr. Basquiat looked stunned. "Fine. I apologize, ma'am. We just have to ask certain questions when we suspect trouble. That's all." He pulled out the discharge papers from his clipboard and reached over to Mama to hand them to her. But like the evil, lying, manipulative bitch she was, she snatched them out of his hand. Dr. Basquiat looked at me, shaking his head. "Good luck in school, Andrew. What do you want to be when you get older?"

"A doctor," I replied.

"Good. Stay in school. Make your mother proud," he said, and then exited out of the room.

Soon as the door was closed, Mama glanced over at me and said, "Get your ass up, so we can leave. Got these folks all up in my damn business."

I got out of the hospital room bed and trailed her as we exited out of the ER. Mama, at the last minute, had one of our neighbors to watch after Tay'Quan while we went to the hospital. I didn't know why she didn't make him come with us, but I assumed it was because she didn't want Tay'Quan to accidentally run his mouth to the nurse or even the doctor. Even if he did, I honestly think she would've not done shit to him.

My shirt was soaked from sweat as we trekked through the parking lot. It was so humid outside, even for damn near midnight. That was Miami for you. We got close to Mama's car. Since Tay'Quan wasn't with us, I figured I'd ride up front with Mama. I hated sitting in the back. Before I could open the front passenger door, Mama shouted, "Hell no! Sit in the back! Kids don't get to sit up front!"

I didn't even want to argue with her, so I just opened the back passenger door and got in. I threw my seatbelt on and stared out the back window, my eyes focused onto the big blue moon glowing in the dark, cloudless skies.

"And you ain't going to school for the rest of the week either. I don't want no damn teachers of yours asking a million mothafuckin' questions about what the fuck happened to you," Mama said, starting up the car's engine.

I suddenly got mad. "But I have a bunch of tests this week, Mama!"

Mama turned around in her seat and cocked her hand back as if she was about to punch me. I flinched, throwing my hands up to protect myself.

"BOY! Who the fuck are you raising your voice at?!? You want me to go across your head again!?!?"

"No, ma'am."

"LIKE I SAID! You're not going to school for the rest of the week. You could forget about that school shit. You ain't learnin' nothin' no damn way! Besides, the year is almost over. Why the fuck you got all those tests?!?"

"It's our final exams, Mama!"

"I don't care! You'll make it up! School shit is pointless anyways. You act like you finae go to college. Who the fuck you think can afford to send you to college anyways? Not me! Mostly white folks go to college. Not niggas. Yeah, a few black folks go to college here and there, but that's because they had money. We ain't got money like that. Your teachers – they probably had money. They puttin' all those fucking pipe dreams in the back of you niggas' minds about college and what not. That's stupid. When you get older, you gonna get a real job. You'll thank me later, too. Watch. Don't you even know how much college costs? I bet you don't. Do you?"

"No," I replied.

"Exactly."

"Guess how much college costs?"

"A thousand dollars?"

"No! Boy! See, you stupid as fuck! And you think you know shit? You got them teachers gassing you the fuck up. School costs tens of thousands of dollars. A YEAR. Who the fuck you think got that type of money?"

"But I can get a scholarship!"

"Boy, ain't nobody just gon' give you scholarships like that! Everybody say they wanna get a scholarship. What makes you think you finne get one? Just because you get some good grades here and there? You ain't the only one who gets good grades. Plenty of people get good grades. And it ain't about just good grades. It's about tests. And also about people you know. You don't know nobody who's rich? Who you know?"

I was silent. I didn't know anybody rich.

"EXACTLY! That's what the fuck I thought. Just sit the fuck back, be quiet and take a nap or something. Getting on my last damn nerve, I swear. Boy, sometimes I wish your daddy was out of prison so you could stay with his stupid ass, too. Then, y'all can be dumb together. Dumb and Dumber. Just like the movie. Except, y'all can be Dumb Nigga and Dumber Nigga. Well, for you, Dumber Fat Ass Nigga. And when we get back inside that house, go straight to your room. You ain't gettin' nothin' to eat or drink. You understand me?"

"Yes, ma'am."

"Good."

CHAPTER EIGHT

When it came to fucking with me, Mama always kept her promises. However, she'd lie or renege when it came to everything else. She promised she'd buy me new clothes, but she never bought any. She promised to come to my school's PTA meetings or come to open house night to meet my teachers, but she'd never come. I remember one time, she promised to take me and Tay'Quan to Disney World and Universal Studios in Orlando. But of course, we never went. Well, Tay'Quan went with his cousins on his dad's side one time. Last summer, actually. I couldn't go with him though. Mama said his family didn't want me to go with them 'cause they didn't know me like that. She said his family were some hatin' ass, boujee niggas who thought they were better than everyone else. Crazy thing was Tay'Quan did eventually tell me a few weeks after he went I could've gone, but Mama didn't want to pay for me to go. I kind of figured that was the real reason I couldn't go. Tay'Quan's family was always nice to me the few times I was around them, so it didn't make sense they felt that way about me.

But like I said, when it came to her trying to fuck with me or punish me, Mama definitely kept her promises... So, this week, she kept her word when she told me after we left the hospital that my fat, black ass wasn't going back to school until my head was healed. Said she didn't want those nosey ass teachers asking me a million questions on how I got hurt. I was so fucking mad, too, 'cause I just knew I was going to be so far behind by the time I got back.

I was lying in my bed reading my American History book. Slavery in America was the topic Mrs. Garrison, my 3rd period social studies teacher, had us reading about. Needing a break, I sat up for a moment and opened my window blinds to see what outside looked like. Although I had been at home for days now, Mama didn't even want me to go outside.

From the looks of it, it was an extremely hot and sunny Friday morning. I didn't know exactly how hot it was, but I wouldn't be surprised if it was close to a hundred degrees outside. I swear it had to be that hot 'cause even with the AC blasting freezing air throughout the apartment, my room still felt like an oven. Felt like I was in the middle of Egypt or some shit. Damn, like how do those people even survive over there? My black ass would've been dead already.

Not wanting those blazing sun rays to fry me to death, or even worse, make me even blacker, I quickly closed the blinds. My eyes then flew right back to the last page I left off reading in my American History textbook. "...The rapid development of the cotton industry in the Deep South after the creation of the cotton gin significantly boosted the need of labor. For this reason, Europeans enslaved Africans..."

Reading about slavery had me so shocked. All of this information was so mind-blowing to me. Like, I knew slavery existed, but I never realized there were so many Black people that had been kidnapped and brought to America as slaves.

And slavery lasted for so long. Over four hundred years. That was a long time. Like, how though? How could people let themselves be held captive for so long without doing anything? Then, again, Mrs. Garrison did tell us that slaves would revolt from time to time. Like Nat Turner – he led a big revolt and killed all these white slave masters and whatnot. However, not every slave rebelled. In fact, a lot of Black people during those times who were born into slavery knew of nothing else but slavery. To them, well, they just accepted their enslavement as facts of life.

Shit.

Now that I think about it, it sounded like I was a slave, too. And I was accepting my enslavement and torture by my wicked ass mama as facts of my life.

However, that shit was only gonna last for so long. I wasn't gonna be her slave forever. One day, I was gonna be free. I was gonna revolt. Hell, I almost killed her Monday night. But I promise you this; let her put her hands on me again and I was gonna do some Nat Turner shit to her. And I meant it this time. That bitch was really turning me into a coldhearted, ruthless rebel she was gonna fear one day...

"DRU! ANDREW! Come here!"

Speaking of the mothafuckin' devil...

That evil, stupid ass bitch was calling my name. What the fuck did she want? I got up from my bed and walked into the den where I saw her buried in the couch, her feet kicked up on the coffee table. A cigarette in one hand, the TV remote in the other, her eyes were glued to the TV blaring an episode of Jerry Springer.

Now that I'd been home with Mama for almost a week, I realized she definitely didn't have a job. I didn't even know how she was managing to pay rent and other bills. However, for some reason, she always seemed to have money. Now that

I think about it, maybe Michael or Randy was helping her out… or maybe that baldheaded light-skin dude she was snorting cocaine with last Saturday was giving her money. Either way, the bitch didn't have a job, so some nigga she was fucking obviously was giving her lazy ass money. My guess was Mike though. Yeah, it was definitely him 'cause I could tell that nigga was in so much love with Mama. Then again, he hadn't been around in over a month. Maybe it wasn't him then…

"Yes, Mama," I cautiously announced myself as I stood off to the side of the couch. I had to keep my distance because I absolutely hated the smell of cigarettes. Mama took a puff from her cigarette then casually blew smoke from her nose.

"Go outside and go get the mail. I got my settlement check coming. I'm too tired to get up," she muttered.

Settlement check? "What's that?" I asked.

Mama cut her glassy, red eyes at me. "Boy, I swear, you always asking a million questions."

"I'm sorry…"

She cleared her throat. "But since you wanna know, I finally got my money from a car accident I got into a while ago."

My eyebrow raised out of curiosity. "When you get into a car accident?"

"Boy! Just go get the damn mail!" she roared through gritted teeth.

Her sudden angry screech made me flinch and gasp. "Okay, I'm getting it right now," I said, massaging the side of my head where my stitches were at.

"And stop rubbing your head. You can get an infection if you keep touching it!"

"Okay," I replied, quickly pulling my hand off my head as I made my way back to my room to slip my tennis shoes on.

Our mailbox, along with everyone else's who lived in the complex, was downstairs near the entrance of the apartment complex. Now back out in the den, I flew over to Mama with my hand reached out. "Whaaaaaaat?!?" She looked at me, her face screwed up with confusion.

"I need the mail key…"

The anger on her face disappeared just that quick when she realized I needed her keys. "Oh, go look in my purse."

"Where's your purse?"

"On the dining room table."

Dashing over to the dining room table, I opened her black Gucci bag and searched for her keys. My gaze widened with surprise when I saw a bag of what was probably cocaine, a razor blade and a mirror inside sitting next to her wallet. Mama probably knew I knew about her habit, but I had to play dumb and not act shocked seeing her drugs. So, I just pretended like I didn't see anything as I continued rummaging her purse.

"Got em," I mumbled once I quickly yanked the keys out of her purse. I wondered if Mama realized she left her shit in her purse…

"And be right back, too! Don't be talking to none of these raggedy ass, broke ass, nosey ass neighbors. And if they ask you why you ain't in school, just tell 'em you sick! Got it?"

"Yes, ma'am!" I darted out of the front door, cut the corner then approached the staircase. However, before I could make my way down, my gaze landed onto Crackhead Willie slowly making his way upstairs. His head hung low, once he heard me coming down the steps, he lifted his head. Seemed like it took him a moment to register who I was.

He shouted, "SUP, LIL MAN!" A big ass smile then ran across his bony, sunken-in brown face, revealing the few remaining crooked yellow-brownish teeth he had buried in his black-purplish gums.

"Wassup, Mr. Willie! I can't talk. Mama will get mad at me!"

He started coughing, clasping his chest. He was coughing so hard, it sounded like he was choking on a chicken wing bone. "Why you ain't in school, boy?!?" he asked, rubbing his chest.

Now the both of us were halfway in the staircase. I took a quick scan of him, noticing something was off about him. However, not wanting to piss Mama off, I said, "I got sick! I can't talk, Willie!" I kept walking down the steps, feeling kind of bad. Usually, Willie and I would talk for a good twenty minutes or so in the morning before I went to school. I stopped, thought for a moment and then turned around, staring right at him as he moved at a turtle's pace up the stairs. Any other day that nigga would fly up the stairs like it was nothing. When we'd see him walking down the street, his ass would move like he was gliding on water. But on this early afternoon, he was exceptionally slow. What was wrong with him? And that was why I just had one burning question for him. "Willie!" I shouted.

He turned around and gawked at me with his bug eyes. "What? I thought you said you can't talk?" he replied.

With the sun damn near blinding me, I held my hand over my forehead. With a clearer view of Willie, I now realized what was so different about him. He looked skinnier. I mean, he was already skinny, but Willie looked like he was about thirty pounds lighter. "Why I ain't hear you whistling this past weekend? You went to jail or somethin'?" I had to ask, although it was probably none of my business.

He seemed to take in a deep breath, not answering my question immediately. He just lowered his head and then glanced back up at me. "I'm sick as hell, bruh. I had to go to the hospital. Was in that muhfucka for a few days..."

"Oh, you sick, too? What you got? The flu?"

"AIDS... I got HIV/AIDS now...," he confessed. A chill zipped through my fat ass the moment those words effortlessly rolled off his tongue.

Damn. AIDS...

Honestly, I didn't know what to say. How do you even respond when someone tells you some shit like that? This was the first time ever someone told me they had AIDS. I knew about people having HIV/AIDS, but I never really knew anyone who had it. All I could do now was respond by saying, "Oh... I'm sorry to hear that."

"Oh, don't be sorry, my guy. Shit, just don't be stupid like I was."

"Okay... I won't..."

"You promise?"

"Yeah... I promise..."

Willie shrugged his bony shoulders. Scanning him up and down, Willie was so frail. His favorite Miami Dolphins jersey he usually wore now looked like a dress on him. You know, now that I think about, Mama did tell me when people got AIDS they'd lose a ton of weight. I remember one time she told me half the people she went to school with died from AIDS. I remember her telling me that losing weight very quickly was the number one sign somebody was infected with HIV. Fucked up thing was Mama, from time to time, would tell me maybe if I got AIDS, I just might lose all this weight on me.

"...but you're gonna be fine, right?"

Willie smacked his teeth. "Boy, don't you know about AIDS?"

"Yeah, I do."

"So, why you ask me some shit like that? No... no, I ain't gonna be fine. Shit, I wanna be fine, but AIDS is a death sentence, lil nigga."

"Damn... well, I'mma pray for you, Willie."

"Man, you pray for yourself. God's done with me." Willie turned around and proceeded to walk up the staircase. I just stood there for a second, watching him walk down the hallway toward his unit. He threw me another glimpse and said, "You be careful out there, Dru."

"I will..." I then took off to the mailbox.

All two hundred apartment mailboxes were lined in one long row. Our mailbox, Unit #234A, was in the center. Just as I was about to open up the mailbox, out of the corner of my eye, I saw one of my other neighbors, Ms. Washington, walking up to the mailboxes.

Fuck!

Mama must've spoke this hag into existence. Her ass just told me not to open my mouth to any of my nosey ass neighbors and the nosiest neighbor of them all was now strolling up to me. I just knew her ass was about to ask me a million mothafuckin' questions. Mama didn't really like her either 'cause one time when Mama was having one of her kickbacks, she swore it was Ms. Washington who called the police on her for making too much noise. That woman ain't nothin' but an old, naggin' ass bitch that ain't getting any money or dick. Old, fat ass bitch need to get a life! Those were Mama's words.

"Boy, this the first time I seen you home around this time! Why you ain't in school?"

Ughh! Here we go!

I swear, Ms. Washington kind of reminded me of Mrs. Littlefield, my music teacher. She was a bigger, brown-skinned woman with shiny silver hair. Looking at her, I almost wanted to throw up because she had all of these moles and spots covering her saggy face. She had on what looked like a family reunion t-shirt. The nosey ass bitch swiftly strolled up to me, looking me up and down, her thick, wrinkly hands resting on her plump waist. Now that she was a few inches away from me, my eyes darted down to her chest. I was right – the snug-fitting yellow shirt she had on had a big tree printed in the middle of it. The words, "WASHINGTON- JENKINS- COOPER FAMILY REUNION 1995 – A FAMILY THAT PRAYS TOGETHER STAYS TOGETHER" beamed across her long, big titties. I didn't know how old she was, however, I swore she and Mrs. Tubman were identical twins. I knew Mrs. Tubman was 59-years-old, so I presumed Ms. Washington, aka "Ms. Nosetta" as Mama would call her, was the same age.

Quiet and frozen in place, I had to formulate the right response in my head. Yeah, of course, I could tell this lady I was sick, but I didn't even look sick. And then there was this big ass bandage glued to my head.

"You heard me, boy? Why you ain't at school? Are you skipping school?!? Now, you know you can get in trouble for skipping school! You wanna be just like them thugs?" she snapped.

"No, ma'am. Actually, I got sick," I lied and immediately began to fake-cough. Truth be told, I really hated lying but I had no other choice. Her ass would probably call my school and snitch on me, telling them I wasn't sick.

"Sick with what? Boy, it's almost summer. Cold and flu season over," she said. Her beady eyes then analyzed my head. "And what happened to your head?"

"I fell down the stairs the other night," I lied again. Had to keep the lies consistent.

"You fell down the stairs?!? When?!?"

"Monday night, ma'am."

"Monday night? I was home all Monday night. And I ain't hear a dang 'ole thing. And no one else told me you fell!"

Since Ms. Washington was pretty much like the neighborhood watch, she knew everything that happened around the complex. Damn, if I really did fall and hurt myself, truth be told, she kind of would've known. I mean, someone was bound to see me fall, right? Damn near five hundred people lived in our complex. There were always people around at all times it seemed. Hell, even the dope boys that hung in the parking lot would've seen something. And although Ms. Washington always got into arguments with them and would often call the police on them, she was cool with a few of them. And that was only because one of her nephews, Trayvon, was one of those dope boys. He was always hanging out in the parking lot near our unit at night. He would've at least told her I fell and hurt myself really bad. Getting nervous because I sensed she wasn't done probing me, I said, "Yeah, I don't think anyone was around when it happened but I gotta go, Ms. Washington. My mother's waiting for me to get the mail."

Just looking into Ms. Washington's eyes, I could tell she wasn't buying my story though. "Oh, she's home with you, too?" she asked.

"Yes, she is," I responded. Damn, would this bitch just stop being nosey already?!?

"Then again, she don't work," she continued. "I swear I ain't never seen ya mama leave that house 'cept for at night. I always wonder why she always be going out that late. Sometimes at midnight during the middle of the week. Do you know that?"

I shrugged my shoulders. Ms. Washington wasn't lying though. Mama did often leave the house late at night during the middle of the week. I just assumed that she was going to hang out with one of her niggas or her friends.

"What does she do? Where she work at? Y'all get section 8?" Ms. Washington just kept coming with the damn questions.

Silent, I just shrugged my shoulders.

"Hrrrm..." Ms. Washington's eyebrow lifted. "Well, listen,

I don't mean to be all up in y'all business and whatnot, but when I was walking my dog some days ago, I heard ya mama fussin' and screamin'. Everything alright?"

"Yes, ma'am..." Another blatant lie.

She leaned down into my face saying, "Now Andrew, if ya mama ever really tries to hurt you or put your hands on you, you can always tell me the truth. I won't tell anyone. I promise you."

"Okay," I replied, uneasiness now choking my throat.

Ms. Washington continued with her questioning, "So, tell me, has she been hitting you and your brother, Tay'Quan?"

"No ma'am." *Damn, another lie...*

But this was a truth I was ready to tell. And although I would've liked to tell someone what was going on, truth be told, I didn't trust any of these niggas around here. Not even Ms. Washington.

Ms. Washington paused for a moment, her eyes devolving into slits. "Look, Andrew... I promise, I won't tell a soul. If she's hitting you, then she needs to be reported to DCFS. Do you know what that is?"

"No ma'am..." I lied for the umpteenth time. I knew what DCFS was.

Mama always told me that DCFS would take me and Tay'Quan away and put us in some crazy ass foster home if we ever tried to report her. And that was one of the main reasons why I never really said anything to anyone.

Although a lot of times I was scared of Mama, there was still a part of me that felt like I could deal with Mama's cussing, screaming and occasional whoopings. Then, on top of that, I couldn't imagine being taken away from her and being put into foster care. That shit seemed worse. Way worse.

Mama would always tell me I'd get fucked up even more if I had to go live with foster parents. And I believed her, too.

Shit, I even knew a few kids at my school who had foster parents. Marlon and Princess were foster kids and those niggas looked like a hot ass mess. They wore worse clothes than me. Yeah, Mama may have not always bought me the nicest clothes and whatnot, but Marlon and Princess always looked dusty and dirty. Then, I remember at one point, a rumor was going around that Princess had got pregnant by her foster dad. Now, I heard she was going to Hope North, a school for girls that got pregnant.

"It's the Department of Children and Family Services. They investigate child abuse and other things. They will protect you if your mother is hitting you. Now, again, tell me the truth. Is your mother hitting you?"

"DRU! BOY, HURRY UP! WHAT THE HELL IS TAKING YOU SO LONG, GODDAMNIT?!?"

Suddenly, I turned my head in the direction of the staircase. Mama was standing at the top of the staircase, hands glued to her waist. Although I was hundreds of feet away from her, I could zoom into her face and she was thirty-eight hot. "I'M COMING, MAMA!" I screamed. Then, I looked back at Ms. Washington. "I gotta go!"

"Okay," she replied and walked off. I looked back at the staircase and Mama was now back inside the apartment. Guess it was too hot outside for her to stand there and wait for me.

Once I opened the mailbox, I grabbed the mail and began walking back toward the staircase. Although I knew I'd get in trouble for doing so, I started fumbling through letter after letter seeing if Dad had sent me any new letters. He'd write to me from time to time, But now that Mama was divorced from him, Dad did tell me during our last visit that Mama would probably start throwing his letters away. Now that I thought about it, I wondered if Mama had been throwing away other letters he'd been sending me. Some of the mail looked like junk mail. A few others were bills. One pink letter stood out. It was from Florida Power & Light. The top of the letter had the word, "URGENT" in bold. What was that about? But once I got to the last piece of mail, that's when I saw I had an envelope addressed to me. My eyes grew wide with happiness.

I got up the staircase and then made my way back inside the apartment. Before I could even close the door, Mama started cussing.

"What the fuck that old, nosey ass black bitch want?!? See! Didn't I tell you to not talk to them damn fucking neighbors?!? Damn, she always in someone's shit, I swear! I can't wait until that old bitch dies! Fat ass, chitlin' eatin' ass bitch!"

Mama was still in her spot, puffing away on another cigarette, going off into a deep rant about Ms. Washington.

"She was just asking me why I was home and how was school," I said as I moved deep into the den and proceeded to hand her the mail.

"And what you tell her?" Mama asked, taking the cigarette from between her lips and holding it in her right hand. She angrily snatched the mail out of my hands with her left hand.

"I told her I was sick. Like you told me to tell everyone...," I said.

"Good!" Mama took a puff from her cigarette and blew smoke in my face.

I instantly began to cough hard.

"Boy, stop overreacting! Ain't no damn cigarette smoke got you coughing like you about to die or something!"

Mama sat upright on the couch and slapped the cigarette in her mouth. Ash fell down her shirt. She quickly flipped through each piece of mail. When she landed on the pink envelope from FP&L, she opened the letter with swiftness. Her laser-focused eyes scanned the letter. "Yeah, yeah, yeah, whatever. You mothafuckas will eventually get yo lil money. Talkin' 'bout they finne disconnect our lights."

"We're about to get our lights cut off?" I had to ask.

Mama looked at me with a flat expression. She smacked her teeth. "Boy, no! They always do that when I'm like a month or two behind. They ain't finne cut shit off up in here. I'll run down to the check cashing store and pay them."

"Mama, I know you don't like me asking questions and whatnot, but I gotta do a homework assignment for my English class. I gotta write about what our parents do for a living. Can you help me out?" I figured since I was on a roll with lies, I might as well lie and finally ask her what she did to make money.

Mama's face twisted. "And how am I supposed to help you?"

"Well, I just need to know what you do for a living... that's all."

"Ughhh! Just make some shit up! Tell them I'm a call center representative. I work as a supervisor for AT&T!"

"But is that true though?"

"NO! DUH! That's why I said make something up! Damn, Dru!"

"Mama, I'm not trying to get on your nerves or nothing like that, but how are we able to survive if you aren't working?"

"And who said I wasn't working?!?" Mama shouted with a raised angry eyebrow. That was my cue to stop, but she ranted on. "When you get old enough, maybe I'll tell you one day. MAYBE. You still a baby and sometimes you so damn immature. There's just some things you don't need to know yet, boy."

"Mama, I'll be fourteen in a few months..."

"Yeah, and that means what exactly?!? Boy, you still a baby. MAYBE. Keyword – MAYBE – when you turn seventeen or eighteen, I'll tell you But even then, there's just certain shit you don't need to know."

I shrugged my shoulders. "I mean, I know that Dad sold drugs."

Mama rolled her eyes. "Yeah, well, he told you that. He felt comfortable telling you that. And I don't feel comfortable letting you in on all my business. Just focus on being a kid. That's all you need to worry about. Okay?"

"Okay... well, I saw Dad sent me a letter. Can I have it?"

All of a sudden, Mama grabbed my face and yanked me into hers. "So, you went through my shit?"

My eyes popped out of my head with fear, now she was about to fuck me up again. I just knew it. "No, Mama! I just—"

"DON'T FUCKING LIE TO ME! HOW DID YOU KNOW YOU GOT A LETTER FROM YOUR DAD IF YOU DIDN'T GO THROUGH MY SHIT?!?"

Feeling anxious, knowing I was about to get my ass beat again, my body became tight. I clenched my fists. Now, I was ready not to be a slave to her shit no more, so I knew I was gonna have to defend myself. I was gonna have to fight her now. I'd be damned if I was gonna take another beating. My head was already fucked up from her busting that lamp across my head. Bruises were still on my back and parts of my legs from her whipping. I swear to God if this bitch was about to put her hands on me again, she was definitely going to die!

She looked down at me. "Oh, you ballin' up your fists?!? You finne fight me, nigga?!? That's what you wanna do?!?" she shrieked.

My eyes watered. My breathing was deep and fast.

"COME ON THEN! LET'S FIGHT! SHOW ME WHAT THE FUCK YOU WORKIN' WITH! SINCE YOU WANNA BEAT MY ASS SO BADLY, LET ME SEE IF YOU GOT SOME SKILLS, PUNK ASS NIGGA!"

Mama screamed, shoving me toward the coffee table. She instantly shot up from the couch, threw her fists up, swaying her arms side to side like she was a boxer.
BAM! BAM! BAM!
"POLICE! OPEN UP!"

CHAPTER NINE

Mama was squared up with me, just about to ready deliver me a Mike Tyson uppercut. But when both of us heard the three loud pounds on the front door, we both instantly halted what was gonna be our ultimate showdown. We tossed our eyes toward the front door.

BAM! BAM! BAM!

"POLICE, I SAID OPEN UP AGAIN!"

Damn! Did Ms. Washington call the police?!? I just had a feeling her ass was gonna go back to her apartment and call the cops! I knew it! I saw it all in her snitchin' ass eyes. But I was somewhat glad. Now, the fucking police could come in here and see how much of a monster my so-called mother was.

"Why the fuck is the police bamming on my mothafuckin' door!" Mama growled, then cut her eyes at me. She lunged at me, grabbing me by my shirt collar. "You told Ms. Washington I was hitting you?!?"

"NO! Let me go!" I yelled back, slapping her grip away. I was now defiant more than ever.

"WHAT?!? BOY! I SWEAR, I'MMA FUCK YOU UP! I SWEAR TO GOD!"

My rage boiling, I just fucking snapped. "DO IT, BITCH!" Now, I was ready to duke it out with her.

Her face twisted with shock, I guess she never saw my reaction coming. "WHAT DID YOU CALL ME?!?" Mama suddenly cocked her hand back, but she was distracted by another round of pounding on the front door.

BAM! BAM! BAM!

"Open up the door, ma'am!" the police officer roared again, his tone vicious.

Mama froze. She glanced at me and growled. "I swear to God, boy! I SWEAR!" Now, looking thoroughly confused, she trembled with anxiety while scanning the living room. Next thing you know, she rushed to try to tidy up the den.

I ran off near the dining room table, watching Mama go nuts trying to clean up. But no amount of cleaning up was gonna save her ass. *Yeah, bitch! You fucked up now!* I almost wanted to burst out laughing watching her have this unexpected nervous breakdown.

BAM! BAM! BAM!

"Ma'am! I'm not gonna repeat myself! Open up the fucking door! NOW!" Just from the sound of it, I bet some big ass cracker was on the other side of the door ready to arrest Mama's stupid, low-life ass.

"FUCK!" Mama grunted, throwing her hands up in the air. "Coming!" Mama squealed as she lunged at the front door. Her hands quaking with fear, she looked out the peephole. She smacked her teeth, her tense body suddenly relaxing. "OH! That's Rahzel! Why he fuckin' with me?!?" Mama snickered, quickly unlocking and opening the front door. "MAN! You had me nervous like a mothafucka! Why you fuckin' with me?!?"

Rahzel?

Nonstop chuckling entered the apartment as that light-skin nigga Mama was snorting coke with ambled through the door. He was clapping his hands as if he was celebrating pulling off the prank on Mama.

Quiet and motionless, I scanned him up and down, now having a better sight of him. The last time I saw him, I didn't catch a good glimpse of him. But now, I was able to see this new nigga in his entirety. This was the new nigga Mama obviously was fucking. And he reminded me of LL Cool J.

Standing at around six feet tall, he had a shiny, clean-shaved head. A well-trimmed chin strap ran across his wide yet chiseled face. He had a mustache that wasn't too thick but not too thin. Gold-hoop earrings hung from both his ears. As he proceeded to walk into the foyer, he looked around, scanning the apartment as if he hadn't been here before. He took off his gold-rimmed sunglasses and stuffed them in the front pocket of his long-sleeved Versace shirt. I quickly looked down at his right wrist and saw he had on a diamond-studded Rolex or something like that. One solid gold ring was on his right ring finger. That shit was bedazzling. Whoever this dude was definitely was rolling in money. This obviously had to be the dude taking care of Mama, which explained why her lazy ass didn't have a fucking job.

Mama closed the door behind him. All over him, she picked lint and wrinkles out of his shirt. She'd do this same shit to Tay'Quan when she dressed him up in new clothes. "Why you playing fucking games with me, man?!? I really thought that was five-o. Thought I was going to jail?"

"Why?" Rahzel asked, his voice deep like an ocean. The moment he opened his mouth, nothing but gold flashed out of his mouth. However, his gold grill wasn't like my dad's. This nigga had a few diamonds in his shit. Ironically, his flashy teeth didn't stand out to me the most though. This nigga's voice did. He sounded scary as fuck. I really wasn't paying attention to how he sounded that night I heard him talking to Mama. But now that he was standing feet away from me, I carefully analyzed this dude while becoming terrified by the deepness of his voice. Nigga sounded like he'd murdered for fun. He glanced over at me and smiled, once again flashing his gold teeth. "'Cause you was fightin' the young god over there?"

"Boy, no!" Mama laughed.

"So, why were you scared then? What shady shit you doin' up in here?"

"Man, nothing! Just have a seat," Mama said, playfully smacking her teeth. "I forgot you were coming over..."

"How'd you forget?" he asked through a snicker as he still kept his eyes on me. "And aren't you gonna introduce me to the young god?"

Mama then looked over at me, her eyes turned to slits. "Come on over here, Dru. I want you to meet one of my friends. This is Mr. Rahzel."

Cautiously ambling into his presence, my gaze widened with anxiety. This man was built like he played football or something. Like, he was big but muscular at the same time. I looked at his fists and I swear to God they were the size of bricks.

This Rahzel nigga's eyes had a fierceness to them I'd never seen before. It was as if he could stare directly into you and burn a hole in your heart. I genuinely was afraid to even shake this man's hand but had to now that he reached out his meaty, bear paw-like hand. I slowly reached my hand out and shook his. "Hello," I muttered.

Rahzel let out a light laugh. "Don't be afraid, young god. I'm Rahzel. Close friend of the family. What's your name?"

"Andrew... Andrew Geter..."

"Okay, Mr. Andrew Geter... nice to meet you, young god.

As-Salaam 'Alaikum," he replied in his thick New York accent. How did Mama even know a guy from New York City? Maybe she met this man at a nightclub or something...

"Nice to meet you as well, sir." I didn't know what he just said, but I swear I heard it before in a movie. I think in that Spike Lee movie, Malcolm X. Was this man a Muslim or something?

I didn't know how to respond. Rahzel then said, "You're supposed to say *Wa 'Alaikum As-Salaam*. Do you know what that means, young black God?"

"No... what does that mean? I think I heard it before, but I don't know what it means..."

"*As-Salaam 'Alaikum* means Peace Be Unto You. When someone tells you that, you supposed to reply back with *Wa 'Alaikum As-Salaam*. That means, And Peace But Unto You As Well. Say it with me... As-Salaam 'Alaikum."

"As-Salaamalikum," I replied, attempting my best to mimic what Rahzel uttered.

"Good... perfect, young black God..."

Why did he keep calling me that? God? I wasn't God. And I really wish he'd stopped calling me black. And how can God be black? Jesus is white. None of what he was saying really was making sense to me.

"Rahzel, he too young to understand all of that Five Percenter stuff."

"Why is he too young?" Rahzel asked, his piercing eyes still glued to me. "How old are you, young god? Thirteen? Fourteen?"

"Thirteen, sir," I slowly replied, my eyes unblinking.

"Thirteen." Rahzel smacked his teeth and stared at Mama with judging eyes. "This boy old enough to understand the Supreme Wisdom. I can see it all in his eyes. He can learn much more too," he snickered in his deathly, bass-heavy voice.

"One day," Mama said. "Well, have a seat." She smiled, hugging all up on Mr. Rahzel. "I've been missing you so much."

Mentally smacking my teeth, it was obvious by now Mr. Razhell wasn't just a family friend. He was one of Mama's boyfriends.

"Yeah, I bet. I've been missing you, too... although I just saw your crazy ass last Saturday."

"Yeah, but these past few days I've been so lonely."

Mr. Rahzel grinned, playfully smacking his teeth. "Yeah right, Earth. You know damn well you've been messing around with some other goofies while I was gone."

"No, I wasn't!" Mama quickly retorted with a sad, puppy face. Fake ass bitch. I wondered if Mr. Rahzel knew Mama was a two-timing hoe. He'd better not trust her raggedy ass. Then, again, they were both doing coke together, so he definitely knew she was a hoe. And only a hoe would have sex in a bathroom when other people were around. Just like in the movies...

"Yeah, yeah, yeah... anyways, what's up? When you finne move out of this rat hole?" Rahzel inquired as he moved into the den and sat on the big couch, kicking his feet up on the table, stretching his arms out as if he paid rent. Then, again, he probably did. Probably paid for a lot of shit around here it seemed, with the way he got so super-comfortable.

Knowing that Mama would get mad at me if she noticed I was paying too much attention to their conversation, I began to slowly make an exit out of the den.

"Where you goin', young god?" Mr. Rahzel suddenly asked. "I ain't talking about anything inappropriate with your mother. You can stay if you like. Besides, I wanna teach you the Supreme Wisdom..."

"Umm... he needs to go to his room. He's on punishment!" Mama snapped.

"Punishment for what? What he do?" Rahzel raised a brow. "This boy looks smart as hell. And he's respectful. Boy don't even look like he'd fight an ant."

"For back-talking me! That's why!" Mama growled, staring directly at me.

My head hung low out of embarrassment, I didn't say a word.

Rahzel smacked his teeth. "Young black God, lift your head high! Don't let these blue-eyed devils see you walking around with your head low. That's that the first way the white man will psychologically defeat you. Fuck up your self-confidence. Come over here..."

Near the entrance of the hallway, I looked over at Mama. She rolled her eyes. I was starting to like Mr. Rahzel. This nigga was putting up a challenge to Mama's stupidity. And truth be told, he sounded like he read a lot, too. I wondered if he went to college. He was very charismatic with his words. I wondered if he was a lawyer or a professor. I proceeded to walk back into the den and then stood in front of Mama and Mr. Razhell, as they both sat next to each other on the couch.

"Now, what you get in trouble for?" Mr. Rahzel asked.

I looked at Mama, not knowing what exact response to give this man. If I told him the truth, he may not believe it. But then again, he may check Mama, put her stupid ass in her place. However, I was still too fearful of what the consequences would be if I spilled the truth about Mama and her lunacy. But something told me Mr. Rahzel would protect me if I just told him the truth. I could feel it. He kept calling me God, so maybe he saw something in me. Maybe he was smart enough to read my mind, read my body language, read my soul and know all the bullshit I had to go through dealing with this wench.

"Well, asking too many questions..." I knew that was a response vague enough to not be accusing Mama of fucking me up. But it would also trigger him to ask more questions. He'd probably wonder how in the fuck could someone get in trouble for asking too many questions.

"What?!? Asking too many questions?" Mr. Rahzel looked at Mama. But by this point, Mama's attention turned away from me and she rolled her eyes huffing. "Yeah, he asks too damn questions. Things he don't need to be knowing," Mama responded, annoyance laced in her tone.

"That's ludicrous as fuck. Yo, young god, tell me... what kind of questions you've been asking your *muhva*?" Man, his New York accent was so thick, but there was something so alluring about it. Shoot, I wanted a New York accent now. He sounded so slick and cool as fuck. Just like in the movies, too. Like, this dude could really be an actor!

"Well, I just wanted to know about what my father did to go into prison. That's all. Along with what Mama does for a living. I mean, I always have questions, but Mama just shuts me down every time. Says it's inappropriate for a child to ask adults certain types of questions."

"Your father? Andrew Sr.?" Rahzel then glanced back at Mama. "So, all this time the young god don't know about his pops and his history in the streets?"

"No! He don't need to know that!"

"Ahhh, you trippin'! You know I knew your pops. Cool dude. Made some crazy choices, but he's a good dude. Solid head on his shoulder. You visit your pops?"

"When I get a chance to..."

"That's cool. Stay in contact with him. A lot of young brothas need to have a father figure in their life. I wish I had one. I mean, I have one now though. All Praise Be To Allah. But every young black man needs a strong father in their life," he explained. And I agreed. And you'd think Mama would agree too and not be so quick to try to cut me off from trying to have a relationship with my dad.

"I agree, Mr. Rahzel," I replied.

"So... what?!? You wanna mentor my son now?"

"Shoot... why not?!? I got a lot of time on my hands now. Shit, I'm settled down in Miami for good now. Business is booming. I'm looking for a young disciple for my army."

"Nah! He just needs to focus on school. All that other stuff you talkin' ain't for him. Besides, I don't want him to end up like his daddy! You see where that got him!"

"Who said I wanted to take the young god out of school?" Mr. Rahzel shot back. He then looked at me and said, "You got a girlfriend, young god? You gettin' pussy?"

"RAH! DON'T SAY THAT AROUND HIM! GOSH!"

Rahzel playfully nudged Mama with his elbow. "Sorry about that, young god. I don't wanna disrespect your mother... anyways... let me holla at your mother in private for a second and then we'll talk later. Okay?"

"Yessir..."

"Aiight, God."

I walked off and made my way down the hallway. I was tempted to eavesdrop and listen to whatever conversation Mama was about to have with Mr. Rahzel. I stopped for a moment and thought if I should listen to what they were talking about. So, I quietly spun on my feet and crept down the hallway, walking on the tips of my toes. With Tay'Quan's room being the first room on the left side of the hallway, I leaned up against his door and carefully listened.

"So, what's up? You gon hook me up?" I could hear Mama asking.

"Yeah, I am. Here... take this. This should last you for a while. You probably could make twenty-stacks off that. But you not gon rock that up in the house with these kids in here, are you?" I heard Mr. Rahzel ask Mama.

"Hell nah, boy! I'm finne take this over to my girl Shaniqua's spot and rock it up there. That's where we always cook it up at. And then we got her cousin serving for us."

"Good... I'm not a work from home-type of nigga."

"Shit, I ain't either!"

"Yeah, I know..." Then, I heard what sounded like a smack on Mama's thigh. "You can't make your other dollars in this roach motel."

"Boy, fuck you."

"You never answered my other question. When you plan on moving out of this spot?"

"Shit, not anytime soon. Besides, I like to be low-key. Yeah, I could move down south or over to Pembroke Pines, but I like where I stay. Nobody fucks with me over here. You know I love to keep a low profile."

"Girl, you trippin'. This shit ain't low profile at all. If anything, you need to move to where them white folks and rich Cubans are at. That's a low profile."

"Yeah, well, until I start making some real cash, then I'll consider it."

"Well, baby, you already know the moves I'm making. Once I make this trip to Colombia, I'm finne put everyone on. You first..." Then, I heard what sounded like wet kisses being exchanged.

My naïve eyes amplified with confusion and shock at the same time as I continued to listen to the rest of their conversation. I finally got one of my questions answered finally. *What does your mother do for a living?* Sell drugs for a nigga named Rahzel. What the fuck kind of name was that any damn way? By this point, I had heard enough and I didn't want to get into trouble for snooping in their business. So, I cautiously turned around and tip-toed back down the hallway and into my room, quietly closing my door.

This was the second time my mind was blown today. I couldn't believe Mama was selling crack. My heart almost exploded out of my chest now that I knew the truth about what she was doing to make a living. This shit was so unbelievable, but it all made perfect sense. My mama was a crack dealer. Both of my parents were drug dealers. Now that I knew this, I was determined not to do the same.

CHAPTER TEN

There were times I used to pray to God, asking him why he made me black. Why put me in this color of skin if you knew people wouldn't like it? But another thing I'd ask God was why give me the parents I had? Why make me be born to people who seemed to be so irresponsible and reckless with their decisions? I just wished I could've been born in a normal family. I wish Mama was a lawyer or a doctor. Dad seemed like he could be a lawyer himself, too. Or an accountant. He'd probably be a good accountant if he knew how to sell a lot of drugs in the streets. I wished we lived in a big house with a big ass backyard, pool and jacuzzi. Wished we live somewhere far from Opa Locka and Liberty City. Somewhere that was much safer and had better schools. Somewhere that just seemed normal...

Now that I knew Mama was making her own money, not necessarily getting it from guys, I grew kind of mad wondering why in the fuck she kept us here in this raggedy ass apartment. Shit, from the sound of it, Rahzel wondered the same damn thing, too. But that's how I knew Mama was nothing more than a straight up hood rat. She couldn't and wouldn't see the need to leave the hood. Opa Locka was her stomping ground. She swore she was the Queen of this part of the city.

But I wasn't gonna stay here. Soon as I graduated and went off to college, I was gonna move far away from Opa Locka. I'd even leave Miami. I wanna go somewhere like New York City or Los Angeles, where people with real money and power lived. From what I've seen on TV, you go to those cities when you've made it. That was why once I graduated from college, I was gonna become a doctor in either of those cities, never to return to Miami again. I fucking hated the ghetto.

Lying in bed, I stared up to the dusty white ceiling thinking about everything I just learned about Mama. I'd been in my room for about a good hour now while Mama and Mr. Rahzel were still out in the den. I still couldn't wrap my mind around Mama being a drug dealer. Shit was unbelievable, but this was a fact I just had to accept. Honestly, at this point, she wasn't Mama to me no more. I didn't even know what to call her. *Maybe I should just start calling her by her first name.*

"Shalanda. Shalanda. Shalanda," I uttered her first name. "Shalanda Greene." I'd never called her by her first name before, but I should start now just to start fucking with her. And if she tried to fight me, I'd beat that bitch's ass. As much as I just wanted her to be my mother and for her to love me like any other mother would love their son, I had to get over that shit. The little respect I had for her was now gone. She was really no different than any other street nigga. It made perfect sense why she always tried so hard to clamp down on my dreams.

"YOUNG GOD! Lemme holla at you for a sec!" I heard Rahzel shout from the den.

I really didn't know how I felt about this Rahzel nigga

either. Yeah, he sounded like he was all smart and whatnot But clearly, this dude was a drug dealer, which meant he was dangerous. I didn't want any parts to what the fuck he had going on. I turned my gaze toward my bedroom door, contemplating whether or not I wanted to get up and see what the fuck he wanted with me. He did tell me he wanted to speak to me before I left. I didn't want to be disrespectful and I also didn't Mama to get on me again, so I plopped myself out of the bed, stretched and then made my way back into the den.

"Yes, sir," I announced, now standing back in front of Mama and Rahzel.

"Young black God! What you got going on this summer? You going to summer school?"

Glancing over at Mama, she nodded her head to the side and gave me this look. This look suggesting I had to tell him I had nothing going on.

"No, I don't have anything going on, sir."

"Good. 'Cause I talked to your mama and she told me you need a job for this summer. You wanna make some money?"

I looked back at Mama. Her eyes grew wide. That was her look to tell me yes.

"Can I ask you a question?"

Rahzel smiled, his gold grill glowing. "Wassup?"

"What do you do for a living?" I needed to ask, although I knew what the answer was.

Rahzel looked at Mama. "Can I tell him?"

"Sure," she said.

He looked back at me. "I used to be a boxer but now I own a boxing gym. A few other businesses, too."

I hesitated for a split second. "Oh... oh okay." I just knew this nigga was lying, but I obviously wasn't going to continue to press him.

"That's why I wanted to see what you were doing this summer, young god."

"Ain't no need to ask him what he gonna do. He's GONNA do it! Shit, he need to lose that weight! His stupid black, fat ass walkin' around here with diabetes and whatnot. So damn ridiculous."

"HEY! What the fuck is wrong with you?!?" Rahzel barked at Mama. My fat, black ass flinched hearing his heavy voice. Mama shook too. "Yo, don't talk to him like that! All of that isn't necessary! Is that how you talk to him all the time?"

Mama stared off, not looking at anything in particular. She couldn't immediately come up with words.

Without hesitation, Rahzel yanked Mama into his face. "Answer me, bitch! Is that how you fucking talk to him all the time?"

"Oww! Let me go! You're hurting me!" Mama cried.

"ANSWER ME! Don't fucking try to act all scared now! Why the fuck would you say some shit like that?!?"

I started to get scared 'cause now it looked like he was about to fuck Mama up on site. A part of me wanted to get ready to fight him 'cause this was my mother and I was supposed to defend her, but there was another part of me that wanted to see him beat the shit out of her. And I knew he'd do it, too.

"No... no... not all the time," Mama mumbled.

"Bitch, look at me when you talking to me! Don't look away! Look at me. I think you're fucking lying!" Rahzel snapped. Rahzel then looked at me. "Yo, young god, your mother talks to you like this all the time?"

I didn't know what to say. I was afraid, but I was also willing to snitch on this evil ass bitch. My nervous eyes danced between the both of them. Mama looked at me like she was ready to cry. Rahzel looked at me as if I really needed to tell the truth. If not, then he'd fuck me up. So, I went ahead and told the truth. "Yes. Yes, she does."

Suddenly, Rahzel cocked his hand back.

"NO! NOO! No, Mr. Rahzel!" I charged at Rahzel and grabbed his arm. "Don't hit her!"

With his wide-open eyes glued to my hand on his arm, he glanced up at me. Then, this demonic smile stretched across his face, once again revealing his full set of glimmering gold teeth. He began chuckling and released Mama from his grip. He shoved her then started clapping, laughing uncontrollably. "Damn...you really love your mother, I see. You know the Fifth Commandment then. You know that the Fifth Commandment is, young god?"

"No, sir."

"Honor thy father and thy mother that thy days may be long." Rahzel then stood up, stretched then adjusted his expensive ass Versace shirt. With a mean mug on his face, he looked down at Mama saying, "Shalanda, I'mma give you a call before I swing by and pick up the young black God. And clean up this mothafuckin' apartment. It smells like shit up in here."

"Okay," she replied. I could hear the nervousness in her voice. Damn, I ain't never heard Mama sound so terrified before in her life. Rahzel must've really been a dangerous ass nigga for her to act this way.

Rahzel then turned his attention toward me, once again grinning. "Young god, I'mma be here on Saturday to pick you up. You and I are gonna hang out."

"O-okay," I stuttered. I was nervous as shit, too.

Rahzel reached his hand out. "Give me dap, young god." Reaching my hand out, he pulled me in and then hugged me. He leaned down into my ear and said, "Next time she start some shit with you, you have my permission to beat her ass. Understand, young god? Just because she's your mother doesn't mean she has the right to talk to you like you're a piece of shit."

"Yes, sir."

"Good. Now, go back to your room and study. Why aren't you in school?"

I quickly looked at Mama and then back at Rahzel saying, "Well, I'm sick. Mama didn't want me to go to school."

"Boy, you ain't fucking sick. You're going to school tomorrow. Early and prompt, too." Rahzel threw his lethal gaze back onto Mama. "Ain't that right, Shalanda? He's going to school, right?"

"Yes. Yes he is," she replied, obvious fear still etched in her voice.

Rahzel then looked back at me. "Young black God, you like school, right?"

"Yes. Yes, I do, sir."

"Good. Don't be like the rest of these deaf, dumb and blind niggas. That's the eight-five percent. You are a God – that means you're supposed to know everything. Stay your ass in school."

"I will, sir."

"And stop calling me sir. Call me Rahzel."

"Okay, Rahzel."

Rahzel grinned then snickered, shaking his head as he began to walk toward the door. "I'll be back on Saturday. Word is bond."

"Okay, Rahzel," Mama replied, snatching a pack of cigarettes off the coffee table. She fumbled trying to get a cigarette from the pack. Just before Rahzel was about to open and walk out of the door, he punched the door; the entire walls of the house quaked. Both Mama and I gasped and shook. "I don't want you smoking those death sticks around these young gods, either. Throw that shit away," he commanded.

"Yes!" she screeched, suddenly throwing the loose square and the pack of cigarettes back onto the coffee table.

"Good,!" roared Rahzel. He looked at me again while opening the front door. Blinding, blazing sunlight filling the entire foyer. All I could see was his wide silhouette, but I heard him say, "As Salaamu Alaikum, young god."

"Wa 'Alaikum As-Salaam," I returned the greeting.

Rahzel proceeded to walk out. But just as he was about to close his door, he stuck his head back inside and said, "And Shalanda. Stop stripping. That shit is dead. You work for me now one-hundred percent. I don't want you shaking your ass and titties in that raggedy ass nightclub anymore. You understand?"

"Yes..." Mama screeched, clasping her chest as she was caught by surprise. Rahzel slammed the door. I dashed up to the window in the den and pulled the blinds back to see what kind of car he was about to get into. Looking from side to side and wiping his head free of sweat, he casually walked up to a cream-colored Mercedes two-door S-Class sitting on gold rims. My eyes ready to pop out of their sockets, I knew Rahzel wasn't just some regular drug dealer. He had to be selling lots of dope. There were three types of niggas that I knew drove those types of whips: athletes, rappers and actors. Rahzel was neither, but he obviously had money as if he was one of those types of niggas.

"SHIT! What time is it?" Mama rasped, shooting up from the couch. She dashed into the kitchen. "Shit! I gotta go get Tay'Quan! I'll be back later tonight 'cause I gotta go to this mandatory meeting at Tay'Quan's school!"

I still stood at the den window, peering out into the parking lot as I watched Rahzel take off in his car. Damn, I really wanna drive something like that when I get older. Everyone would like me and respect me if I drove around in the streets with a fresh ass ride like that. Mama's words went through one ear and out the other as my eyes latched onto the spinning gold rims on Rahzel's coupe.

"Andrew! Did you hear me?"

I turned around. "Yes, Mama," I replied.

"Okay, good," Mama said in a strange, tender voice. She then rushed down the hallway to her room. She had to be nervous as fuck. Her entire demeanor was different. It was as if at the snap of Rahzel's fingers, she turned into a completely different woman. A woman I didn't recognize at all. Damn, Rahzel really put the fear of God in her.

As much as I kind of didn't trust that nigga, I liked the fact that he put her ass in her place. Too bad Dad wasn't here to do that. I knew he would've checked her ass, too. And Mama knew that, too. But because Dad was locked up and couldn't check her ass behind prison bars, Mama acted like she had the absolute power to do any and everything she wanted to do. Even abuse me. But now it seemed like the days of her fucking with me were over. Although I knew little about Rahzel, I hoped he stayed around long enough to keep her ass at bay. After all, he did give me the permission to fuck her up. Yeah, I think I'm gonna like that nigga...

Mama scurried back down the hallway, then dashed over to the dining room table. She grabbed her keys and purse and flew to the front door. But just as she was about to open the door, she paused and looked at me. "Are you hungry, Andrew?"

I didn't know if this was some trick question or not, but I didn't want to agitate her 'cause I knew her nerves were fucked up. "Not really, Mama. I'm fine..."

"Okay, well, if you get hungry, I'm gonna leave $40 on the table. Order you a pizza or something if you get hungry, okay?" She rummaged her purse and then pulled out two, twenty-dollar bills and put them on the dining room table.

My eyes exploded with shock. I couldn't believe Mama

was giving me forty-dollars to order anything I wanted. "Okay, Mama."

She stared at me for a moment, her lips pursed. For a second, I thought she was gonna utter words I never thought I'd hear out of her mouth. She slowly opened and began to fix her lips as if she was gonna say them. Then, she shut her mouth and rushed out of the apartment, quickly locking the door.

CHAPTER ELEVEN

Amirah.
That was her name. Amirah Paschal.
I had no idea what her name meant, but one thing was certain to me – her name was just as beautiful as she was. My unblinking eyes were gifted the sight of the most beautiful girl I'd ever seen before in my life. On God, I wasn't lying.

Amirah was dark, but a different type of dark. Her complexion possessed a tinge of mahogany. Long jet-black hair ran down her back, damn near touching her plump ass. She wasn't skinny nor fat – she was the perfect size for the type of girl I'd like. But what really drew me in were her glowing, caramel doe eyes. I swear they were putting a spell on me. I wondered where she was from. She didn't look Cuban or Dominican. Then, again, she could be Cuban or Dominican, maybe even Panamanian, but she looked Indian. Maybe she was Jamaican... or even Trinidadian. I didn't know, but I hoped to ask her. Her looks was not what made her seem different from the rest of the girls at school though. Truth be told, there were a lot of fine girls that went here. Nyla was cute. Tashianna was fine, too. But most of the fine girls were straight-up hood rats. Amirah seemed like she had class though. Something told me she wasn't from Opa Locka. Probably not even from Miami. I hoped to ask…

I hadn't noticed her when she first wandered into the classroom moments earlier. I was too busy trying to get caught up on some reading. But when I heard Mrs. Tate announce, "Oh, you must be my new student. Amirah. Amirah Paschal, right?", I looked up and instantaneously froze in place, all of my mind, heart and soul kidnapped by her presence. *Was this love?*

"Yes, ma'am," she had replied.

Then, Mrs. Tate said, "You can sit anywhere you like… class will be starting shortly." Mrs. Tate glanced at me smiling and then uttered, "That is Andrew over there. He's nice. He won't bite."

"Good morning," I mumbled to her, still motionless but my hands trembling with anxiety.

"Good morning. Nice to meet you," she said back to me in her soft voice. She picked a seat a few seats up from me. She looked around, seeming a tad nervous. She took her purple JanSport book bag off her shoulders and sat down.

I was in love. Well, I think I was in love… shit, I ain't really know what love was, but I could *feel* it now. Felt it deep down in my chest and stomach. My anxious hands still somewhat shaking, I kept staring at the back of her head. I knew I wouldn't feel this way if I wasn't in love.

Still starving myself to lose this damn weight, I had been hungry all morning. But now, I wasn't hungry anymore. Amirah kept me full just thinking about how pretty she was.

This morning was the first time ever I woke up at 4 am. Especially for school. At first, I thought maybe it was just the thrill of getting back here. God knew I didn't wanna stay at home another day with Mama's crazy, trifling ass. And now that I thought about it, I was so damn thankful Rahzel came by and got Mama's rotten ass in check. Hell, he was the one who scared her into making me come back here. If I wasn't in school now, I wouldn't have the chance to see Amirah. I just knew all of this wasn't just mere coincidence. This had to be my destiny. Amirah and I were going to be together.

The first period bell hadn't even rang yet, and she and I were now alone in the class. Mrs. Tate was out in the hallway monitoring the hall. Since I was in Honors English, not too many kids were in my class anyway.

I closed my textbook and then thought for a second if I should say something. But I was so scared. But maybe now was the time to stop being so shy. Then, again, I was fat, ugly and black as fuck. Why would she even give me the time of day?

Kendrick, one of my classmates, strolled into the classroom. Although Kendrick was this lanky, goofy dude, he was cool and he usually kept to himself. Playing with the small twists in his hair, he said, "Oh, we got a new kid." He made his way over to his usual seat in the back of the first row. Looking over at me, he asked, "Where you been at, Black?"

"I was sick," I started the lie up again. Although I hated it when people called me out of my name, Kendrick and I were kind of cool, so I didn't get pissed when he called me black.

"What happened to your head?" Kendrick asked, I guess noticing the bandage on my head.

"I fell down the stairs at my house," I told him.

"Shit! Boy, that had to be a hard ass fall!"

"Yeah, it was. I had to get eight stitches," I said while shaking my head, turning my attention back to Amirah's head. I needed to stop staring at her before she thought I was a stalker or something.

"DAYYUMMM! I ain't never had stitches!" Kendrick shouted. "Excuse me! What's your name?" he hurled over at Amirah.

She slowly turned around and looked at Kendrick. "I'm Amirah."

"Where you from? You new or something?"

"Yeah... I'm from Orlando," she said. "Just moved down here recently."

"Oh, okay. Cool. Well, I'm Kendrick. Nice to meet you."

"Nice to meet you as well," she said then turned back into her seat, lowering her head. Now that I had an opportunity to hear her speak more, she sounded a tad sad. I wondered what was to that.

Some moments later, more students trickled into the room.

The school bell rang.

Mrs. Tate, who was a short, blonde white woman, the only white teacher in the school, bumbled back into the classroom, closing the door behind her. She happily strolled over to her podium and whipped a bunch of packets from underneath. "We're gonna be reading some Shakespeare starting next week. We'll be starting with Romeo and Juliet," she said. "But before we begin, I wanna introduce the class to a new student. Her name is Amirah."

The rest of the day had been a blur since I had my mind focused on Amirah. I tried so hard to get that girl's face out of my mind, but I couldn't. Damn, this feeling I carried had to be love. It just had to be.

I saw her in the cafeteria during lunch, but she was busy talking to a bunch of other girls. I had to approach her during the right time. I didn't know when that time would be though. But hell, what was I even thinking trying to talk to her? I just knew she had to be into guys like Tyrone. My intuition kept telling me that she had a thing for light-skin niggas.

That was why when I got home, I needed to bleach myself again. I think if I started giving myself a second round, it might make me lighten up faster.

I had just got out of my fourth period class and I was making my way to Ms. Reid's class. Zipping through the crowded hallway, I got to her classroom about a good ten minutes before the final bell would ring. I walked in, noticing I was the first one in the class. Ms. Reid was sitting at her desk when she glanced up at me and said, "Andrew! You're back. Let's talk for a second!"

"Yes, ma'am," I responded, walking over to her desk.

"Have a seat next to me. Let's talk," she instructed, looking over my shoulder toward the door. I took my book bag off and sat in a seat next to her.

Staring deep into my eyes, I could tell she probably had a million questions about why I was gone and why exactly my mother didn't want me to go to MAST Academy. Taking a deep breath, she pursed her lips and her eyes turned into curious slits. "Andrew... I want you to know that I really care a lot about my students. Honestly, out of all the students, I really think about you the most. That was the only reason why I wanted to go over to your house the other night. I'm sorry if I was intrusive, but I just felt like it was the right thing to do, considering I want to see you go to MAST Academy."

"I understand," I replied solemnly.

"I'm glad you do. You're so smart and you have a bright future ahead of you. You're exceptionally talented when it comes to math and science. It would be such a shame if you didn't go to that school, too, because not too many children of color get into that school. And not too many black boys get into schools like that, too."

"Why is that?"

"Because... sometimes, those schools are set up in such a

way to keep boys like you out. Have you ever heard of the saying, 'You have to work twice as hard to be half as good'?"

"No... what does that mean?"

"Well, you're a young black boy about to become a man. And unfortunately, in our society, racism still exists. I am sure you know that. I'm sure your mother tells you that all the time. And because of racism, black people have to really work hard to prove that we are even fifty-percent as good as white person. There's a white boy out there right now who is not even as smart as you are and, yet, he will be able to get into any school he chooses simply because of his race. Especially if his parents know the right people. But young black kids like you have to damn near be Einsteins just to get into certain schools." She continued, "Anyways. Enough about that. I'm glad you're back in school. I was about to call home and ask what was going on. I heard you were sick." Ms. Reid stole a quick glimpse of my head and then stared back at me. "What happened to your head?"

"I fell," I had to lie. Ms. Reid was nice and all. I knew she meant well. But at this point, seeing how Rahzel had control over Mama, there was no need to worry about telling Ms. Reid or any other person about what was truly going on. For starters, I still felt like it was none of their business. And now that Rahzel was going to be a constant presence around the house, I figured I'd rather let him deal with Mama than the police or DCFS.

"You fell? How?"

"I fell down the staircase at my apartment complex."

"How did that happen?"

"My shoes were untied." I kept telling lie after lie.

"You're not lying to me, are you? Andrew... I really care for you. If your mother is hurting you, you can tell me."

"I understand. There's nothing going on. I really did fall."

"So, what were you sick with?"

"I had a little cold. That's all."

"And you're fine now?"

"Yes, ma'am."

Damn, Ms. Reid must've been related to Ms. Washington with all these fucking questions she kept asking me. I should've seen this coming though.

"Well, Andrew, if there's anything that's going on at home, you can always tell me. I promise you I won't go back and tell your mother." Although my back was turned toward the door, I could hear students strolling into the classroom. Ms. Reid looked over my should saying, "Y'all just have a seat. I'm talking to Andrew for a moment."

"I will," I lied again.

Ms. Reid got quiet for a moment and then exhaled. "Well, that's all I wanted to tell you. I hope you had a chance to do all the reading while you were out."

"I did."

"Good. You can go back to your seat now."

Soon as I stood and turned around, I instantly froze in place.

Amirah...

She was inside the classroom... and she was sitting at the table I usually sat at. Each table inside the science classroom was wide, long and black, seating two people. She was sitting on the right, her gaze glued to the inside of a black and white composition book.

Suddenly, my heart began to flutter all over again. My hunger pangs were on a roller coaster all day, but even they came to a screeching halt once that fuzzy, warm sensation returned to the bottom of my stomach.

I slowly strolled over to the table. She looked up at me and produced a smile. "Hey... you're Andrew, right?"

"Hey... yeah. I'm Andrew. Amirah, right?"

"Yeah. Is there assigned seating?" she asked, still smiling at me. By now, I almost wanted to throw up.

"Ughh, n-no. No. Not really," I stuttered, my mouth flung wide open. Shit, I hope I wasn't drooling.

"Oh, okay. Cool."

"I usually sit here though," I said nervously. I didn't want her to get up and find another seat.

"Oh, do you mind?"

No! Don't get up! Don't get up!

"Nah. Not at all. You can sit there. I was just saying... just in case you were wondering why I was sitting next to you," I replied as I pulled the seat out from under the chair and sat down. I tossed my book bag down to the side of the desk, opened it up and pulled out my science book.

"Is this class hard?" she asked, her flowery scent streaming into my nose. Damn, she smelled beautiful, too.

"No... well... I don't know. I guess it depends. I mean, it is almost May. School will be over in less than two months. I mean, are you good in science? Ms. Reid is kind of hard to the other kids. But I love science."

"I love science, too," she stated.

"That's a good thing. You wanna be a doctor?"

"Yeah... you?"

"Yeah, I do. I wanna be a surgeon."

"Oh, that's cool. I wanna be an oncologist."

"What's that?"

"They study and treat cancer."

"Oh, wow. Why you wanna be that?"

"Well, my mother had breast cancer. She just died from it. That's why I moved down here. To stay with my grandparents. My grandparents on my dad's side."

I fell silent for a second, not knowing what to say. "Oh, I'm sorry to hear that. I, umm—"

"It's okay. It's not your fault. No need to apologize."

"I heard you tell Kendrick you're from Orlando. Is that where you were born and raised?" I had to ask.

"Yeah... well, my mother was from Trinidad. My dad is Black. But he's in prison, so that's why I'm staying with my grandma and grandpa," she explained.

"Oh, yeah. Well, my dad's in prison, too."

"Yeah?"

I lowered my head to the table out of slight shame. Shit, I didn't even know why. I think it was just an automatic reflex, given I was still so embarrassed knowing my dad was in prison. Granted, I knew other kids had fathers in prison, but there was just still something so embarrassing having to reveal that to people. I always felt like people would judge you and look at you differently if they knew that about you. In fact, anybody at my school who I talked to from time to time didn't know that. If they asked about my dad, I just told them he lived in a different state for work.

"Well, looks like we already have something in common, right?" she asked smilingly.

"I guess," I somewhat chuckled.

"SHABBA RANKS' SON! YOU'RE BACK!"

I looked up and saw Tyrone sauntering into the classroom with this devilish grin plastered across his face. "Bruh, I miss your black ass! You look like you got a bit lighter!"

"Tyrone! Sit your ass down before I send you to CSI! I'm getting sick of your mess! Leave Andrew alone! This is my last warning to you!" Ms. Reid shouted.

Tyrone glanced over at Amirah. "Damn, we got a new student. Hey, sexy. What's your name?"

Amirah didn't respond. She quickly looked at me and then back at Tyrone, seeming nervous.

"Damn! It's like that, shorty?"

"TYRONE!" Ms. Reid shouted. "That's it! Leave my classroom! The bell hasn't even rung yet and you're already starting your mess. I told you earlier this week to be on your best behavior, but you obviously are hard-headed! For someone to be as smart as you are, you sure are dumb! GET OUT NOW!"

Tyrone smacked his teeth. "Ahh! Come on, Ms. Reid! I was just playing, man!"

"Well, sit your behind down now and SHUT the hell up! And that goes for the rest of you all!"

Every Friday afternoon when the final school bell rang, it seemed like the entire school would shake with a joyful fury. Obviously, everyone was ready to go home and get a break from school.

Mrs. Littlefield was in the middle of giving us weekend homework assignments when she was interrupted by the final bell. All of a sudden, everyone in the classroom exploded out of their seats, quickly packing their book bags to take off.

"AND DO NOT FORGET TO WRITE YOUR ESSAY ABOUT YOUR FAVORITE SONG!" she screamed to the top of her old lungs, hoping every would hear her. But not a single student was paying attention. Not even me. Shit, I was too excited to dash out into the hallway and hopefully catch up with Amirah before the weekend. I had to get one last glimpse and maybe even a conversation out of her before I went home.

I didn't know why I didn't ask for her phone number earlier in Ms. Reid's class. Granted, it probably was a bit too early to make that move. I mean, she did just move down here. And she was living with her grandmother. Her grandma probably wouldn't want anyone, especially a boy, calling her house. And on top of that, asking her for her phone number might actually scare her. She might think I was a stalker or something. Honestly, I still wasn't too sure if she would even be into me like that. With my size, skin color and old clothes, she'd probably just write me off as a nice guy and throw me into the friend zone. Deep down, I just had this feeling I wasn't someone she'd find attractive. And for that reason, this bursting motivation had me energized more than ever to really lighten my skin and lose this damn fat. She was now gonna be my sole reason for transforming myself into the pretty, light-skin nigga I knew she craved. Once I got back home, I was gonna take my ass right back into the bathroom and start another round of bleaching. Then, I was gonna start doing sit-ups, push-ups and jumping jacks in my room.

Now out in the hallway, I zipped through the crowds of students, hoping Amirah was out in the front lawn waiting for her ride. She told me earlier her grandfather was going to be picking her up.

Getting closer to the door, I started to feel nauseous. My stomach was still twisted with so much hunger pain by now, I almost felt like I was about to throw up. But fuck that. I just had to man the fuck up and stop thinking about eating food. Truth be told, the only thing I ate this week were a few apples and water. And I was still fat. So, that meant I had to take up the starvation by a notch or two.

I was now near the front building exit. A sea of students poured out of the open doors and onto the front lawn. Once outside, I paused for a moment, scanning around to see if I could find Amirah. I kept looking around, hoping she hadn't left yet.

Boom! There she was, standing a few feet away from the entrance of the staff parking lot. Dashing in between folks, I made my way over to her. She just stood there by herself, staring off at nothing in particular.

"Hey Amirah," I announced once I strolled up to her.

She turned my direction and smiled. "Hey, Andrew. What's up? What you got going on this weekend?"

"Just hanging out with one of my mama's friends. He wants me to work for him. What about you?"

"Well, I got a bunch of reading and whatnot to do obviously. Besides, my grandparents are strict and they stay up in church. So, I'll probably be going to church all weekend, too. You go to church?"

"Nah. Not really."

"Oh, okay. Yeah, I mean, my mother really wasn't going to church like that when we lived in Orlando. She was actually a Muslim."

"Word. I think Rahzel is a Muslim. As-salaam 'Alaikum. That's a Muslim thing, right?" Damn, I felt kind of stupid.

Suddenly, Amirah exploded into laughter. "Oh, my God! Yes! That is a Muslim thing. Who is Rahzel?"

"That's my mama's friend."

"He's Muslim?"

"I believe so."

"Sunni or Shi'a?"

I shrugged my shoulder, not knowing a damn thing she was talking about. "Ehhhh..."

"Don't worry. Not a lot of people knows what that means... but that's cool you know some things. You know how to return the greeting?"

"Yeah... Wa 'Alaikum As Salaam, right?"

"YUP!" Amirah smiled. "Man, that's cool. You're really cool."

"Thanks... you're cool, too."

"So, is your name Muslim, too, then?"

"Yeah... it is."

"What does it mean, if you don't mind me asking? I mean, I've heard the name before, but I always wondered what it meant."

"Oh, it's Arabic for princess. Amir means prince. Amirah means princess. I know a little Arabic. When I was in Orlando, my mother made me go to Islamic school on the weekends."

"Oh wow. That's dope. It's different?"

"Yeah... but a lot of things are the same. It's just like Islamic Sunday school."

Honk! Honk!

"Amirah! Come on now!"

Both Amirah and I suddenly threw our attention toward the silver Cadillac DeVille idling across the street. An older, brown-skinned black guy with a head full of thick gray hair and a gray goatee began waving.

"Oh, that's my grandpa. Gotta go, Andrew! I guess we'll see each other on Monday!" She smiled.

"Okay... well, I got a quick question for you," I said nervously. Okay, Dru. *This your time. Be a man. Stop being scared. Ask her. Stop being a pussy. Be a man.*

I hesitated for a moment. Amirah's eyes widened with curiosity.

I looked over her shoulder and stared at her grandfather, who even from a hundred feet away looked mean as fuck. *Don't do it. She's gonna say no. Be patient.*

"Nevermind. I'll see you on Monday. Take it easy," I said.

"Take it easy, too. As-Salaam Alaikum," she softly replied with the most angelic smile stretched across her beautiful mocha face.

"Wa 'Alaikum As-Salaam," I replied, feeling gushy. I'm in love. I know it.

Amirah. Princess...

But she ain't no princess...

She's a queen. She's gonna be my queen. Watch and see.

As I watched the Cadillac take off and barrel down the street, I began walking back home, imagining one day me and

Amirah were going to be King and Queen. I could already see it, too. We were gonna get married outdoors on the beach. It would be a perfect day. With not a single cloud floating above, nothing but pure turquoise would fill the skies. The sun would be out, but it wouldn't be too hot. Ocean breeze would keep us all cool. She was gonna walk down that rose petal-filled aisle and be right by my side. I was going to take her hand and slide a million-dollar platinum ring on her finger. Then, she was gonna be mine forever. And I was gonna be hers forever....

I didn't even have one foot in the apartment when I already heard mama yelling at me. "Damn, Andrew! What in the hell took you so long to get back home! You had me worried!" She was standing in the middle of the den dusting the ceiling fan when she saw me stepping into the apartment. "And take your shoes off! I just vacuumed!"

"Okay," I replied, still standing in the door shocked for moment. It was almost as if I was thrown into a sudden dream. The entire apartment looked different. Even smelled different. Truth be told, while we weren't the cleanest people, we weren't the dirtiest either. Honestly, I think Rahzel was somewhat exaggerating that day he came over. But I guess now that it seemed like he was gonna be running things around here, the apartment had to look spotless. The door still open, I took a quick scan of the apartment just noticing how immaculately clean everything was. Damn, did Mama hire someone to come by and clean up?!? I knew she didn't do all of this by herself.

"Boy, are you gonna walk in or what?" she asked, grumbling. I gawked at her, noticing she wasn't even dressed in one of her usual stripper hoe outfits. Aside from selling drugs, Mama being a stripper was still so unbelievable to me. I kind of still didn't want to believe any of this shit. Why in the fuck couldn't she just be a normal mother like everyone else?!?

Anyways, I took a step into the apartment and, following her instructions, I took my shoes off. "Sorry, Mama. Where do you want me to put my shoes at?"

"So much damn dust!" Mama sneezed then smacked her teeth, cutting her eyes over at me. "You still ain't answer my question! What took you so long? And put them inside that Publix plastic bag right next to you."

"I had to stay behind and talk to my teachers about some of the missed assignments," I lied as I pulled my shoes off and placed them in the Publix bag sitting on the freshly vacuumed floor. Damn, I hated that I kept having to tell these lies. I hated liars.

Suddenly, her somewhat angry face turned flat. Rahzel's voice must've been going off in her head when she realized her tone sounded a bit harsh. "Oh, okay. Cool," she replied softly and then returned to cleaning the ceiling fan with a duster in her hand. She paused again and looked at me with tightened lips. She took a deep breath then exhaled saying, "Dru. You know I'm just hard on you 'cause I don't want you to end up like your father."

"I understand, Mama."

"Okay, 'cause, you know sometimes I know I can be a bit much. Things just been so hard around here and I try my best to take care of y'all the way I know best."

"It's okay, Mama. I get it," I told her, although deep down I felt like she was only running me this bullshit because of Rahzel. She would've been totally different had he not got her ass right.

"Are you hungry?" she asked, putting down the duster on the coffee table and strolling over to me. I was now standing between the kitchen and the hallway, ready to go to my room and take a nap before I began my bleaching and exercise.

"No, ma'am."

"Dru... ughh, before you go to your room... I know you got homework and whatnot, I wanna talk to you for a second, okay?"

"Okay," I said as I looked at her nervously wondering what in the hell she wanted to talk about now. This newfound change was actually starting to irritate me 'cause I just felt like it was so fake. She would've been calling me all types of names and whatnot by now. And if not that, I would've had a slap across my head or a punch thrown to my chest.

"Let's sit down and talk," she said, grabbing my hand.

I gasped and flinched for a second, thinking she was about to hurt me. She looked at me and said, "Boy, I'm not finne hurt you. Just sit."

"Okay," I responded. I trailed her over to the long couch and we sat next to each other.

"Look, I know I ain't been the best of mothers But like I said, I've been trying, okay?"

"I hear you, Mama... I understand," I said, not looking at her. My eyes were glued to the television blaring a Puff Daddy music video, but I wasn't paying attention to that either.

"Look at me, Dru," she screeched, gently grabbing my chin and turning my face toward hers. "You believe me, right?"

Staring deep down into her shady hazel eyes, I knew exactly what the fuck she was doing right now. She was trying to manipulate me by showing me this sudden fake love. Since Rahzel was gonna be coming by tomorrow to take me to hang out with him, I guess she didn't want me to run my mouth around him.

"Yeah, I do," I mumbled.

"Okay, good then. You know, it wasn't like I was dancing

all the time and whatnot. I mainly was just a cocktail waitress. That's it," she confessed.

"Okay," I replied again.

Her eyes got a tad watery. And seeing that almost wanted to make mines swell with tears as well. Although I wanted to believe her, I still couldn't shake the thought that this was all fake. It had to be. It shouldn't take another nigga to make you treat your first born with respect. Truth be told, I should tell her how the fuck I was really feeling right now. I should lay it all out on her. She began sniffling and grabbing her nostrils as if she had something stuck up in her sinuses. Yeah, see, I knew it. This bitch was also probably getting high as fuck.

"I got a question for you, Mama."

"What's that?"

"Do you love me?"

Mama paused for a moment and stared at me. Awkward silence came between us. "Umm. Dru, why would you ask me some shit like that?"

"Like what?"

"Boy, stop playing! That's a crazy question to ask your mother," she said, shaking her head. She quickly popped up from the couch and dashed into the kitchen. "Anyways, I gotta continue cleaning up before I head out tonight. I gotta take care of some other business. And, no, I'm not going to the strip club. So if and when Rahzel asks you tomorrow, you can tell him the truth," she groaned as she began fumbling with glasses in the sink.

I stood up from the couch and grabbed my book bag off the floor. "Okay," was all I could keep replying with because I was so floored that my own fucking mother had to think about that question. And that was how I knew right then and there this bitch was no longer a real mother to me. She gave birth to me, but she wasn't a mother. A mother wouldn't have to hesitate expressing her love to her child, especially her first born. She knew deep down all I wanted was for her just to say she loved me. I knew that bitch saw the desire for her to say so buried in my eyes. She hated me. She hated everything about me. And, now, I truly hated everything about her. Now, I realized I had to really transform myself for Amirah. Why? Well, if no one was going to love me, I now had to put all my efforts into loving someone. And my heart was set on loving Amirah, my future queen to be.

CHAPTER TWELVE

Exercise sucked. But it was a necessary evil. I needed to get in shape.

I had just got done doing a round of push-ups. On my bedroom floor, I sluggishly rolled over onto my back and got into sit-up position. My breathing was hard like I had asthma. My entire tank top soaked, I was sweating like I was in the middle of Africa. "Damn. Fuck," I grumbled, throwing my clammy hands under my head. The hunger pangs intensified, but I didn't care. I had to lose this weight.

It was around seven pm now and, after I got done bleaching myself and showering, I went straight to my room and began working out.

Mama and Tay'Quan were in the living room watching television and eating Domino's. That was their typical Friday night routine. Ironically, Mama invited me to come eat and chill with them. But I declined. Fuck that bitch. Without a doubt, I still believed she was showing me fake love. Even though the aroma of pepperoni pizza filled my room, I wasn't tempted at all. I'd rather starve than to fill my fat ass face with food Mama was giving me because she was forced to do so. Fuck that bitch.

Staring up at the slowly moving dusty ceiling fans, I gave myself ten seconds to get my breathing under control. Then, I went right into my first round of sit-ups. My goal was to try to do at least a hundred. Coach Martin often made us do sit-ups and push-ups in PE. So, following his normal routine, I divided up the hundred reps into ten sets. It took me forty minutes to complete the push-ups. Hopefully, it wouldn't take me that long to do sit-ups. Honestly, the hunger pangs were fucking me up and I just felt like I was really about to pass the fuck out. But I had to endure this shit.

"Come on, Dru. Get your fat ass up," I muttered harshly to myself. "AHHH!" I groaned, going right at it. "One... ahhh-hhh... two... three... four... AHHHH!!! Five," I kept moaning, struggling to power through each rep. But once I got to the sixth rep, I couldn't take it anymore. All the muscles in my stomach began to cramp up. My back suddenly collapsed to the damp floor. I was now staring up at the ceiling fan once again, gasping for air like I smoked a pack of cigarettes a day. "Fuck!"

Wiping my brow, a part of me wanted to give all of this shit up so badly. *Man, get your fat ass up and go get something to eat. Starving yourself over this bitch that probably don't even like you. She don't want your big, black fat ass. She's just being friendly to you 'cause you come off too nice. You're a geek. Don't nobody want your geeky, fat, black, ugly ass. Fuck that. Man, don't you smell that pepperoni pizza? Mama said you can have some. Get the fuck up and stop starving yourself for nothing. All of this isn't necessary.*

With this persuading voice going off in my head, I was seconds away from bursting up to the floor and running into the den to slam a pizza slice in my mouth. *Dru, be a man. You got this. Don't give up. You want the girl of your dreams, right? You* want to be her King, right? Be patient. Be disciplined. Success ain't gonna come overnight. Stop being so weak. Stop being a punk. Even Dad would tell me this. *Man the fuck up. Stop being a mothafuckin' chump. Get your fat ass up! Now!*

Sweat covering my forehead and a few tears trickling out the corners of my eyes, I was going to conquer this exercise shit. "AHHH!" I growled, pushing myself to complete the sixth rep. "SIX! AHH! SEVEN! EIGHT!" All of a sudden, the stomach muscle cramps got worse. My chest and stomach felt like one big, overstretched rubber band about to pop. "FUCK!" I growled, collapsing back onto the floor.

I needed help. I needed a boost. I needed something that was gonna allow me to power through all of this. I wasn't quite ready to give up yet, but it was going to take a big jolt of energy to make me endure this shit.

I wiped my brow and face again, thinking for a moment of what I could do. Then, an idea hit me...

Cocaine.

Maybe if I could just take a small hit of Mama's cocaine, I would feel energized.

Still breathing hard, a great debate went off in my head about what I should do next.

Should I sneak into her room and try to find her stash?

Or should my fat ass just give up?

Yeah, I think I should just give up. Why in the fuck would I do some crazy shit like use some of Mama's cocaine?

But then again, curiosity kept me contemplating why exactly people even used cocaine in the first place. What did it feel like? Did it give you energy? Did it make you feel smart? Fast? Mama used cocaine. Rahzel used it, too, obviously. Shit, most of Mama's friends used it. I knew drugs were bad, but none of them looked like crackheads though. So, obviously, there had to be a huge difference between using crack and cocaine. Shit, maybe there was a big difference between what was in cocaine compared to crack. Even before I found out Willie was dying from AIDS, the nigga already looked damn near dead. So, obviously, crack was a fucked up drug that made you look like shit. Cocaine had to be different...

I kept wrangling with myself until I finally realized I had nothing to lose at this point. What was the harm in trying it at least once? I mean, trying it once couldn't do anything bad to you, right? Besides, I knew I wouldn't and couldn't get hooked. I was too smart to let myself even go down that path.

I could hear Mama and Tay'Quan still in the living room. Mama did tell me she was gonna be leaving later tonight to go handle some business. Not stripping business though. Probably drug business. She was probably gonna take her stash with her so, if I was gonna really try this shit out, I needed to stop being a punk and go get some now before it was too late.

I quickly got up off the floor and dashed out into the living room. Mama's room was directly across from mine. *Stop being a bitch, Dru. Go in there and find that shit.* But damn, where would her stash even be? Last time, she hid it under the sink in the hallway bathroom. The other day, she had it in her purse. Damn, it probably would still be in her purse, I bet. But I had to check her bathroom anyway.

Quickly glancing down the dimly lit hallway, it sounded as Mama and Tay'Quan weren't going to be getting up off their asses anytime soon. I could hear an episode of Family Matters booming from the den's television. Funny thing was, I would've been in the den watching TV as well but fuck that corny ass show. With me on the verge of going to high school in the fall, I needed to stop watching those corny TGIF shows any damn way.

With the coast clear, I tip-toed across the hall and slowly cracked Mama's bedroom door open. The room was dark. I flicked on the light switch and saw her entire room was cleaned up as well. Even her bed was made up. Although the smell of cigarettes was still somewhat glued to the walls, mama had scented candles burning all throughout the apartment. I crept past her bed and made my way into her bathroom. I turned the lights on. The bathroom was spotless. Smelled like fresh bleach and Pine-sol. Damn, Mama was really changing shit up because of Rahzel. What the fuck kind of terror did he put on her? Yeah, that nigga still was a bit shady to me, but I had to be like him when I got older. I wanted people to respect me like that if they talked down to people, especially kids.

My eyes zeroed in on the sink cabinet. I dashed to it, quickly opening it up. All I could see was a bunch of hair care products, combs, brushes, and some cleaning supplies. "Damn it!" I whispered to myself. I closed the cabinet door and then flew over to the bathroom linen closet. I pulled the doors apart, quickly scanning the closet from top to floor to see if I'd see the stash. Nothing. Damn, where would that shit be at? Probably her purse I now assumed. But something told me she kept this shit inside of her room. She just wouldn't walk around with it on her like that. And if she was selling drugs, she was keeping most of it inside the house.

"DRU! COME HERE!" I suddenly heard her scream. My eyes exploded with fear. I quickly closed the closet door, turned off the lights and dashed out of her room. "DRU! COME HERE, BOY!" I heard mama yell again.

"Coming, mama!" I yelled back to her But then, I forgot just that quick I left her bedroom light on. Fuck! I spun around and dashed back to her room, turned the bedroom light off, and then sprinted down the hallway and into the den. She was standing up, adjusting her shirt and jeans. Tay'Quan was still sitting on the couch. Her face screwed up with surprise, I guess, when she noticed I was in nothing but some shorts and a sweaty tank top. I probably smelled musty as hell, too.

"Damn! Why are you sweating like that?!?" she asked, skimming me from head to toe.

"I was in my room working out," I somewhat lied. I mean, I was working out But now, I was looking for your shit, bitch.

"Oh... oh, okay. Well, there's still some leftover pizza if you want any. I'm about to head out now. I should be gone for a few hours. I don't want no mess out of y'all. By the way, I finally got a new cell phone now. If y'all need to call me, I left my phone number scribbled on a piece of paper on the fridge."

"Mama, you got a cell phone now?!?" Tay'Quan asked, sounding excited.

"Yes, I did!" She grinned.

"Can I see?!?" he asked.

"Boy, calm down! A cell phone ain't a toy. But I might let you see it maybe when I get back. But anyways, like I said, I don't want no mess out of y'all. Y'all understand me?"

"Yes, ma'am," both Tay'Quan and I replied together.

"Good... anyways, I'm about to head out now," she said, strolling over to the dining room table. Her purse sat next to the open Domino's Pizza box. She snatched the purse off the table and threw it over her shoulder. She threw her hand inside the purse, rummaging for her keys. She pulled them out, along with a pack of Newports. My eyes glued to her purse, I wondered if her coke stash was in there. Probably was, I bet. But I just knew she had some cocaine around the house somewhere. I was gonna find that shit once she left.

Mama sauntered over to the front door and then looked

at me saying, "And take a damn shower before you get all musty. I do not want my damn house smelling like ass!"

Fuck you, bitch.

"Okay, Mama," I said, fake laughing.

Mama rolled her lying eyes and smacked her teeth. "For real... ain't nothing funny about that. Rahzel won't let you in his car smelling like that either," she said, then opened the front door and walked out, slamming it behind her.

Once I heard her lock the door, I glanced over at Ty'Quan and said, "I'm gonna be in my room working out and then studying."

"Well, I'mma go get my Super Nintendo and hook it up to the TV out here! Mama got me a new game. You wanna play with me?"

"What game she got you?" I asked, although I didn't play with shit.

"Super Mario Cart. You can play with two players."

"Nah, I'm good," I said. "Maybe later."

Not saying a word back to me, Tay'Quan flew his punk yellow ass off the couch and rushed down the hallway to his room to grab his Super Nintendo.

Time to resume my mission to look for Mama's cocaine stash. However, before starting up the search again, I needed something to drink. Strolling over into the kitchen, I quickly grabbed some water. Then, I made my way back into my room to chill out for a few seconds. I didn't want Ty'Quan to hear me going into Mama's bedroom.

About a good ten minutes passed. I was sitting on my bedroom floor stretching my sore legs out. I could hear Tay'Quan's gay ass giggling out in the den. Hopefully, he was deep into his new video game. Now, it was time to go back on the hunt for that coke.

I got up from the floor, crept out into the hallway, quickly looking down it just to make sure I was in the clear. Go.

Tip-toeing across the hall, I quickly opened Mama's bedroom door and walked in, closing it behind me. I flicked the light switch on. *Think, Dru. Think. Where else would she put this shit at?* I scanned the room; my wide eyes morphed into snooping slits.

Under her bed...

My eyes focused towards the bottom of her queen-size bed, I just knew under it would be a perfect hiding spot. I lunged at the bed and dropped to my knees. I leaned down and looked under the bed. Although it was very dark underneath, my gaze zoomed in a single shoebox sitting in the center. I crawled halfway under the bed then reached for the box, pulling it out. It was an old ass Adidas box. Anxious as fuck, I opened it and immediately my eyes grew wide with surprise. A bunch of yellow-top vials filled the entire box. "Shit!" I couldn't help but gasp when I stared at what looked like hundreds, if not thousands of vials damn near spilling out of the shoebox. Butterflies filled the pits of my empty stomach, increasing the slight nausea already holding me hostage.

How many should I take? Maybe one.... or maybe I should take two, in case I liked it. Then again, if I did like it, I'd need more than two. So, maybe I should take four. There were just so many vials, I knew Mama wouldn't notice.

I grabbed four vials and quickly stuffed them in my right pants pocket. I closed the box then pushed it back to the center of the floor. Hopefully, Mama wouldn't know the box had been moved. I crawled from up under the bed then quickly stood up, shaking dust and dirt from off me. Mama obviously forgot to vacuum under there.

Damn, I was crazy as fuck for doing this, but I just had to try to see what the hype about cocaine was all about. Time to experiment.

I dashed back over to the bedroom door and, just as I was about to head out, I took a quick scan making sure the entire room looked the same as I entered it. If Mama knew I was in her room, let alone in her stash, she was gonna kill me. And at that point, she wouldn't even care about Rahzel. She'd definitely fuck me up, even if he stood to her side watching her. Everything inside her bedroom looked the same, so I turned the lights off, closed the door, and rushed into the hallway bathroom.

Once inside, I locked the door and stood in the mirror. I pulled the vials out of my pocket and sat three of them down. With the one vial in my hand, I lightly shook it, closely analyzing it. More anxiety filled my insides. *Don't do it, Dru. Don't do it. Just go put this shit back, dude. What the fuck are you doing?* Suddenly, I got scared. I couldn't do it. My conscience was begging me not to give this shit a try. *Boy, stop being a bitch. Everyone you know is doing this shit and they are fine. Trying one time ain't gonna hurt.* Now, my mind was telling me to go ahead and give this shit a shot. There was no harm in trying at least once.

Fuck it.

I pulled the top off the vial and gently placed it next to the other vials.

Staring at myself in the mirror, I carefully inserted the vial into my right nostril. With my left index finger, I pressed against my left nostril.

My heart was pounding rapidly, ready to explode out of my chest. My eyes widened. *Don't do it, Dru. Put it down. Put this shit back.*

I closed my eyes and took a snort.

"AHH!" I gasped, quickly pulling the vial out of my nose. Then, I started sniffling and sneezing uncontrollably. Clutching my chest, I thought I was about to pass out feeling the rush of powder fill my head.

But once the sneezing stopped, this weird, warm, fuzzy

feeling flooded my entire body. It was that same feeling I felt when my eyes first landed on Amirah. It was love.

I was in love. This coke set my heart and soul on fire.

Putting the vial back into my nostril again, I took another snort. Within seconds, the feeling of love got even greater. I was in heaven. I felt like God. Now, I see why Rahzel kept calling me God.

CHAPTER THIRTEEN

You ever wondered how it feels to get struck by lightning?

That was a question I always wanted to ask Ms. Reid.

Some months ago, I remember reading in my science book that Florida had the highest number of lightning and thunderstorms out of all the states in the country. We got close to eighty to a hundred days of thunderstorms a year. I also read on average about twenty people get struck by lightning a year, and half of those people lived in Florida. I wondered what they felt. Obviously, I knew that shit had to hurt. But what if it didn't? What if it felt like you really had super-powers? Super-powers that were too strong for your body to handle, so that was the reason why you'd explode into a million pieces.

The questions kept popping up in my head while I stared at myself in the mirror. This cocaine was filling me with super-powers. Breathing hard, sweating, my heart beating out of my chest, I swear lightning was flowing through my entire body. Electricity buzzed at the tips of my fingers.

I swear to God I could fly the fuck away. Shit, wings were

ready to pop out of my back. Unstoppable and limitless I was, I swiftly floated out of the bathroom and back into my room.

I paced my room in a circle, wondering what I could do next. Throwing light punches and jabs in the air, the strength and power of Mike Tyson was in me. I could fuck someone up if they fucked with me. Including Mama...

"AHAHAHAHAHAH!" I erupted into nonstop laughter.

Then, a million thoughts invaded my head. All I could see now was Amirah's beautiful face glowing in my head. "Hey, Andrew! Give me a kiss! Lay down on the bed. Let's have sex. Let's make babies," I heard her soft, sensual voice utter. I closed my eyes and reopened them. Her face was gone.

Shit, I was tripping.

Man, this cocaine had me in a whole different dimension. Yeah, now, I fully understood why people messed with this shit. Words couldn't describe the overpowering feelings flooding my entire mind and body.

My mood blissfully energetic, I had the will and power to conquer these damn sit-ups. I flew down to the floor and quickly got into sit-up position. Throwing my hands under my head, I took a deep breath, hoping I truly did have superpowers. "LET'S GO!"

I shouted so loud that Tay'Quan's punk ass probably heard me. But I didn't give a fuck at this point. My mind was dialed all the way into getting the rest of these sit-ups done. In fact, I was gonna start all over from scratch.

"One. Two. Three. Four. Five. Six. Seven. Eight. Nine. Ten," I counted, damn near going to twenty.

I was unstoppable. Nobody was gonna fuck with me. I'm a God. I'm a black God. All the power of the universe was in me now. I was unconquerable.

I spent the next twenty minutes or so knocking out those sit-ups. Then, like a rocket, I blasted up from the floor and went straight into doing jumping jackets. Beads of sweat rushed down my face and now my entire outfit was soaked with my own sweat. I was gonna lose this goddamn weight. I was gonna get skinny.

"One. Two. Three. Four. Five. Six. Seven. Eight. Nine. Ten," I kept counting, going all the way to fifty. I stopped for a moment to catch my breath and then right back at it. Fuck it. I was gonna do two hundred jumping jacks.

Although everything around me was beginning to look and even feel like a blur, I didn't stop. I kept going until I hit my goal.

"YES!" I was unstoppable.

I sat down on the floor for a moment and stretched. I cracked my neck and knuckles. Jumping back onto my feet, I was ready to go at these push-ups all over again. I hopped back down onto my feet and got into push-up position, beginning another round, pushing myself until I couldn't take it anymore. But I took it, completing close to fifty push-ups without a struggle. I got back onto my feet, but now soreness was starting to kick in. That was my cue to give it a break for the night. I'd already pushed myself unbelievably hard.

Mama wasn't lying though about my sweat and must. I was drenched all over and smelled like a stray dog. It was time to take a shower. I flew over to my dresser and pulled out some fresh underwear and a tank top. My feet still feeling light, I soared out of my bedroom and into the hallway bathroom.

Now that some time passed from my first bump of coke, the rush of energy was beginning to fade. Shit, I thought the high would've lasted much longer. But I still had so much left in that first vial though. So, once I got done showering, I was gonna fly back to my room and take me another hit.

I stepped in the shower and let the hot water beat my body. I closed my eyes and just thought about Amirah. Damn, did love make you this infatuated with somebody?

Going off into Lalaland, I could see us both being doctors, living in some big mansion and having a bunch of nice cars and shit. With so many happy thoughts flooding my mind, I just leaned against the shower wall, going into the deepest dreams about my future. My future with Amirah. My destiny...

BOOM! BOOM! BOOM!

My eyes exploded open with surprise when three booms damn near busted the bathroom door down.

"ANDREW! GET THE FUCK OUT THE SHOWER, YOU FAT, FUCK BLACK NIGGA! HAVE YOU BEEN GOING THROUGH MY SHIT?!?!?" That was Mama screaming.

Shit! I'm dead!

She must've known I had gone through her stash. Fuck! Fuck! Fuck!

My fear and anxiety mixed with the cocaine still running in my system. My heart was beating out of my chest.

"OPEN UP THE FUCKING DOOR, GODDAMNIT!"

"Mama! What happened?!?!?" I acted as if I didn't know what she was talking about. I tried to come up with the best excuse I could give her. I quickly turned off the shower and hopped out.

"ANDREW! I'M GONNA FUCK YOU UP! GET THE FUCK OUT OF THERE NOW, GODDAMNIT!"

"Mama! What happened?!?" I yelled back to her, quickly drying off. I threw my tank top on and then put on my underwear. Hesitant, I didn't know if I was prepared to open the door. She could've been on the other side of the door with an extension cord in her hand. Or even another lamp.

"OPEN UP THE GODDAMN DOOR, ANDREW! IF YOU DON'T OPEN IT UP, I SWEAR I'M GONNA FUCKING KILL YOU. I MEAN THAT! I AM GOING TO KILL YOUR FAT, BLACK, WORTHLESS ASS. YOU

LYING, ROTTEN PIECE OF SHIT! GET THE FUCK OUT OF THERE NOW!"

Shivering, I was about ready to cry, but anger and rage began to fill me. Hearing her call me all of those nasty words was triggering the monster in me.

"Leave me the fuck alone, Mama! Get away from me! I'mma tell Rahzel!"

"WHAT?!? BOY, YOU AIN'T GON TELL SHIT ONCE I FUCKING KILL YOU! IF YO FAT ASS DON'T OPEN THIS MOTHAFUCKIN' DOOR, I WILL. AND I WILL BEAT YOUR ASS TO DEATH WITH THIS BELT IN MY HAND! NOW, OPEN THE FUCKING DOOR! I'MMA GIVE YOU TILL THE COUNT OF THREE!"

Gasping, I stood in the center of the bathroom, my fists clenched.

"ONE!"

I couldn't move.

"TWO!"

"THREE!"

BOOM!

The bathroom door flew open. Mama kicked the door open with her right foot, busting through the doorknob's lock. A long, black belt was gripped in her left hand. The second she had her foot back to the floor, without hesitation, she lunged into the bathroom and started throwing a mix of punches and whips at me.

"YOU WENT THROUGH MY STASH?!? THE FUCK IS WRONG WITH YOU?!? WHY THE FUCK WOULD YOU GO THROUGH MY STASH?!? DID YOU USE THAT SHIT?!?" She kept screaming, kicking and whipping me with the belt.

"GET OFF ME!" I cried, balling up and trying to protect myself from the nonstop belt lashes. Mama was using the belt buckle to whip me. "HELP!" I screamed at the top of my lungs. "SOMEONE HELP!" But I couldn't take it anymore. It was either kill or be killed. This bitch had to die. I lost it and fucking snapped. This sudden burst of energy gripped me, making me throw the most vicious upper-cut. My fist connected under her chin and she flew back toward the door.

She stood in the door for a moment motionless, holding her chin. Her reddened eyes amplified with shock. Guess she didn't see me doing that.

"OH, NO THE FUCK YOU DIDN'T! NIGGA, I'MMA KILL YOUR FAT ASS!" She lunged back at me But this time, I wasn't going down like that.

"BITCH, GET THE FUCK AWAY FROM ME!" I roared, ducking a swing she tried to drill into the side of my face. I lunged at her and tackled her out into the hallway, using all of my weight to slam her against the wall. Her back and back of her head hit the wall and all I heard was air escaping her lungs.

Although the cocaine high seemed to be fading from my body, suddenly, I felt like I had another bump. My super-powers returned to me. And my number one super-power now was the ability to turn the years of all the fucked up shit this bitch did to me into bricks and kill her with them.

"NO! NO, ANDREW! NO!" she cried, as I released all of my wrath and fury onto her trifling ass.

"BITCH! I'LL KILL YOU! I'M GONNA FUCKING KILL YOU!"

"ANDREW! NO! STOP, ANDREW! GET OFF, MAMA!"

I didn't see Tay'Quan, but he tried to pull me off Mama, but I wasn't having any of his shit either. I spun around and knocked him out. He flew to the ground crying and clutching his face. "GO TO YOUR ROOM, FUCK NIGGA, BEFORE I KILL YOU, TOO!"

Tay'Quan hopped back up and then lunged at me, swinging. Then, he and I started to go at it.

"NO! Y'ALL STOP!" Mama screamed. Out the corner of my eye, I could see her trying to slowly stand up.

Tay'Quan, at first, threw some fast blows to my face, but they were nothing to me. I reached in, grabbed him by the neck, and slammed him against the wall. Then, squeezing as hard as I could, I was determined to choke him to death.

"NO! ANDREW, STOP! HE CAN'T BREATHE!" Mama wailed as she tried to quickly limp over to me and pull me off him.

"GET OFF ME!" I spun around and threw my fists back up.

Mama, this time, threw her hands up in surrender. "ANDREW! NO! PLEASE! DON'T HIT ME. I'M SORRY!"

"GET THE FUCK AWAY FROM ME!" I cried to the top of my lungs.

"ANDREW! I just wanna know did you go through my stuff?!? Did you use that stuff? You're high now! You used it! I can tell!"

"GET THE FUCK AWAY FROM ME, BITCH! I SWEAR TO GOD I'LL KILL YOU!" The murderous monster inside of me was off its leash and, if this bitch made the wrong move, I swear this was it. Her life was over. I meant it this time.

A small trail of blood leaked from Mama's nose. Her entire body shaking, she held her side. I hoped I broke one of her rips or busted one of her kidneys. Tay'Quan was huddled against the wall crying nonstop like a little bitch.

BOOM! BOOM! BOOM!

"What's going on inside there?!?"

Mama and I suddenly threw our attention to the front door. Sounded like Ms. Washington was at the front door. That old, nosey ass bitch knocked again.

"Tay'Quan, go to your room and be quiet!" Mama instructed bitch ass mama's boy. He got up from the wall and dashed into his room, immediately closing the door and locking it.

Mama then looked at me and said, "Go tell her everything is okay. Tell her that was just the TV."

I stood there for a second with my fists still balled up, ready to go at it again with Mama. Not saying a word to her, I ran over to the front door and opened it. "WHAT?!? What the fuck you want, Ms. Washington?!? Bitch, you always in our shit! Get the fuck out of here! Mind your own damn business, old ass bitch!" I snapped.

Ms. Washington gasped, clutching her chest. Her eyes flew open with surprise at me cussing her out. "Boy! Who you talkin' to like that!"

"I'm talkin' to your mothafuckin' ass, bitch! Get the fuck away from our shit! Always up in our shit! That was the TV, you rotten ass hoe! GET THE FUCK AWAY FROM HERE!" I slammed the door in that old bitch's face then stormed back over to Mama. Lunging back into her face, I cocked my fist back and grabbed Mama by her shirt collar. "Bitch! If you ever put your hands on me again, I swear to God, I will fucking kill you! YOU UNDERSTAND ME?!?"

"YESSS!" she cried, flashing her bruised hands over her face to protect herself.

I let her go and stomped down the hallway.

"ANDREW! Please! Just tell me why you went through my stuff! That's not my stuff! That's Rahzel's! You took like a hundred dollars away from me!"

"BITCH, I DON'T CARE!" I yelled back to her, my back turned to her. I rushed into my room, slammed the door shut, and locked it.

Pacing my room, I didn't know what I was gonna do next. But I was certain of one thing: a massive headache started pounding my skull. As each second went by, the cocaine's magic disappeared. The walls of the room were spinning. Nausea from not eating all week returned But this time, it was stronger than ever. I stood still for a moment and grabbed my stomach. Next thing you know, I threw up watery vomit all over the place.

    I fell to my knees and more vomit came up. The headache seemed like it was getting worse. I wasn't afraid of Mama no more But now, I was afraid of death. What the fuck was going on?

CHAPTER FOURTEEN

Someone's hard coughing echoed into my bedroom, waking me up from weird, deep, dreamless sleep. My hazy, heavy eyes opened. The window's white curtains didn't stop rays of light from filling my room. The morning sun was cooking the side of my face.

Last night's headache was gone, but every single muscle in my body was on fire. I was tight and aching all over. Hunger pangs were stabbing me in my stomach. My throat was drier than the Sahara Desert. With nausea still keeping me hostage, I just wanted to go back to sleep. But I couldn't since Rahzel was going to be over here soon. For a split second, I thought about telling Mama I wasn't going with him. Then again, I didn't want to spend another second in the house with her or Tay'Quan. But shit, I just needed at least another minute or two of rest. So, I rolled over, crawled into the corner of my bed, and closed my eyes. However, I still heard someone coughing up their lungs outside of my bedroom window.

That had to be Willie.

My eyes back open, I slowly got out of the bed, walked

over to the window, and looked out of it, staring right at the backside of Willie. He was leaned over the walkway's guardrail, damn near looking like he was about to fall over and kill himself.

Damn. Willie's happy whistling didn't wake me up this morning... it was his constant, painful cough.

Man, I felt so bad for him. I mean, he and I weren't necessarily *cool* like that, but he was a good guy. Actually, he was probably the only nigga I trusted around here. Everyone else was just on some shady shit or were nosey as fuck like Ms. Washington.

Slightly pulling the curtains back, I knocked on my window to see if I could get Willie's attention. But he just kept coughing away. I wondered how long he had left to live now that I knew he was dying from AIDS.

I knocked again. His coughing quickly ceased. He slowly lifted himself up and then turned around, staring directly at me. "What's happenin', big boy?" he mumbled, wiping his mouth with a lime green washcloth.

"You aiight, Willie?" I asked, although I knew he was just as fucked up as I was. Well, he was even more fucked up than me. I wasn't dying. At least I didn't think I was.

"Yeah... I'm straight, boss. This bug just tearing me up."

"You take medicine, right?" I had to ask. I remember when Mama was telling me about HIV/AIDS, she told me there was no cure. Ms. Reid even said the same thing.

"Yeah, they got me taking some things here and there. But there ain't no cure for this, young blood. I just gotta deal with it until my body ready to go," he muttered, walking closer to my window.

I shook my head. "Damn. That sucks... you afraid to die?"

"Hell yeah. Who isn't? But we all gotta die one day, young blood."

"Why are you afraid?"

Willie tightened his cracking lips. Suddenly, he began coughing again and quickly pulled the lime green rag up to his mouth. I noticed the rag was spotty with blood. Damn, he was really dying. He clasped his chest and, within seconds, was able to contain his cough. "Shit. Goddamn!"

"You alright?"

"Yeah, I'm fine... But I ain't afraid of death. I'm afraid of going to hell. I did a lot of fucked up shit in my life, bruh. Don't be like me. Stay out them streets and stay righteous."

"Okay," was the only response I could give him before he walked off, disappearing into the blinding Miami sun.

Just as I was about to turn around and get ready, this sudden tingling feeling swamped my entire body. Then, I got weak and even more nauseous. "Shit, what the fuck?!?" I groaned, holding my stomach. Felt like I was about to vomit all over again. I leaned over, still holding my belly. The throw-up sensation traveled from my stomach and was now up into my throat. My mouth exploded open, but I didn't throw up anything.

I wondered why I was feeling this way. Was it the cocaine? Or was it because I hadn't been eating all week? I had to stop whatever was causing me to feel this fucked up 'cause now I felt like I had traded places with Willie.

Within seconds, I started to feel better again. I shook off the lingering nausea and made my way over to my dresser to find an outfit to wear today. Since I couldn't wear shorts at school, I usually wore them on the weekends. I grabbed a pair of my Levi's, some boxers, a tank top, and an old pair of Cross Colors shorts and made my way into the hallway bathroom to shower.

Before I walked in, I could hear the den's TV rumbling. That was either Mama or Tay'Quan watching TV. They had better not fuck with me.

I strolled into the bathroom and quickly locked in. I

didn't know exactly when Rahzel was coming over, but I didn't think it would be this early. Before I left my room, I saw on my alarm clock that it was 8:45. Rahzel probably was gonna be over here around 10 or 11, I bet. So, with a good hour or so to get ready, I opened up the sink cabinet and pulled out the bottle of Clorox. As usual, I needed to apply my daily round of bleach to get this skin right. I turned on the water faucet in the sink, then dashed over to the tub to turn on the shower. Both now running hot ass water. Within seconds, the entire bathroom became steamy. I took off my tank top and underwear, getting completely naked. I grabbed a washcloth off the towel rack and walked over to the countertop, grabbed the bottle of bleach and screwed its top off.

"YOUNG GOD! You ready to go?!?"

"Shit!" I gasped when I heard what sounded like Rahzel's deep voice traveling into the bathroom.

"Yeah! Just give me a few minutes and I'mma be done!" I yelled back. Goddamnit! I screwed the cap back onto the bottle of bleach and put it back in the sink cabinet. Obviously, with no time to spare, I turned the sink water off and then hopped in the shower. A good ten minutes later, I was out of the shower and back in my bedroom. Once I had my outfit on, I checked myself in the body mirror hanging on the back of my door. Man, I wish I had some better clothes. I looked like a fucking bum.

Although the shower seemed to make some of the body aches disappear, I still felt slow and now slightly agitated. Fuck it. I needed something to eat. I'd just grab an apple or two and try to quickly eat it down. But then, I thought to myself, *maybe I should take another hit of the cocaine*. I still had some left in the first vial. What should I do? It felt good... so good. I ain't never felt like that before in my life. But I didn't want to become an addict. Now, I could see how people got hooked to that shit. But right now, I felt like shit. Maybe if I just took a smaller amount, I wouldn't get so blasted. *What should I do? What should I do?* The question kept running in my head.

"YOUNG GOD! WHAT'S UP?!?" Rahzel's shouting snapped me out of my temporary daze. Fuck it. I'd take a bump.

"COMING! Just give me another minute!" I yelled back, dashing over to my closet and quickly pulling the doors back. I hid the vials in a Payless shoebox on the top shelf, all the way in the far left-hand corner of the closet. I was still curious how Mama even found out I went through her stash because I hid the vials right before I showered last night.

I reached for the box, pulled it down, and opened it. I yanked the vials out of one of the shoes. Mama had bought me these ugly ass shoes about a year and a half ago. I only wore them once 'cause kids at school made fun of me for wearing them. The shoes were gray and brown and had Velcro straps for shoelaces. The only kids I'd see wearing shoes like this were the retarded kids that went to my school. Just looking at them made me cringe. I just kept thinking about this one nigga, Ryan, who wore shoes like this all the time. His ass was so damn out there, he couldn't tie his own shoes. Mama bought me these shoes actually out of punishment. She said because I smacked my teeth hard at her once, I didn't deserve to get any new shoes because I was an ungrateful piece of shit. These shoes were an exact reminder of why I hated the fuck out of Shalanda. Yeah, I decided I wasn't gonna call her Mama anymore.

With the vials in my right hand, I grabbed the first one I used last night with my other, then threw the other vials back into the shoe. I quickly put the shoebox back up into the corner, closed the closet door, and made my way over to the body mirror. I stood there, once again thinking whether or not I should do this. But fuck it. I had nothing to lose. A little bump probably wouldn't hurt. It wasn't like I was going to be doing this all day any damn way.

I took the top off, plugged the vial into my right nostril, and took a fast, light sniff. I sneezed and sniffled. My eyes flickered and my sinuses burned. I should do another hit just in case. I put the vial back into my nostril again and, this time, took a much bigger hit. Within seconds, the blissful energy returned and lightning zipped through my body. My super-powers were back. I looked at the vial and noticed I had about a quarter of cocaine left. That was probably enough for another three or four rounds, I presumed.

For a second, I debated whether or not I should bring the shit with me. Fuck it. I slipped the vial into my pocket then floated out of the bedroom, down the hallway, and into the den. Rahzel was sitting on the smaller couch, his arms stretched out, looking like he didn't even wanna go anywhere. Mama and Tay'Quan were on the other couch sitting upright with their arms folded, their faces glued to the television. Teen Summit was on. Ananda Lewis' sexy ass was yapping off at the mouth about teenage pregnancy. Damn, now that I think about it, Amirah reminded me so much of her. But Amirah was sexier.

"Hey," I announced my presence, my trembling, clammy hands in my pockets. Damn, this coke was making me jittery and sweat.

"Hey?!?" Rahzel looked over at me with a raised eyebrow. "You forgot already?"

"My bad... As-Salaam 'Alaikum," I said nervously.

"Wa 'Alaikum As-Salaam," he replied, producing a wide grin and revealing his glistening gold teeth. "Young black God, you ready? What took you so long? In there beatin' yo meat?" he snickered.

"Nah," I laughed back, still nervous. "Sorry, but I didn't know what time you were coming over," I apologized. I was getting anxious wondering if Shalanda told him about what happened last night. Not saying a word, she looked at me and I looked right back at her. She then threw her eyes back onto the television.

Rahzel looked at Mama then back at me. "Damn, what's going on? Why y'all all quiet and shit? Acting like y'all just heard someone died."

"My stomach was kind of hurting from the pizza last night," I lied, my heart pounding out of my chest.

Rahzel raised an eyebrow. "Pork?"

"Yeah."

"See, that's why you gotta leave that shit alone, young black god. That pork ain't nothing but rat, cat, and dog. Shit gonna put worms all in your system," he laughed as he stood up. Today, Rahzel wasn't dressed in all Versace. He had on a tight-fitting V-neck muscle shirt that had his shoulders exposed. His arms were massive and muscular like he started lifting weights since the day he was born. He had this big number seven encircled in what looked like a sun or star tattooed on his right shoulder.

"So, you saying pork isn't healthy?" I asked, my eyes not letting go of his crazy looking muscles.

"Hell yeah! You should only be eating fresh fruits, vegetables, and the best meat. Even then, all of that meat ain't good either. The black gods only need to eat once a day," he smiled as he walked up in front of me. Now hovering over me, he extended his hand out so we could dap up. He gave me a tight hug then released me. He gently squeezed my neck and said, "I'mma put so much knowledge in you. Knowledge, wisdom, and understanding." He playfully punched me in my shoulder asking, "You ready to learn?"

"Ughh... yeah, I guess," I nervously replied.

"NAH! Not no guess. Yes or no. I don't do no gray area shit."

"Yes. I'm ready to learn."

Rahzel looked over at Mama. "See, I told you this boy is smart as fuck. I can see the thirst for knowledge in his eyes. We got a long day ahead of us."

Still trembling from the cocaine, my eyes widened with curiosity. "Where are we going?" I asked.

"Plenty of places." He grabbed my chin and turned my head right then left, analyzing my hair. "First thing's first though – we need to get you lined up," he said, still looking at my nappy ass uncut hair. "Don't nobody who works for me gonna look like that crackhead neighbor of yours."

"Who? Willie?"

"Yeah... Whatever the fuck his name is. That nigga looks sick as fuck, too. Look like he got AIDS. Stay the fuck away from him. You touch that nigga, you might catch that shit."

"I don't think you can get AIDS that way though," I said. "You can only get it through needles, sex and blood transfusions."

Rahzel chuckled. "Young god, I know. My uncle died from that shit. But still, stay away from that sick ass nigga. You don't want his energy to get inside of you. You may not get AIDS from him, but you'll get his ignorance. Let's go though, because time is already slipping away from us. And time is money, young god. I got much to show you."

I nodded and replied, "Okay."

"Good." Rahzel glanced over at Mama. "Shalanda... I'll call you when I'm on my way back with him."

"Okay," she responded nonchalantly, her eyes still glued to the television.

"Damn...Y'all acting weird around here. Let's go, young god." Rahzel threw his arm around my shoulder and escorted me toward the door. I didn't even give that bitch a glance, but I could feel her eyes burning the back of my neck.

Once outside, Rahzel and I coolly strolled down the walkway. From afar, I could see Willie outside of his door. He lived in the unit a few feet away from the staircase. Humming and doing a two-step, a pipe hung from his mouth. He held a lighter up to the pipe and flicked until a long flame cooked his rock. Luther Vandross' *Here And Now* echoed from a small black radio next to his bare feet.

"You see what the fuck I mean?" Rahzel asked, his voice now deep and murderous as if his eyes landed on someone who tried to rob or kill him.

Not saying anything back to Rahzel, we got closer to the staircase. Willie must've heard us coming 'cause he immediately took the pipe out of his mouth and then tried to act like he wasn't smoking. "Big man! What's up!" He grinned. His yellow bug eyes shot over to Rahzel. "Wassup, brotha?!? You his uncle or something?"

"Man, get the fuck away from me before I put a bullet in the back of your head, fuck nigga!" Rahzel growled, reaching in his back.

I gasped, not knowing if Rahzel really had a gun on him But from the sound of it, he did.

"Sorry, bruh!" Willie screeched, throwing his hands up in the air. He looked at me and then back at Rahzel, as we trekked past him and made our way downstairs.

Damn, I felt so bad and even embarrassed. Willie was cool and Rahzel didn't need to scare him like that. I had the sudden urge to turn around and look at Willie and mumble an apology But I knew if I did that, Rahzel would probably put a bullet in my head. So, I kept my nervous, unblinking eyes straight ahead as we moved down the staircase and into the parking lot.

"You saw all the black scars all over the nigga's face and arms?"

"Yeah," I replied, looking up at Rahzel.

"That ain't just from using crack. That's also from using that scag."

"What's that?"

"*Her-ron*."

"How you know?"

"My daddy was a dopefiend. I can spot a dopefiend from a mile away. New York got crackheads and dopefiends now. Shit is truly the wilderness now. Beasts and savages everywhere."

I shook my head mumbling, "Damn, that's crazy."

"But I love it. Easy money, young god. Easy fuckin' money."

As usual, the dope boys who lived in the complex were hanging out. Saturdays seemed to be their primetime working hours. A few of them were leaning up against their candy-painted box Chevy's, puffing on blunts and sipping on 40s. Biggie Smalls boomed from one of their car's speakers, filling the entire parking lot with thundering bass. As we walked past them, a few of them had their reddened eyes on us. Damn, I hoped they didn't fuck with me and Rahzel. But then again, I think these guys were cool and weren't on no bullshit. Mama told me they were just about making their money. That was it.

"Sup, boss," some fat, brown-skinned nigga with dreads muttered. A half-smoked blunt hung from his mouth. I'd see him from time to time, but I didn't know his name. Didn't even know if he lived in the complex. He looked like he was probably in his late twenties or thirties.

"What's good?" Rahzel replied.

"Shit, chillin," the dreadhead mumbled. "You still gon' holla at us later, right?"

"Yeah, I gotchu. I'm just gonna show my guy here around the city to take care of some shit."

"Bet," the dreadhead replied, blowing smoke from his

wide nostrils. He looked at me and smiled while saying, "Damn, boy, you look just like yo daddy."

Not saying anything back, I just nodded. Rahzel hit his car alarm. I walked up to the back passenger side and proceeded to open the door, but before I hopped in, Rahzel shouted, "Hey!" I looked at him scared as fuck. "Why you getting in the back?" he asked, his face screwed with confusion.

Shrugging my shoulders I said, "'Cause... you didn't say I could sit in the front."

"Young god, I ain't your mothafuckin' chauffeur!" Rahzel said, playfully smacking his teeth then grinned. "You better get your ass in the front seat so I can drop this knowledge on you," he commanded.

Without hesitation, I quickly closed the back passenger door and opened the front. I got in and quickly put my seatbelt on. Rahzel chucked up the engine and, before he threw the car in reverse, he looked at me and said, "Stop with the shy shit and stop acting scared. If you're gonna work for me, I don't want no mothafuckin' scared ass niggas on my team. And speak the fuck up. All of that weak boy shit is over. You're a man now. You almost fourteen, right?"

"Yeah, I am."

"Okay then. So stop with the weak shit. When I was your age, I was getting plenty of pussy and money. You want pussy and money, right?"

"Yeah."

"Well, then stop acting like a hoe ass nigga. You're a God. Everything around you is your domain. Your kingdom. Your universe. You supposed to rule this shit. Now, sit back and let me drop this supreme wisdom on you."

"Okay," I replied and watched him throw the car into reverse.

I had no idea what the fuck I was about to get myself

into, but I knew I had to quickly dead whatever weakness I was showing Rahzel. He saw that shit in me from a mile away and I didn't want him thinking I was weak or anything like that. Shit, I didn't want anyone thinking I was weak. He was right though. If I was going to get Amirah, I had to be a man.

Once we were out of the parking space, Rahzel slowly drove as he fumbled with his car radio. "You like Wu-Tang?" he asked.

"Yeah, they dope as hell."

"Good. Those are my niggas. They Gods, too," he said as he pushed a CD into the car's CD player. Within seconds, Wu Tang's *Ice Cream* boomed throughout the entire whip. Leaning back in his seat, Rahzel held the steering wheel with his left hand and held his chin with the other, his elbow resting on the glove compartment. "It's a hot ass day to get this ice cream, too, young god. You hungry, young god?"

"Yeah. I didn't even get breakfast," I said, looking out the window.

"Good. I'mma feed you food and knowledge today, young god. Sit back."

Following his command, I sat back and drowned myself in the rumbling bass. The cocaine still running a million miles through my veins, I killed off any anxiety within me. Rahzel was a real ass dude. I wonder what it would be like to have this dude to be my father. Shit, my life probably would've been so different. Maybe it would be different now.

CHAPTER FIFTEEN

With cocaine electrifying every square inch of my body, my brain cells were fired up with a million burning questions. Since Rahzel said he was going to teach me everything I needed to know, I hoped he was ready to get drilled by me. Do you sell drugs? Where are you from? Why are you in Miami? Have you ever been to jail before? Have you killed someone before? Why are you messing with Shalanda? How long have you known her? How do you even know my dad?

Shit, since he told me to man up just some moments ago, I was gonna man up and ask him the shit he thought I'd be too afraid to ask. No doubt I was still terrified of him, but what was he gonna do? Kidnap me and kill me? Throw me over a bridge? He seemed like he was with the shits, but I knew he wasn't that crazy. Besides, if he wanted me to work for him, then I needed to know exactly what I was getting myself into this summer.

Truth be told, I didn't want to sell drugs. I wanted no part of it. Then, again, I was high off his shit right now and I was tingling with ecstasy I'd never experienced before.

Damn, I was beginning to feel like a hypocrite.

We had been cruising in his fly ass whip now for about a good fifteen minutes. His Mercedes was decked the fuck out on the inside, too. The coupe had cream-colored leather seats. Glossy wood paneling lined the sides of the door. This was the first time ever I'd known a nigga with a CD player in his shit, along with BOSE speakers. Man, this dude had to be making some serious cash selling drugs. Speaking of which, that was another question I had for him. How much do you make? Two hundred thousand a year? Four-hundred thousand? Maybe a million? I knew he couldn't have been making more money than a football player or a rapper. Shit, if he was, he wouldn't be driving his own car right now. We would've had a driver driving us around and whatnot.

Still not knowing where we were going, I figured he was going to first take me to a barbershop. Earlier, he did tell me I needed a haircut. Usually, when I did get my haircut, Mama would take me to Mr. Harper's Cuts over in Liberty City; however, we weren't headed in that direction.

With the music still blasting from the car speakers, Rahzel hadn't begun to drop his knowledge just yet. Bobbing his head, he was mumbling the lyrics to a song by Raekwon. His eyes were focused on the light traffic ahead of us.

"What do you believe in? Heaven or hell? You don't believe in heaven cause we're livin' in hell..."

Rahzel looked at me. "You hear that, young god? What do you believe in? Heaven or hell?"

"What do you mean?" I was confused by his question.

"You heard the God, right? Heaven or hell. What do you believe in?"

I shrugged my shoulders. "I don't know."

"Then, you must believe in hell then since you don't know."

My eyebrow lifted with more confusion. "What makes you say that?"

"Cause your ignorance is hell. You still in the mental grave of ignorance, young god. But I'mma pull you out of it. You got a lot of potential. I can see one day you're gonna be my top right-hand man."

This dude was throwing me deeper and deeper into confusion.

"Look around you, young god. You see where we at? You think this is Heaven?"

"No. It can't be."

"Why not?" he asked, turning down the music.

"Cause... you gotta die to get to heaven," I replied.

"Says who?"

"The Bible."

"Why do you gotta die to get to heaven when there are people living in heaven right now?"

Silent, I just shrugged my shoulders. I didn't know what response to give him. This dude was confusing the shit out of me even more. But didn't he know the Bible said you can only get to heaven once you die? And not everyone went to heaven, especially those who didn't believe in God, so what the fuck was he talking about?

'I'm confused."

"I know you are. That's why you're in hell right now."

"So, you're saying you don't have to die to get to heaven? You can go to Heaven right now? How?"

"Look around you, young god. Don't you see all of these broke, dumb ass niggas around here? Look at how niggas live. Look at all of these dirty ass niggas walking the streets," he said, pointing to people walking along the sidewalk. "They don't have no money. No power. No respect. Look at all of these busted ass piece of shit hoopties people are driving. Look at them."

I scanned all of the older cars on the road. Many of them did look like they were on their last limb. Then, an old ass maroon Accord passed us by. Aside from noticing the fading and chipping paint on the car, I also saw the car's side view mirror dangling and blowing in the wind.

"I mean, look at the conditions of all these people out here. Think about your own neighborhood. Think about the school you go to. Mostly everyone you know is poor, right?"

"Kind of," I replied, thinking about what he was saying. I wanted to see where he was going with all of this.

"Look at all the raggedy ass houses niggas living in. You think the white man lives in these fucked up conditions? You think the white man out here riding around on the bus? Riding around in busted ass cars? Wearing clothes from K-Mart and shit?"

"No."

"People out here suffering and struggling. My mother always used to tell me niggas are so 'PO', they can't even afford the letters O and R in the word poor. Young God, that is hell. You don't have to die to experience hell. Likewise, you don't have to die to experience heaven. That's why I asked you what do you believe in – Heaven or hell?"

"But none of this lasts forever," I retorted. "When you die, heaven lasts forever. So does hell."

"Says who?"

"Says the Bible."

Rahzel smacked his teeth then let out a loud chuckle. "Young God, when you die, that's it. Ain't nobody ever come back from the grave to tell you if Heaven and hell is real. Have you met anyone who came back from the dead?"

"Of course not."

"So, why in the fuck would you believe that Heaven and hell exist once you die? Sometimes, the things you read in the Bible are an allegory. You know what that means?"

"Yeah... an allegory is like something is symbolic of something else, right?"

"Exactly... heaven and hell are states of the human mind and experience – right here and right now. No need to die to experience the finest things in life. That's why I wanna teach you Islam."

"Islam? Like the other religion that people practice in the Middle East?"

"Not that Islam, young god. That's the old Islam. I wanna teach you the new Islam. Islam taught by Father Allah. The real Islam. The real Islam stands for I-SELF-LORD-AM-MASTER."

Everything Rahzel was starting to somewhat make sense... to an extent. This Islam stuff now was starting to sound weird.

"See, young god, when you realize you are God, you become the master of your own destiny, master of your own universe. You create your own heaven. Just like those blue-eyed devils that live on Star Island. You think those crackers are going out there worshipping Jesus and bowing down to a spook God? Hell fucking no. Those crackers realized a long time ago their true power. They came into self-knowledge."

"So, you are saying I can master my own reality? How? It ain't like things can just pop up," I said. This dude was really starting to talk a lot of gibberish, but I was actually quite entertained.

"Yes, you can. And I'm gonna teach you."

"So, Rahzel, I got a question for you."

"Sup, young god?"

"So, you don't believe in the Bible?"

"Man, fuck a Bible, young god. Don't you know the Bible was created by a cracker named King James?"

My eyebrow raised and I tapped my chin with a finger. "Nah... I never knew that," I said back to him, looking out onto the road in front of me. Seemed like we were now headed for I-95. Maybe we were going to South Dade.

"Where do you think the name King James comes from?"

"Shit, I don't know... I guess some white man."

"Yeah, some blue-eyed devil from Europe. Now, I'm not saying there ain't wisdom in the Bible. Don't get me wrong. There's plenty of wisdom. But those blue-eyed devils tampered with the Bible to enslave niggas and make us deaf, dumb, and blind. And that's why we're living in hell."

"So, what religion are you, if you don't mind me asking?"

"I don't follow a religion. Gods don't need religion."

"So, you don't pray?"

"Why the fuck would I pray if I'm God?"

"So... I mean... if you're in a bind or you got a problem, you don't think there is a higher power—"

"The power is within me to change my reality, young god," he interrupted. "And it's in you, too. Niggas been praying to that white Jesus for over four hundred years. You think God was listening to them when that cracker was busting their backs out with whips and chains? Where was that God they were praying to when all of that was happening?"

I shrugged my shoulders and fell silent. Although I was doubtful about some of the things Rahzel was saying, much of it was truly starting to make sense. I just read that slaves often prayed for God for help. If God was out there, why would he let them suffer for so long?

Rahzel chuckled when he saw I couldn't give him an exact response. "Exactly. Ain't no spook God out in the sky. The God is within you. That's why when we call on Allah, we not talking about some mysterious force in the sky or somewhere off in the far corners of the universe with a long white beard and a pitchfork in his hand. We talkin' about the original supreme being – the Asiatic black man – Arm, Leg, Leg, Arm, Head. That's what Allah stands for, young god."

The more he kept talking about Islam and Allah, the more I wondered if this was the same Islam Amirah practiced. "I met this new girl at my school. Her name is Amirah. She's a Muslim."

"Yeah? Where she from?"

"She told me she's half black, half Trinidadian."

"Damn, she sounds sexy as fuck. You wanna fuck?"

I laughed and lowered my head out of slight embarrassment. "Yeah, I guess."

"What you mean, you guess? You ain't never fucked before?"

"No."

"How old are you again?"

"Thirteen but I'll be fourteen in August."

"Yeah, you kind of young But when I was your age, I was getting all types of pussy. Puerto Rican. Haitian. Dominican. Even Trinidadian. What Amirah look like? She look like she got some Indian in her, huh?"

"Yeah. How'd you know?"

"Young God, I just told you I had all the pussy back in my day. Shit, the only type of pussy I wouldn't touch is white pussy. I wouldn't touch that shit with a ten-foot pole. And you shouldn't either. Those white bitches will put a rape charge on you."

I suddenly exploded into laughter.

"For real, young god. All them ball playin' niggas in the league always end up messing with them white bitches and end up in trouble. Stay away from them. Plus, they smell like dogs."

"Hahahaha! Yeah, one of these guys I know at school said that once. Mama says that all the time, too."

"Yeah. Everyone knows that, young god. Anyways, this Amirah. You like her?"

"I mean, I just met her. She's new to my school, like I

said."

Rahzel glanced at me with eyes now turned into curious slits. He then smiled saying, "Yeah, I can tell your ass is in love. Tell you what, young god. Once we get your cut, we're gonna head to the mall and get you some new threads. You can't be going to school looking like you get your shit from the Salvation Army. I'mma also drop you some knowledge about how to deal with the ladies. But one thing is for certain, you gotta get rid of that shy shit, young god. Bitches don't like no shy nigga. You man the fuck up and take what you want. And when I say take, I don't mean you snatch a bitch and try to rape her. I mean you tell her how you feel about her and let it be known to her you want her heart. You feel me?"

"Yeah."

"Good."

Rahzel turned his attention back to the road and zipped in and out of traffic until we got to the on-ramp for I-95. Now silent, I guess he was done dropping his wisdom on me for now. But I still had my questions to ask him. Time to man up.

"Rahzel... I don't mean to be all up in your business, but can I ask you a question?"

"What's that, young god?" he asked, staring at me.

"Do you... do you sell drugs? You don't have to answer that if you don't want to."

Rahzel threw his eyes back onto the road and pursed his lips. He looked back at me and asked, "Well, what do you think?" He sounded a tad nervous. I must've caught him off guard.

"Yeah... you sell drugs."

Rahzel nodded. "Affirmative."

"So, is that what you gonna have me doing for you? Selling drugs?"

"Maybe. Maybe not. I'll let you decide. I can't force you to do shit, young god. Remember, you got the power to control your own reality."

"Aren't you afraid?"

"Afraid of what?" he asked, not giving me eye contact.

"Like going to jail? I mean, you said you knew my dad. That's the reason why he's in jail now."

"Yeah... I knew your old man. And, yeah, I know that's the reason why he's in prison now. But there's a big difference between your father and me."

"And what's that?"

"I never killed anybody."

I froze for a moment, my eyes widened with shock. "Huh? What are you talking about?"

"Your pops...yeah, they got him on some trafficking charges. But they also got him on a few murders. You didn't know that?"

"No... no, I didn't know that. He didn't tell me that."

"Yeah... and that's another big difference between me and your pops. I'm not reckless, he was. I'm the CEO of an organization; your father was just a hotheaded street nigga, young god. I hate to break it down to you like that, but it is what it is."

"Damn," was all I could say. I sat back and folded my arms. I didn't know if Rahzel was lying or not. But why would he lie about something like this? There was no incentive for him to lie.

"I'mma let those jewels marinate first before I go back to dropping some more knowledge on you, young god. Just sit back. We'll be at the shop in a few," he said and then turned the music up.

Rahzel took me to a barbershop in Overtown, which was a neighborhood a few blocks away from Downtown Miami. Afterwards, we rolled down to Dadeland Mall. I hadn't been here in years actually. This mall was so different from the mall Shalanda would usually take me to up north. Down in this part of Miami, most people were rich Spanish people. The houses were nicer, bigger and you'd see more BMWs and Mercedes on US-1.

As time passed, so did the cocaine high, and I became agitated and slightly depressed thinking about the shit Rahzel told me about my dad. I still didn't believe it. I mean, why wouldn't Dad just come out the gate and tell me what he did? Why lie about something like that? Was he ashamed to admit that he murdered somebody? Earlier, I had a million questions for Rahzel, but now I had a million questions for Dad. Now, he seemed to the nigga I truly needed to be probing.

Now armed with a fresh fade, Rahzel and I roamed the crowded mall, making our way to Macy's. "When's the last time your mother took you shopping?" Rahzel asked as he kept gawking at fine ass Spanish women walking past him.

"Shoot. Maybe like two summers ago," I said. "She said I needed to start wearing men's clothes and they were too expensive."

Rahzel shook his head. "No disrespect but that bitch needs to be decked in her fucking mouth. I'mma get her right," Rahzel huffed as his eyes kept wandering at the sexy ass Latina chicks who kept walking past us.

If Shalanda wasn't such a fucked up person to me, I would've probably tried to fight Rahzel right here and now for disrespecting her. But seeing as how I damn near had to beat her ass last night and she wasn't a mother to me anymore, I didn't care. He could kill her and I wouldn't shed a single tear. That bitch was already dead to me.

We walked inside the Macy's store, walking straight to the men's section. "Now, you're a bit on the heavy side, so we're gonna have to buy you some shit from this section. But I'mma still have you looking right, young god," Rahzel explained. "What size pants you wear?" he asked as he started picking through some expensive ass Karl Kani jeans.

Was he really gonna drop all this money on me? Feeling a bit embarrassed, I answered, "34."

Unfazed by my response, he kept picking through jeans until he found my size and yanked as many as he could off the rack. "Come on, let's go get you some matching shirts. Man, I'mma have you fresh and iced the fuck out, young god," he said, then walked us over to the shirts section. He grabbed a bunch of shirts, still not even giving a fuck with the price was.

Some moments later, we trekked over to the dressing room area. Once we told the old Hispanic dressing room attendant how many pieces of clothes I had, I went straight to a dressing room all the way in the back while Rahzel waited for me near the front.

Once inside the dressing room, nausea and lethargy began to bog me down. The cocaine was wearing off. Before I took my clothes off, I stood in the dressing room mirror staring at my fat, black ass contemplating whether or not I should bump another hit. Be a man. Make a fucking decision. My eyes latched onto my fly ass fade, I quickly whipped the vial out of my pocket. Once I had the top off, I plugged the vial into my right nostril and took a deep blast. Twenty seconds later, I was energetic and peppy again.

Soon as I put the vial back into my pants pocket, I quickly took my clothes off. But as I continued to stare at myself in the mirror, the thought of what that dreadhead nigga said in the parking lot back home had me curious. 'Damn, boy, you look just like yo daddy.' Now, that had me wondering how much of a reputation did Dad really have.

How many people really knew him? Was he a big-time drug dealer like Rahzel? And who the hell did he kill? Shit, how many people did he kill? All of these questions were beginning to make me a tad angry. I really had disdain for liars and now I was starting to think that Dad was a liar himself. He should've just been upfront with me and told me what the deal was instead of trying to hide shit from me as if I was still a baby. But fuck it – if Rahzel was telling the truth, which he had to be, then I didn't care anymore. Truth be told, the next time I had a chance to visit him or send him a letter, I was going to outright ask Dad what the fuck was really going on. I had the right to know the truth.

Anyways...

As I continued staring at myself in the mirror, it seemed like all those push-ups were starting to pay off just that quick. Although I had titties, I could see my chest muscles were looking bigger. Even my biceps were popping out. Shit, just looking at myself was now giving me the motivation to get my ass back home and go right into my workout routine. If I kept this shit up, I was gonna drop this weight by the end of the summer and look like a completely different person.

"Damn! Young God! Boy, you look like a different man!" Rahzel shouted and jumped up in the air when he saw me walking out in the front of the dressing room area. "Boy, you look fresh as hell! Well, aside from them bogus ass shoes on your feet. But we gon take care of that!" he chuckled.

Smiling back, I asked, "Can I get some Jordans?"

"Young God, what kind of question is that?!? Of course! We gon get you some Timbs, too!"

I tried on a few more outfits and, once I got done, Rahzel

bought everything without hesitation. Bought everything in cash. Although I was still leery about being around this nigga since he was a dope dealer, I didn't give a fuck anymore. Honestly, he was doing more for me than both Shalanda and my dad. As bad as they may sound, fuck them. From here on out, Rahzel was right. I had to be a man. I had to make my own decisions. Look out for me. Do for self. I had to be a master of my own world. Master of my own universe. With several shopping bags in my hand, we rushed over to Foot Locker. Once we got inside, Rahzel went even crazier with buying me shoes. And I could get my hands on any pair I wanted.

About a good two hours later, we were back in Rahzel's car, cruising through Coral Gables. Man, I swear this part of Miami was so different from North Dade. Down here, people really had money. Like serious money.

Glancing out the window, someone driving a red drop-top Lamborghini approached us. "Damn, that whip is fly as hell," I commented with my eyes attached to this older white man behind the steering wheel.

"Hell yeah. You like that, huh?" Rahzel asked.

"Hell yeah. I would buy one of those once I get money," I replied, still staring out of the window. The white man adjusted his Ray-Ban Aviators and then looked at me. He nodded his head and smiled, then sped off like a bat out of hell.

"You see what I mean, young god? That white man is living in heaven. You think he's living in hell?"

"Nah," I replied, thinking that Rahzel was right. Why in the fuck would you need to die to experience something that we could have right here and now?

I had no idea where we were going now, but we were headed northbound on US-1, making our way closer and closer back to Downtown Miami. Still glancing out of the car window,

Tupac's music booming in my ears, I saw a partial reflection of myself. I smiled, seeing how much a haircut and new clothes made me look so damn different. Before we left the mall, Rahzel made me change into one of my new outfits and shoes. Honestly, I couldn't lie – I was feeling really good about myself.

We just finished eating some Pollo Tropical, which was a grilled chicken spot popular all over Miami. I had never eaten there before. Shit was like the Burger King of Cuban food it seemed. Rahzel said he only ate once a day because that's what Elijah Muhammad said. I had no idea who that was though. I guess either I was gonna have to ask or he would eventually tell me.

But I still had questions. So, I turned my head his way and asked, "Rahzel, how long has my mother been working for you?"

"Years," he replied nonchalantly.

"And she's never gotten in trouble before?"

"No. Never. Anyone who works for me won't get in trouble."

"I'm so confused. How come my dad didn't try to work for you then?"

"We were partners once… but he decided to go off and do his own thing," Rahzel said as we approached a red light. Looking around, we were now in what looked like a neighborhood of mansions. Gawking out the passenger window, my vision zoomed into a row of big ass castle-like mansions hidden behind tall black metal gates and plush, tall palm trees.

"Damn, where are we at?" I had to ask, my mouth flung wide open. Heaven?

Rahzel chuckled, "Heaven, young black God. This area is called Brickell. Looks different, huh?"

"Hell yeah. Much different. Shit is almost unreal."

"You like what you see?"
"Yeah."
"Are you dead?" Rahzel laughed.
"No."
"See what I mean. So, what do you believe in? Heaven or hell?"
"Heaven. Shit, I wanna live in Heaven."
"That's what I thought. I'mma show you how to get there."

Rahzel pulled into a backlot of a warehouse sitting in the middle of Downtown. I'd really never been down here like that, so a lot of these buildings were very unfamiliar to me. But I never would've imagined a big ass warehouse would be sitting among these tall high-rises and skyscrapers.

Rahzel threw the Mercedes into park and turned it off. Stuffing his keys into his pocket, he said, "I'mma show you how this game is really played safely. I know you got your doubts and reservations, but I'mma show you the difference between a CEO and a street nigga." He reached over to the glove compartment, opened it, and pulled out a gun. He quickly stuffed the glock in his waist then got out of the car, slamming the door behind him. My gaze wide with fear, I got scared, wondering why he needed a gun. "Get out the car," he instructed.

Without hesitation, I opened the car door and gently closed it. Looking around, my wide, nervous eyes scanned the area. By now, it was around six and the echoes of traffic began to simmer down. All of this shit was too surreal to me. Like, was I dreaming or something? "What is this?" I nervously asked, trailing Rahzel as we made our way toward the loading dock's steps.

Rahzel spun around. "If you wanna work for me, you'll be working here," he uttered. He leaned down into my face and said, "Now look, young god. You ain't a kid no more. What you are about to walk into isn't some kiddy shit. You understand me?"

"Yes," I responded, my unblinking, scared eyes peering into his.

"Now, whatever you see in here is my business. And I don't want my business out in the streets. You know what a confidentiality agreement is?"

"No."

"It means whatever I tell you and whatever I show you is secret or confidential between you and me." Rahzel brushed his hand against the gun resting in his waist and said, "There are serious consequences when you breach a confidentiality agreement. You understand?"

"Yes." I gulped.

"Good, young god," he smirked, his gold grill twinkling. He stood up and threw his arm around my shoulder. We walked up the steps of the loading dock and approached a rusting maroon double door. Rahzel pulled out a set of keys from his pocket and unlocked the door. We walked into a dark foyer. With the lights completely off, I had no idea what the fuck we were about to walk into. But I knew whatever I was about to see could get me killed if I opened my mouth. With the door closed behind us now, the silence made my heart rate race like the Lamborghini I saw earlier. Rahzel took a step over into a corner and flicked a light switch on. My gaze suddenly exploded with surprise.

CHAPTER SIXTEEN

I swore I was gonna see nothing but mounds of pure cocaine sitting on tops of tables throughout the warehouse. And I just knew sexy ass chicks with their titties hanging out were gonna be cutting up and bagging up the coke. But that wasn't what I saw when Rahzel flicked the lights on in the warehouse.

Pies.

That's what I saw. Pies packaged in plastic containers were sitting on a maze of assembly lines running throughout the warehouse.

I was really fucking confused. I looked up at Rahzel and said, "So, I'm confused. I thought you were—"

"You thought what?" he interrupted.

"Thought you sold dope. Where's the drugs and shit?" My hands trembled in my pockets.

Rahzel laughed. "I do... but you think I'm just gonna keep that shit all out in in the open and whatnot?"

"Oh... no... but what's this? What's all these pies about?"

"This is my new venture I want you to help me with. Shabazz Baked Goods. What you are seeing, young god, are

Shabazz Bean Pies. Gonna try to get these bad boys into Publix and Winn-Dixie soon."

I flinched. "Bean pies? People eat bean pies?!? That sounds nasty as hell," I said, laughing.

Rahzel chuckled as he threw his arm back around my shoulder and walked me deeper into the warehouse. "Bean pie doesn't taste like baked beans or black beans and shit, young god. These pies are made from navy beans. They're boiled down, blended and then mixed with nutmeg, cinnamon, brown sugar, butter and other special ingredients." He asked, "You ever had pumpkin pie before?"

"Yeah... like during Thanksgiving."

"Bean pies kind of taste similar... except better," Rahzel said as we walked over to one of the assembly line belts. He grabbed one of the pre-packaged pies off the line and opened it up. "Here, smell it," he said, gently pushing the pie into my face so I could get a sniff of it.

And he was right. It smelled sweet and spicy – almost like a sweet potato pie. I looked up at him saying, "Damn, this does smell good."

"You wanna try?"

"Sure."

Rahzel took me over to a small office that sat off about a hundred or so feet away from the main assembly line. Windows wrapped around the entire office, giving whoever was inside a wraparound view of the warehouse floor.

We strolled inside. Rahzel trekked over to a small fridge in the right corner of the office and pulled out another pie. "Have a seat at the desk," he said as he walked over to a small kitchenette over in the other corner. I sat down and kept quiet while Rahzel rumbled through a drawer, pulled out some silverware, and then walked back over to the desk. Once Rahzel sat down, he opened up another pie, this one smaller, and then handed me a silver fork. "Here, try it. Tell me what you think, young god," he said smiling.

I took the fork out of his hand and slowly dipped it into the pie. Once I scooped up a good amount onto the fork, I slipped the fork in my mouth, afraid of what I was about to taste. My eye brows suddenly raised out of shock. "Damn, this do taste good," I replied.

"Exactly," Rahzel replied.

I was just about to dig in and take another bite But suddenly, Rahzel snatched the fork out of my hand and closed the pie container. "It's getting too late to eat all that sugar. Besides, remember, only eat once a day," he said.

"Okay," I said and sat back in the seat.

"So, wait, I'm confused, Rahzel. I thought you sold dope."

Rahzel chuckled. "I do, but this is a front company. Do you know what that is?"

"Nah... what is that?"

"See, this is why you need to learn the difference between a CEO and a street nigga. Anyways, a front company is like a shell. People see one thing and think one thing is happening when really, on the inside, there's something else completely going on."

"Oh... so, you use the company to hide the fact you're selling dope?"

"Yeah... that's what any smart businessman should do in this game. You think America's number one addiction is coke? Think again – it's sugar. Plenty of fat ass people out there in the world who need their daily sugar fix," Rahzel explained. "Anyways, I'mma have you learning the ins and outs of how to run this bakery. Finance. Operations. Management. Marketing."

"But I wanna be a doctor," I replied back. All of this sounded kind of cool and all, but I still didn't really want any parts of it.

"That's cool. I wanted to be a doctor, too, when I was around your age. A cardiologist, in fact."

"Really? 'Cause I want to be a heart surgeon."

"Yeah, that's cool... I can dig it. Just sucks that doctors don't really make money though."

"They don't? I thought doctors made serious bread."

"I mean, some do. Surgeons do. But look at how long it takes to become a doctor. How much school do you think it takes to be a doctor?"

"Well, I know you gotta get a college degree first. Like your bachelor's. Then, you gotta go to medical school. That's another four years and then that's it."

Rahzel snickered and said, "Yeah, and then what about your internship and your residency? It takes much longer to become a surgeon, young god. You looking at almost fifteen years' worth of education. And then don't even get me fucking started on just how expensive college is. Gotta take out loans for undergrad. Then loans for medical school. And by the time you get done with all that college and become a surgeon, you'll be making money, but half of your income is going to paying off all them student loans. Shit, I got doctors begging me for money right now."

"Well, how much do you make, Rahzel... if you don't mind me asking?" I flat out asked.

Rahzel pursed his lips, his eyes turned to slits. "Get up. Let me show you something." He and I both stood up and he, once again, threw his arm around my shoulder. Walking out of the office, he escorted me down the end of the warehouse and to a staircase leading to what looked like a basement. With nothing but a single red light illuminating the long, dark staircase, I grew afraid of what I was about to see. *Bodies?* I gulped, hoping that wasn't what it was.

Our footsteps echoed as we trekked carefully down the metal staircase until we reached the end, where we were met by a solid steel door. Rahzel pulled his keys out of his pocket and unlocked a door. He gently shoved me inside of the dark room and, once he stepped in, he flicked on a light switch.

My nervous eyes once again widened with shock.

All I could see were mountains of money neatly stacked on long foldable tables spread throughout the vast basement. Over in another corner, one small square foldable table was home to stacks of plastic-wrapped white bricks. That had to be the dope.

"How much money you think is in this room, young god?" Rahzel asked, staring down into my unblinking and gigantic eyes.

Nervous, all I could respond with was a silent and slow-moving shoulder shrug. I threw my eyes back onto the money, trying my best to guess just how much was in the room. "I don't know," I finally mumbled.

"Take a guess, young god," Rahzel said, laughing.

"Ehh... maybe like a million dollars?"

"Try again... go up a little bit higher though."

"Like two million?"

Rahzel laughed again. "Higher."

"Five million?"

"There's about forty million dollars in this room, You still wanna be a doctor?"

The moment he said that, I swore my eyes grew to the size of Saturn. I didn't want to believe there was that amount of money in the room, but why would he lie? He had to be telling the truth. Had to be. He had no reason to run me some bullshit story, especially if he pretty much threatened to kill me if I opened my mouth.

"I mean, yeah, I guess." I had to think again for a second. *Do I still wanna be a doctor?* This was now becoming a pressing question because truth be told, if I had my hands on a million dollars, let alone forty million, why would I even wanna work?

"This is... unreal... like I'm in a dream. This is like some Scarface type shit," I said, scanning the room once more just to see if I wasn't seeing shit.

"Nah... this ain't a dream, young god. This is heaven. This is my kingdom. Could be yours too if you would stop acting like a bitch and take what's rightfully yours," Rahzel replied as he threw his arm around my shoulder and walked me deeper into the room.

"So, you made all of this selling drugs? Like how?"

"Young God... I told you already... I'm the CEO of an organization. Not a street nigga. The shit you see those dope boys doing in the parking lot back at your crib is low-level peon shit. I told you I'm a God, right?"

"Yeah," I replied, my eyes fixed on the Himalayan mountain ranges of cash. Although the coke was once again fading from my body and I was in bad need of another hit, I was getting so much mothafuckin' energy by absorbing the smell of nothing but fresh green dollar bills. That shit was a high in itself.

"Exactly. Gods are unlimited. Gods are powerful. Gods are omnipresent and omniscient. You know what omnipresent means?"

"No."

"It means you're everywhere."

"You know what omniscient means?"

"No."

"It means you know everything."

"So, you know everything?" I asked, looking up at Rahzel.

Rahzel didn't say anything. He just let out a dark and deep laugh and then spun me around, leading me out of the room. He turned the light off, closed the door and locked it, and we made our way back to the main warehouse floor. As we sauntered across the floor, I was still so confused as to what all of these damn pies had to do with Rahzel pushing dope. But I guess that was gonna be some knowledge he was bound to drop on me at some point.

We got back inside the office and then both sat down. "Anyways... Shabazz Baked Goods, as I was saying, is one of my new ventures. I have many others, of course. But this is the one that's gonna expand my kingdom. Your kingdom. You ready to rule?" Rahzel asked, looking me dead into my eyes.

I didn't know what to say. A part of me wanted to obviously say yes but another part wanted to say no. In fact, I still wasn't even trusting of this nigga. And just the idea of even being around drugs made me cringe to a degree. It just seemed so dangerous. How did the government not know what he was doing? Yeah, I get Rahzel said he was a CEO, but how could I even trust that? Another thing that didn't sit right with me was the fact that he would even sell something that was clearly destroying our community. Like, what about all of the bad shit that happened to people as a result of them using or even selling drugs? So many people got killed and got locked up as a result of selling and using drugs. I didn't want to go down that path. The money may have been tempting, but it seemed too good to be true.

"I don't know, Rahzel. I mean, I hear you and all, but I just think it's still too risky."

"I had a feeling you'd say that," he replied, fiddling with an ink pen in his hand.

"Why you say that?"

"Cause everyone says that. You think you were the first to think that this here game isn't dangerous and risky?"

Silent, I didn't know how to respond to that 'cause that was a good question.

"Yeah, I mean, that's a good point. But still...what about all the crazy shit that happens in the streets as a result of people using drugs and selling it?"

"And? That's a part of life, young god. People eat sugar all day and get diabetes. Is it the grocery store's fault that a mothafucka can't stop feeding themselves?"

"No," I said.

"People drink all the time. Niggas get pissy drunk and beat the shit out of their wives. Is it the alcohol maker's fault that people do crazy shit?"

"No."

"People hop in traffic without wearing their seatbelts. Is it the car maker's fault that a mothafucka didn't wear their seatbelt?"

"No."

"Okay, so why is it my fault that a muhfucka gets high and decides to do stupid shit?"

"I see your point."

"Exactly," Rahzel said and then he fell silent and stared at me with his unblinking gaze. "I'll tell you what though... I'll give you a few days to think about it. In fact, I'll give you till the end of Friday next to make a decision. Time is money and money is time so, if you wanna get down, I'll welcome you to the game. But if not, then you can go ahead and be a broke ass doctor. How about that?" Rahzel produced a wide, Joker-like grin, revealing all of his gold teeth.

I took a deep breath. "Okay... I'll think about it," I said, exhaling.

"Good... well, enough of the business talk. So, tell me... we talked briefly about this new girl of yours. You really feelin' her, huh?"

"Yeah... she's fine. I really like her. She wants to be a doctor, too."

"That's cool, that's cool. I like what I'm hearing. You two sound like you're meant for each other. So, you think you got the balls to spit that game at her?"

I lowered my head and bashfully responded with, "I don't know."

"YOUNG GOD!" Rahzel suddenly snapped. I damn near jumped out of my seat when his voice boomed throughout the office. "That's a yes or no question. Are you gonna spit that game at her?"

"Yes," I nervously responded.

"You know... I got just what you need. Let me make a phone call right quick. Something to slap that indecisiveness, low self-esteem bullshit right out of ya, young god. Sit tight," Rahzel said, yanking a cell phone from out of the desk drawer.

Rahzel quickly dialed a number, threw the gray brick cell phone up to his ear and waited for someone to pick up. Within a few seconds, Rahzel uttered, "Wa 'Alaikum As-Salaam. Yo, listen. I'm down at the warehouse. Have the team to meet me down here in an hour. I got my new mentee with me. We going to see some ass and titties tonight."

Ass and titties?

Rahzel hung up the phone and smiled. "You need to taste test some pussy first before you eat the whole thing."

"Where are we going now?" I anxiously asked, my eyes once again exploding with surprise.

"We going to the strip club."

CHAPTER SEVENTEEN

When Rahzel told me he was the CEO of an organization, I didn't doubt him anymore.

I actually knew it.

And that was because once he made his phone call, within an hour, his entire organization rolled up to the warehouse.

Seemed like Rahzel rolled with at least a hundred niggas, if not more. And these guys didn't look like your typical dope boy niggas. They all looked like straight-up gangsters belonging to the mafia. And with the menacing looks etched on all of their faces, I knew they'd do any and everything to maintain their clout and power. Their auras were absolutely terrifying. Shit, now I realized Rahzel wasn't just the CEO of an organization; he was the general of an army. I had never seen a nigga manage to have this much power over men in my life. And, honestly, I was infatuated and intrigued.

It was around ten pm when Rahzel and I, including his entire crew, pulled in deep into the parking lot of *Juice*, one of the biggest strip clubs in Miami. This time, though, Rahzel and I weren't in his Mercedes. We were actually in the back of a black Chevy Suburban with all tinted windows. A big black nigga by the name of Kareem, who was the size of a Sequoia tree, was driving in the front. Another nigga named Samir was in the front passenger seat. Rahzel and I sat back in the back. Malik, one of his other guys, was driving the Mercedes.

Nervous more than ever, I couldn't believe I was about to step foot inside of a strip club. My heart raced with anxiety trying to figure out how in the hell I was going to even get inside. I wasn't even eighteen and I knew I still looked young as hell. *How is Rahzel going to get me inside?* I thought as we parked, my eyes landing on the thick line already forming outside.

We proceeded to get out of the truck and the Miami heat and humidity began to cloak me. Sweat beginning to drip from my face, I wiped my brow, hoping I wouldn't get in trouble for being underage. But then again, why did I need to worry? Rahzel obviously was that nigga and he wouldn't bring me here if he didn't think I could get inside.

"*Juice* got some of the baddest bitches up in Miami," Rahzel laughed, wiping his head. He then looked at me. "You ready to get a taste?" he asked.

"Yeah," I replied nervously and gulped.

Rahzel laughed. "Young God finne get a taste of the black man's real heaven... pussy. Let's go." He threw his arm around my shoulder and then a bunch of niggas from his team encircled us, forming a wall of security. And we moved as a unit, marching through the parking lot as an army. As we approached the club's doors, bass rumbling from the club intensified. I could hear what sounded like the Notorious BIG's *One More Chance* playing. I looked around to see the crowded line standing off to the side of the club, but it was so many niggas from Rahzel's crew blocking my view. Once we approached the doors, we didn't get stopped by security and strolled right in.

The club's foyer was long with mirrors on each side of the wall, reflecting the dark red lighting inside the club. The music got louder and so did the cheering and shouting of niggas. I still couldn't see shit But once we got inside the actual club, the crew broke apart and my eyes landed on nothing but a bunch of sexy ass chicks walking around naked from head to toe. My dick was starting to get somewhat hard looking at the titties and pussies on some of these broads. This one tall and slender light-skin chick with blonde hair threw her attention directly at me. At first, I wondered if she was staring at me because of my age, but she simply smiled and waved at me. My eyes widened with a rush of excitement, and I damn near collapsed.

"Oh, that bitch giving you the eye, young god! Be careful, she might wanna take you up to the champagne room," Rahzel said among the den of music and roaring.

Rahzel exploded into laughter yelling, "Young God, the champagne room is where boys become men."

I was still confused, but I think I knew what he meant. That was where I would go to lose my virginity.

Rahzel took his arm from around my shoulder and dapped up with a few more guys in the club. One of them, this tall, light skinned nigga with curly hair and a thin mustache, looked at me with a menacing scowl asking, "Who the fuck is this lil nigga?"

"This Dru, my new mentee," Rahzel replied. Rahzel then looked at me and said, "Dru, this one of my top lieutenants... this is Gino."

I reached my hand out to dap up with him. We shook up and then he scanned me up and down. "Boy, you look like you about thirteen or fourteen. How the fuck you get in here?!?"

I didn't say anything. I just looked at Rahzel with fearful eyes and kept my mouth pursed. Damn, now, I was about to get into trouble. Suddenly, Gino smiled and then said, "Lil nigga, I'm just messing with you. Boy look scary as fuck. Shit, I was twelve when I saw my first piece of ass," he laughed and playfully punched me.

Rahzel looked at me with this slight frown. I figured that was his cue for me to man the fuck up and stop acting like a little bitch. So, now I had to play the part. I didn't want to further make Rahzel think I was weak or anything like that. "Man, I wanna see some ass, y'all holding me up," I playfully grumbled.

Rahzel burst into a roaring laugh, slapping his chest. "Young God said we holdin' him the fuck up! I love it!" He threw his arm around my shoulder again and said, "Young God, we going to our VIP room. That's where the best bitches are at. These bitches down here are some gutta hoes with scars, bullet wounds, and stretch marks," he snickered, and we made our way deeper into the smoky nightclub.

The strip club was filled with a lot of dudes that looked like hood niggas and dope boys. A few white guys were in the mix, but for the most part, nothing but straight up goons occupied the surrounding area. I didn't feel intimidated though. Shit, I was too caught up in the haze of seeing so many titties, ass and so much pussy around me. I looked over to the right and saw this Latina-looking stripper with long, pink curly hair gliding down this shiny silver pole in the middle of the well-lit stage. Flashing lights danced all around the stage, making the chick look like she was made out of glitter.

Eventually, Rahzel and I made our way over to another door in the room that was guarded by two buff ass security guards, both of them wearing sunglasses. These onyx statute-lookin' niggas and their forty-inch biceps folded as they stood still, not making a move. You could spray these niggas down with a gat and they wouldn't flinch.

We were still surrounded by a few guys from the crew.

Rahzel coolly strolled up to one of the security guards and dapped up with him. He leaned into the guard's ear, and the two exchanged a few words. The guard then patted Rahzel on his shoulder and mumbled something to the other guard. Once he slowly opened the black door, dark green light escaped from the door's creak. Now I was back to being very nervous as we slowly strolled in. Once the door closed behind us, my eyes adjusted to the new forest green lighting beaming from golden chandeliers hanging from the low ceiling. Although I could still hear remnants from the music coming from the outside, now all I heard was Wu-Tang playing. This room was built like the inside of a genie's lamp. One big, long ass couch shaped like a half-cut circle wrapped around the entire room. A small stage with a single silver pole sat in the circle. It was illuminated with neon blue light. Scanning around, I also noticed there was a small DJ booth over in the corner occupied by some chubby bald dude. And next to it was a small bar tended by some older-looking nigga dressed in a long-white sleeved shirt and a bow-tie. On the far end of the couch, a few guys were being entertained by two chicks that were giving them lap dances.

"The fuck?!?" Rahzel groaned and suddenly clapped his hands twice. The thunder claps caught the attention of the two guys who threw their gawks over at us. They threw the strippers off them and then immediately stood up. Rahzel walked me over to one of the sections of the couch and told me to sit down and wait. He walked over to one of the guys and, without hesitation, slapped one of them across the head. I couldn't hear what he was telling them because the music was so loud, but he sounded mad as fuck. The two guys suddenly took off running out of the room. Rahzel rushed back over to me and sat down next to me, throwing his arm around my shoulder. "I swear, this is why sometimes you can't help niggas. They always on bullshit," he groaned, shaking his head.

Rahzel clapped his hands again and the Wu-Tang song came to an abrupt stop. Seconds later, Luniz' *I got 5 On It* began to play. Rahzel looked down at me and said, "You need to learn the power of feminine mystique, young god." Within seconds, a small door inside the room that I hadn't noticed before, opened up and then the room flooded with all types of fine ass chicks. All of them completely naked, I knew I was about to have the time of my life. This was the best night ever.

While guys from Rahzel's crew started dancing with some of the chicks, some of the baddies approached Rahzel and me. Both of them were light-brown with long black hair running down their backs. One, in particular, caught my attention 'cause she kind of reminded me of Amirah. *Damn, is she Trinidadian, too?* I wondered as I could feel my dick get hard. Scanning her up and down, I couldn't believe I was seeing a full ass naked woman in front of me. One sat on Rahzel's lap and the other one sat to my side and put her arm around me. "You ready to man up?" Rahzel asked smiling, looking directly at me.

"Yeah, I am." I grinned as I looked at the chick to my side. Gosh, she was so damn sexy. But as much as I was tempted, a part of me felt kind of weird. Kind of regretful actually. Was this the right thing to be doing? I felt like I was somewhat betraying Amirah. I mean, she and I weren't boyfriend and girlfriend, but I just felt kind of bad 'cause I felt like I was cheating on her.

Rahzel looked at the girl to my side and nodded. "Take care of this young god," he commanded and, without hesitation, she grabbed my hand and stood up, forcing me to stand up with her.

My eyes widened with fear. "Umm... what's going on?"

"She's gonna show you how to be a man, young god. Go on and do your thing. She's gonna give me a report card at the end."

A million butterflies instantly filled my stomach. My breathing got fast and deep. I didn't know what the fuck I was about to do. I didn't even know how to have sex. I mean, I've seen a few pictures here and there in Playboy Magazine of naked girls, but I had no idea what pussy even really felt like!

But I had to be a man. Especially if I was gonna try to ask Amirah out. I didn't want to come off as scary or punkish. Trying to muster up some self-confidence, I asked the chick holding my hand, "What's your name?"

"Candy," she said, escorting me through the middle of the room to another door.

"Where are you taking me?" I had to ask as we got close to the door.

"To the champagne room."

My throat became tight with anxiety as she opened the small door and pulled me into the small room that was literally the size of a tiny bedroom. The room was dimly lit with a red light bulb centered in the ceiling. A small, black leather loveseat sat up against a wall. Candy shoved me to the couch, then spun me around and sat me down. "Just relax, lil guy. I'mma make you feel really good," she purred as she began to dance to the song still booming outside.

I swear to God my heart was about to explode out of my chest. I couldn't believe this was about to happen right now. I was about to have sex for the first time. Now, I had millions of questions running through my cloudy mind. What would her pussy feel like? Would it be wet? How would she feel? Would she make sounds? Would I nut fast? Would I get her pregnant?

As Candy kept dancing and shaking her ass, she slowly

moved toward me, grabbing her brown titties and squeezing them together. Now an inch away from me, she leaned down and grabbed my pants, trying to tug them down. "Help me out here," she said, laughing.

My hands trembling, I unbuttoned my pants and pulled them down. Now, I was just in my boxers. Candy stood back up and then straddled me, her nice titties hanging in my face. "You're a little cutie pie. So round and chocolate," she uttered, running a finger down my face and my chest. I swear it seemed like I took another hit of the cocaine because I was high all over again. As she moved her hand down to my stomach, my heart beat faster and faster. Yeah, I was gonna have a heart attack. I was gonna die. But at least I'd die getting pussy.

She leaned her face into mine and planted a kiss on the side of my cheek. "Just relax. You look so nervous. My pussy won't bite."

My mouth suddenly flung wide open. "Ahhhhh! Oh, My God!"

CHAPTER EIGHTEEN

"What's wrong?" Candy asked when she saw my eyes shoot wide open with surprise.

Humiliated, I hated to have to admit this. I felt like such a letdown. "I... um... I think I nutted," I confessed.

She took a quick glance down at my boxers then looked back at me. "Boy! Get yo young ass up!" she said, exploding in laughing. She stood up and yanked me out of the couch. "Can't believe I even let Rahzel's crazy ass pay me to do this," she huffed.

I quickly pulled my pants up and buttoned them back up. She grabbed me by my shoulder and playfully pushed me toward the door. "I knew this was gonna happen. Happens all the time. I just thought yo thug lookin' ass would've lasted longer," she said, shaking her head.

Embarrassment couldn't even describe what I felt right now. Now I knew Rahzel was gonna laugh at me and poke fun of me in front of all of his guys.

We exited the room and sauntered back over to Rahzel, who was deep in the middle of a lap dance. I guess he saw us walking up to him out of the corner of his eye. "Damn, that was quick! You used a condom?" he asked, scanning me up and down. The other sexy ass chick was still grinding on him.

I looked the other way, afraid to answer. Candy smacked her teeth and said, "We didn't even get that far. Lil boy punked out. I hate it when you do this to me, Rahzel. This like the third or fourth lil ass boy you brought up in here like this. Gon get me in fucking trouble."

Rahzel smacked his teeth back at Candy. "Bitch, whatever. You still made your money. Now, go suck one of these other nigga's up here." Rahzel looked at me. "Young God, let's jet out of here. I should've known you were too green," he said, shaking his head. He threw the other chick off him and stood up.

He threw his arm around my shoulder and we exited the VIP room. Kareem and Malik, who were his two top guards in his crew, trailed us as we made our way back out onto the main floor of the strip club and over to the exit. Now outside and trekking back to the Suburban, Rahzel proceeded to lecture me.

"Young God... so, tell me, what happened?"

"I... I just came a lil too early, I guess."

Rahzel let out a small laugh while shaking his head. "Young God, you mean to tell me you still didn't proceed to tag that ass?"

I thought for a second. Damn. Why did I stop? But the embarrassment combined with the guilt had me paralyzed with fear. I just wasn't capable of going on.

"I, umm... I don't know, Rahzel. I just feel like this is just a bit too much for me right now," I confessed. "I mean, can I not practice with someone else?"

"No, young god. There's no such thing as practicing with pussy. Like coke, pussy ain't nothin' to play with. Both are powerful drugs that can mess up a man's mind. Speaking of which..." Rahzel suddenly stopped dead in his tracks and, without hesitation, he angrily searched my pockets. He yanked out the vial of cocaine and nudged it in my face. "You think I didn't know, huh?"

"Rahzel! I didn't—"

"Don't act stupid, young god! I watched your lil round ass twitch all mothafuckin' morning and afternoon. You think I can't tell a junkie from a mile away?"

Caught and scared, I couldn't say anything back to him. He leaned down and looked me dead in my eyes. "I was gonna let you have fun, but it's obvious you can't handle nothing. When you get back home, you're gonna run right to your room, get those other vials you stole from ME and you're gonna hand them right back to your mother," Rahzel growled as he yanked me close to his face with his right hand. "And if I ever hear about you stealing from me again or using this shit, I'll kill you. YOU UNDERSTAND ME?!?"

"Yeah!" I screeched, a tear escaping the corner of my eye.

He shoved me in front of him and said, "Now walk... I'm taking your scary, green ass back home. I thought you would've at least handled the pussy, but you can only handle books and twinkies, I see. You're still a little ass boy, young god. Damn near fourteen-years-old and can't even hold a nut in."

bout an hour later, the Suburban pulled into the parking lot of the apartment complex. Rahzel didn't say another word to me the entire car ride.

Once the truck came to a stop in front of my unit, Kareem looked in the rearview mirror and asked, "Is this it, young brotha?"

"Yes, sir," I replied, glancing out the window up to my unit. I could see that the lights in the den were on, which meant Mama was home, probably watching TV with Tay'Quan.

Rahzel, sitting on the other side of the Suburban's back seat, glanced over at me and reached his hand out. "Give me some love, young god. Sorry I went off on you earlier. I just don't wanna see you get hooked to that shit. All it takes is a couple of blasts and you'll be on that shit for the rest of your life."

"I understand," I replied, my head lowered out of shame. I reached over and then both of us dapped up. Truth be told, I was gonna stop using that shit anyways 'cause I didn't like the constant highs and lows. I didn't understand why someone would use that shit if you had to constantly rely on it like that. Then and there, a crazy realization hit me. It made perfect sense why selling drugs was such a lucrative ass business. Once you got hooked on something like coke, you just didn't want it, you needed it. In fact, you were held captive by it. Drugs obviously turned people into slaves. And I'd be damned if I was gonna be someone's slave.

"Get your bags and shit, young god. I'll chop it up with you later. But you can't work for the organization. Just stay in school. I'll still drop by from time to time to check up on you and drop you some knowledge, but you ain't built for this shit."

"Why is that?" I asked.

"Cause your heart is elsewhere. And your heart is too warm. You need to be cold."

"Cold?"

"Yeah... cold. Solid. You too warm. Too much of a nice guy. Nice guys don't survive in this business. Go on and do your doctor thing though... and you and that Amanda chick, or whatever the fuck her name is, can go off and save the world. Me... I wanna run the world. Even if I destroy it in the process."

My eyebrow raised. "Damn… why do you wanna destroy it though?"

"Your mother was right. You ask too many questions sometimes."

"But isn't that the sign of a good student? Ask a lot of questions?"

"Yeah… in certain instances. But sometimes, the answers you're looking for are right there in front of you. Sometimes, you just gotta learn how to keep your mouth shut and move with silence. You can't let everyone know what you thinking all the time, you feel me?"

"Yes. That's a good point."

"Anyways… I was leery at first, but I guess your mother was right. Your brother is built for the game. I swore I thought you were the one who was built for this shit, but your brother proved he was really the young nigga I needed on my team," he said.

"But Tay'Quan is younger than me though," I replied.

Rahzel smacked his teeth. "And? Age ain't nothing but a number."

"Okay," was all I could reply with as I looked away from him and slowly opened the door. "Well, I'll holla at you later, Rahzel. Thanks for the haircut, clothes, and the knowledge," I said and slammed the door. Fuck him and fuck his knowledge, was all I kept thinking as I made my way to the back of the Suburban. Kareem popped the trunk and I grabbed all of my shopping bags. "Thanks again, Rahzel," I said and slammed the trunk. I dashed upstairs, not looking back. Out the corner of my eye, I saw Willie come out of nowhere. Suddenly, he flinched, throwing his hands up in the air.

"WHOA!" he yelled, his entire slender body trembling.

"It's okay, Willie. I'm not gonna do shit. That was just one of my Mama's friends earlier. He's kind of an asshole," I explained.

"Yeah, well, I don't want no problems, bruh."

"It's cool though." I smiled. "You cool with me, Willie."

"Appreciate it, young brotha," Willie responded while smiling, his wide-open jaundiced eyes skimming me up and down. "But damn, you lookin' sharp as hell! You got a haircut and a new fit! Boy, you look like a million dollars!"

Laughing, I said, "Thanks." "You doin' alright though?" I asked.

"Yeah... just maintaining. That's all I can do at this point," he said. "Just maintain."

"That's good though, Willie. Anyways, I'mma head back inside," I said, feeling bogged down with extreme exhaustion.

I trekked down the walkway and made my way to the apartment. I knocked on the door three times and, within seconds, I could hear footsteps rumbling toward the door.

Mama unlocked and opened the door and then scanned me up and down. "You became a man?" she asked dryly.

Glancing down, I didn't know what to say. "Yeah," I lied.

"Hrrrm... yeah, whatever. Come in," she mumbled, letting me into the apartment. "And take your shoes off," she instructed.

Doing as she said, I put the bags down and took my shoes off and put them up against the wall next to the door. Tay'Quan wasn't here in the living room I noticed. "Where's Tay'Quan?" I asked as I picked my bags up.

"His grandma came down and got him. He's gonna be staying with his other peoples for a while until I get some things together," she said.

"What?!?" My face screwed with confusion. "This just happened all of a sudden?"

"DRU!" Mama snapped. "I don't need all of the questions right now. PLEASE!"

"Okay," I said, shaking my head.

Without saying another word to her, I went straight to my

bedroom and put my stuff down. I shot over to my closet and pulled down the shoebox where I kept the three other vials. Once I grabbed them out of the ugly ass shoe, I walked back into the den and handed them to Mama. She looked at me with a weird stare mumbling, "Thank you."

"You're welcome," I replied nonchalantly and proceeded to make my way back to my room.

But before I could make it out the den, Mama uttered, "Dru. Don't leave just yet."

I stopped and turned around and looked at her. "What?" I asked with a raised brow.

"I know you lied to me. You didn't become a man. You're still a little ass boy. Have a good night. I'm going outside to smoke a cigarette," she muttered, rolling her eyes at me.

CHAPTER NINETEEN

My eyes blasted wide open to the ear-cracking buzz coming from my alarm clock. My vision hazy, I turned over and saw that 5:45 am beamed in red. Time to get up to start this brand new day 'cause it was time to be a new me.

Time to be a man.
Man up, Dru.
Man the fuck up.
Stop being a kid.
No more little ass boy shit.

Since Saturday night, I came to the realization that everyone was right. I was a boy. I was weak. I was a punk. So, it was time to change that shit up.

With my new mantra telling me to man the fuck up singing in my head, I sat up in my bed, wiping crust out of my eyes. Still somewhat dark outside, nothing but pigeons singing and chirping could be heard outside.

For a moment, I just stared off in my dark room, thinking about everything that happened on Saturday night. Razhel was right – I wasn't cut out of the streets. I'm a geek. I loved science. But one thing he was wrong about was me not being a man. That shit didn't sit well with me at all. I was a man. I was gonna show everyone I was a fucking man.

See, I hated the fact that everyone could take a glance at me and write me off as a boy or a punk. That meant that I walked around carrying so much self-doubt and low self-confidence. That meant I projected weakness.

But how could I not?

For most of my life, Shalanda (I refused to call that bitch a mother or Mama anymore) made me feel so ugly and unwanted. But I got so used to Mama drilling her hatred into my head that I believed in. However, the one thing that now drove me crazy was the fact that Rahzel said Tay'Quan was more of a man than me. And that he was ready for the game. That shit truly pissed me the fuck off and now I was destined to change that perception people obviously had about me.

First thing first, my goal now was to wake up really early every morning and do as many push-ups, sit-ups, and jumping jacks as I could in thirty minutes. Doing exercise early enough before getting ready for school would shape me up quickly.

"Let's get it," I growled and yawned. I hopped out of the bed, dashed over to the light switch near my door and turned on my room light. Shit, it felt so different being up this early, but this was something I was going to have to get used to. I was determined to now make this a habit every day.

First starting with jumping jacks, I went straight to it. Although I was still sluggish from the craziness of the weekend, I powered through my first set. After that, I went straight to my push-ups and sit-ups.

Once I got done, I flew into the bathroom and took a quick shower. Fuck that bleaching shit. I was done with that. It seemed like it wasn't working and, on top of that, I was just gonna have to be comfortable with my skin tone. My weight could change, but my skin tone was set for life. And if people didn't like, then oh well.

It was close to 7:30 now and, after zipping back to my room, I threw on my new outfit and shoes. Now, I was standing in the mirror in my room, staring at myself wondering how people were gonna react to my new look. With a fresh fade, clothes, and shoes, I knew I was bound to make some heads turned. But I didn't care about anyone else's reaction. I just cared about Amirah's. I wondered how she'd react to my new look.

As the sun began to light up my room, I realized I didn't hear a single whistle from Willie this morning. Bet you he didn't have the energy to even get up and whistle anymore. I felt so bad for the man and I truly hoped maybe he'd find a doctor who'd give him some medicine that would make him live longer. Maybe then he'd stop smoking dope, get clean and change his life around.

Dope...

Speaking of dope, Saturday night taught me a lot actually – I wasn't built to be a dope boy or a nigga kicking it in the streets. That was just never me and never will be me. Call me corny, geeky, or lame – but it is what it is. This was who I am. A science nerd. I loved school. I loved books. I wanted to be a doctor and help people. That's it. All that extra shit was for the birds.

Now granted, I was thankful for Rahzel for helping me out and getting me new clothes and a haircut, but he was right – I didn't have it in me to work for him. And truth be told, I never really wanted to work for him. He and Shalanda were just trying to force that shit on me.

Still staring at myself in the mirror, I realized my dad was right all along. Although I was still upset and curious about the real reason why he was in prison, it seemed like he knew I wasn't cut out for that street shit. And I was glad he warned me not to get involved in any of that mess. But damn, I still couldn't shake the idea though that Dad possibly killed people. But with everything that transpired Saturday, I wonder if Rahzel was just bullshitting me. I wondered if he was just trying to see if I would fold and see him as more credible than Dad. Who knows but still – I wanted no parts of the drug game or street life. Period.

Nonetheless, I will say though that one thing Rahzel saw in me that I knew I needed to change was the fact that I needed to stop being so scared. I needed to be more fearless and go after what I wanted... and that was exactly why once I got to school, I was going to ask Amirah out. I knew it might be kind of pushy or maybe even too early, but I had to ask before someone else did. Then, I knew she'd put me in the friend zone.

I took one last glance at myself. Ready. With my heavy ass book bag slung over my shoulder, I rushed out of my room. Marching down the hallway, rumbling from the den's TV filled my ears. Shalanda's trifling ass was up already. I got into the den and saw her sitting on the couch smoking a cigarette, her hazy eyes glued to the morning news. She looked over at me. "Hey... you want me to take you to school?" she asked.

"I'm good," I replied, making my way into the kitchen to grab a piece of fruit. I was pining for banana this morning.

"Why not?" Shalanda asked.

Staring her screwed up face, I grabbed a banana from a fruit bowl and said, "Cause I'd rather just walk. I'm trying to get in as much exercise as possible... since I gotta lose weight."

"Oh... oh okay," she said, then took a puff from her cigarette. "Well, I'll see you later then."

"Okay," was all I threw back to her and then made my way out of the door.

"OKAY! Listen carefully to me before we go into the library. I am breaking you all up into pairs. I do not want you all hanging out in large groups together!" Mrs. Tate yelled as she scanned the entire English class with her big blue eyes.

We were standing outside of the school library's entrance in the hallway. Lined against the wall, Mrs. Tate was going over instructions for our research assignment.

"As I said before, find one book and then I want you and your partner to identify at least twenty to thirty similes and metaphors. Understand? I want the packet completed by the end of the week!"

"Yes, ma'am," the entire class responded, our tones low and respectful.

"But Mrs. Tate, what if they only have one copy of the book?!?" Jean-Paul, one of my classmates, asked.

"Then, you all will share!" Mrs. Tate shot back. "Okay, first pair... Andrew and Amirah. You all go together."

A rush of a mix of energy and sudden nausea invaded me when I heard Mrs. Tate call Amirah and me. This entire morning I hadn't had a chance to talk to Amirah. She got caught up talking to Cathy, one of our other classmates. Those two seemed like they were becoming the best of friends. But once Mrs. Tate announced Amirah and I were going to be working together on this assignment, my eyes beamed with excitement. Time to be a man...

Standing about four or five kids behind me, we both got out of line and then walked up to Mrs. Tate together. Mrs. Tate handed me our assignment packet and then said, "You all are going to choose a book from the African-American Literature section, okay?"

"Yes, ma'am," the both of us replied then strolled into the library.

"How was your weekend?" Amirah asked, as I led her to the back of the library where I knew the African American literature section was.

"It was cool. Got a new haircut and bought some new clothes," I replied.

"I see," Amirah responded bashfully. "You look good though."

Oh shit! Damn, now that weird magical feeling was coming back again. I glanced at Amirah and said, "Thanks. What did you do?"

"Nothing... just read, caught up on homework, and went to church. The usual stuff," she replied as we found ourselves alone. "What book do you want to read?" she asked.

"I don't know." I ran my hands across the first book I saw in the middle of the shelf. *Invisible Man* by Ralph Ellison stood out. I grabbed it and looked at the weird cover art. "Invisible Man... this looks interesting," I said and flipped through the middle of the book.

"Hrrrm.... Invisible Man. That seems like it's gonna be a long read," Amirah replied. "But we can read it if you want to read it," she said.

"Yeah... I figured since it's a longer book, we can find more adverbs and whatnot. Everyone else might choose something easy, not realizing they will have a harder time finding what Mrs. Tate wants."

"Damn, that's a good point. You're so smart." Amirah smiled.

"Thanks," I replied, staring into her doe eyes. Was now the time to ask? Butterflies filled my stomach.

"Why are you staring at me like that?" Amirah suddenly asked, instantly snapping me out of my daze.

"I'm sorry. I just—"

"You just what?"

"I, umm... I just like your eyes."

Amirah gasped and clutched her mouth.

I quickly grew terrified that I scared her. "I'm sorry. I didn't mean to—"

"No... don't be sorry," she interjected, releasing her hand from her mouth and revealing a bashful smile. "I just... I just never thought you'd say that. That's all."

My eyebrow raised out of curiosity and excitement. "Really? Why is that?"

"Cause I would've thought you didn't like me."

"Really? What makes you say that?"

Amirah looked around for a second. "Well, I think you're cute."

"Really? Me?" I smiled. "That's funny."

"Why is that?"

"Cause I was thinking the same. I think you're cute. I thought you wouldn't like me either."

We both got quiet. Looking into her eyes, I could tell she was nervous. I was nervous, too. Shit, probably more nervous than she was. Then, without hesitation, Amirah leaned down and kissed me on my cheek. "I've been wanting to do that since day one."

My heart exploded. She kissed me. She kissed me. She kissed me.

"Damn..." was all I could say at the moment. "Am I dreaming?"

"No," Amirah said, laughing. "You're not dreaming. I just kissed you."

"Damn..."

"Damn what?"

"From the first day I saw you, I have been dreaming of this," I confessed.

Amirah, still staring at me, said, "Well, aren't you going to kiss me back?"

"Yeah," I replied and closed my eyes, returning a soft kiss onto her cheek.

"We better get started on our work though before we get in trouble," she said.

"You're right."

Some hours had passed from that initial kiss. And I swore with all my heart and soul that I had to be dreaming. This had to be a dream.

But it wasn't... it was all real. Amirah really kissed me. We kissed. We liked each other. This was a dream come true.

It was around eight pm and I was lying in my bed thinking about everything that happened. I was supposed to be reading *Invisible Man*, but I was obviously way too distracted. How could I not be? Like, I couldn't even believe all of this went down today and it seemed like everything happened so effortlessly.

We hung out during lunch and Amirah confessed to me she liked me from the day she met me. She was just waiting for me to make my move. That had me so blown though because she gave me no sign that she was digging me like that. What was even crazier was that I didn't even have to work hard and "man up" to ask her out. After our kiss, I just simply asked her if she wanted to hang out this weekend, and she agreed. The only issue was her grandparents. She told me her grandfather was very strict, but she'd manage to figure out a way to get out of the house. Apparently, her grandparents were very strict religious folks and didn't want her really hanging out with anyone, especially boys. She said her grandfather was very distrustful of the "neighborhood thugs".

She would've given me her phone number, but she said her grandfather would only permit her to speak from five to seven on weeknights to other girls who were her friends. And he'd be on the other line listening, making sure we weren't talking about anything sexual.

But honestly, none of that bothered me. I found love. And it seemed like Amirah found love too. After school, we chopped it for a few, talking about life, our favorite television shows, food, etc. I was still in so much of a daze though because I would've thought my size and skin color would've been a no-no for her. But in our conversation, she did tell me that she liked darker guys and guys with size on them. That was the first time ever I had heard a girl say that.

Staring up at the slowly moving ceiling fan blades, I just kept imagining the two of us running off from Miami and going somewhere big and luxurious like New York City. The two of us would get married and live in a big penthouse where we'd overlook the entire city. We'd be two doctors in love, ready to save the world. I hoped that would become a dream one day, too.

CHAPTER TWENTY

Where is she? I kept thinking to myself. *Was this a nightmare? This was like one big joke God or the universe was playing on me.*

Amirah hadn't been to school for a few days now.

On Monday, I was in heaven. But a few days passed, now I was in hell.

It was Thursday afternoon and I was sitting in Ms. Reid's class barely able to concentrate. Maybe she got sick? Maybe she just has a cold or the flu? I kept trying to come up with excuse after excuse of why Amirah suddenly hadn't shown up to school for the past three days. A part of me was so desperate to go up to Ms. Reid and flat out ask her if she had heard from Amirah's grandparents or anyone else why she was gone. It just didn't seem right that someone who was new wouldn't suddenly be here anymore.

But then again, she was *new*. And that meant maybe her grandfather didn't want her coming to this school anymore. From the sound of it, her grandfather was mean and strict and didn't want her to be in this type of "environment". Whatever the fuck that meant. By now, I had to assume that if Amirah wasn't sick, her grandparents pulled her out of school and sent her somewhere else. And if that was the case, I was going to be completely devastated.

Two pm struck the clock and, once again, I found myself distracted by thinking about Amirah. I was supposed to be reading fifteen pages out of my science book, but all I kept thinking about was that first kiss. And I couldn't believe the first girl who gave me that kiss could be out of my life suddenly... forever.

Twiddling my thumbs, I debated whether or not I should just go up and ask Ms. Reid about her. Fuck it. I closed my book, scooted back my seat and made my way over to her. The entire classroom was quiet as everyone had their heads buried in their textbooks.

I nervously strolled over to Ms. Reid. She was grading some assignments. Glancing up at me, she lowered her reading glasses and asked, "What's up, Andrew?"

"Can I ask you a question?"

"Sure thing," she said, pointing to the seat next to her. "What's going on? Let me guess, your mother finally wants you to go to MAST?"

Taking a seat next to her, I whispered, "Actually... no. It's not about that."

"Damn...well, what's going on?"

I looked around quickly, not wanting anyone to hear me. Then, I leaned into Ms. Reid and whispered, "The new girl... Amirah... she hasn't been to school now for a few days and I'm getting worried."

"Worried about what?"

I shrugged my shoulders. "I mean, she wasn't sick or anything on Monday and now, suddenly, she's gone. Did she withdraw from the school?" I asked.

"I hadn't heard anything. Besides, I wouldn't know until

next week. But I doubt she'd withdraw because the district wouldn't allow that."

"Oh... okay," I replied, then tightened my lips.

"She's your new friend or something?"

"Yeah."

"Do you have her phone number?"

"No... no, I don't. She was gonna give it to me, but she said her grandfather is strict."

"Oh okay... well, if I hear anything, I'll let you know. But anyways, don't worry about her and worry about those grades." Ms. Reid held up one of my pop quizzes she just graded. "You got a B minus. This ain't like you. What's going on?"

Lowering my head out of shame, I said, "I'm sorry. Just had a rough weekend."

Ms. Reid leaned into my ear. "Is it your mother? Is she hitting you?"

"No," I said, shaking my head.

"Oh okay. Well, let me know if you need anything else from me, okay?"

"I will," I said, standing up. Before I made my way back over to my seat, Ms. Reid grabbed my wrist and pulled me close to her. Skimming me up and down, she whispered, "You look like you're losing weight though."

"Thanks, Ms. Reid," I replied with a smile and then walked back over to my desk, my eyes attached to the empty seat that Amirah would've been sitting in.

The final school bell rang for the day and I slowly marched out of the classroom, trailing other students out into the noisy, crowded hallway. My head hung low, a million thoughts swarmed my mind. Where was she? I hoped she was okay. God, please don't play this game with me.

Continuing to walk down the hall, I had absolutely no motivation to go home. Besides, with the amount of homework I had piling up, I figured I could just stay behind an hour or so and read at the library before going back home.

Once I cut a few corners and made my way to the library, I went straight inside looking for a table. It seemed like there were no other students inside. As I kept walking, to my right I saw Ms. Bainbridge, the school librarian, sitting at her desk inside of her office. Her office door wide open, she looked like she was busy typing up some paperwork.

Once I found a table, I sat my book bag down and pulled out all of my books, diving right into reading. Now, I had to distract myself with something else other than Amirah.

Some time had passed and I didn't know exactly how long I had been in the library. This reading proved to be a good distraction. Closing my English textbook, I glanced over at the clock sitting on a wall to the right of me. It was nearly five pm. Usually, I would've had my ass home by now 'cause Shalanda would've tried to fuck me up for being late. But I didn't give a fuck about her anymore. She could kiss my ass from the back, so she could also suck my dick. I couldn't wait until I got old enough to leave home and get far away from her and everything else she put her hands on. And speaking of which, I wondered why Tay'Quan suddenly left. Him just up and leaving seemed suspect as fuck to me. However, I wasn't gonna ask any questions. I didn't like his punk ass any damn way. I felt like he was just as culpable as Shalanda when it came to all the abuse I had to endure.

Ready to head back home, I slowly stuffed my bookbag, trying to pass some time. Then, the sudden urge to pee came. "Fuck," I grumbled to myself, wondering where the bathroom was at. The school library didn't have one, so I would've needed to quickly leave and run down to the hall. I knew there was one by Ms. Reid's classroom, which wasn't too far away.

Once I slung the book bag over my shoulders, I rushed out of the library and down the hall to the first boys' bathroom I could find. However, the moment I strolled inside, my stomach started to grumble. Felt like I needed to do more than pee. So, I found a stall all the way toward the end of the bathroom. Once inside, I threw my book on the door hook. Then, I quickly took my pants off and underwear off, sat down, and did what I had to do. There was no one else in the bathroom at the moment.

My stomach still felt a bit queasy, so I spent more time than usual on the toilet. But some moments later, I heard the door open and then a few boys trickled inside.

"Man, I wanna smoke some weed. Lock the fucking door," I heard the recognizable voice say. Then, I heard whoever else this person was with lock the door.

I could hear both of them step closer and closer to the stall. As they kept talking to themselves, that was when I recognized one of the voices. It was Tyrone.

"So, what were you telling me about the new bitch? What's her name again? Amirah?" the other voice asked. I tried my best to make out this other guy's voice. Sounded like this nigga named Jerrell. But the moment I heard Jerrell drop Amirah's name, my gaze became wide and curious.

"Bro, I raped that fucking bitch. Stupid ass bitch knew she wanted it, but she was giving me problems."

"Nigga, you crazy! What do you mean by you raped her?!?"

"Just like what the fuck I said! Caught her ass lackin'! She was walking in the neighborhood. I didn't even realize she lived that close to me. So, I started talking to her. Next thing you know, she was all over me, kissing me and shit. So, I thought she was going. I was gonna take her back to my place and shit, but you know my pops was home. And then, she told me her people wouldn't let no one over. So, I took her ass to this abandoned house not too far away on York Street. Man, we got inside and started making out even more. I was fingering her lil pussy and sucking on her titties. And, then, once I pulled my dick out, she gon tell me no. I was like 'What?!? Bitch, you gon give me some!"

"Damn, G! She let you do all that and then she wasn't gonna let you fuck?!?"

"Exactly! That's what the fuck I'm saying! She gon run me this bullshit story asking me for a condom and what not. I was like 'Bitch, we ain't need no condom. I'll just pull out and skeet all in yo mouf!'. She was like, 'Nah. I can't do it. I'm a virgin' blah blah blah'."

"Yoooo! So, you just took the shit then?"

"Hell yeah! And then she tried to fight back, but I fucked that bitch up and left her unconscious. That's why she ain't at school."

"YOOOO! You crazy as fuck, Tyrone! Damn, did you kill her or somethin'?!?"

"Shit, I don't know, but ain't nobody gonna know 'cuz I just left her lil stupid slutty as there. You got a lighter?"

"Yeah, I do. Hold on..." I could hear Jerrell rumble through his book bag, then he asked, "so what you gon do if she snitches?"

"I'mma kill her fuckin' ass. Bitch better not fuck with me. I know that for sure," Tyrone answered, snickering.

My stomach became tight and my heart damn near exploded out of my chest hearing Tyrone go back and forth in detail about how he'd raped Amirah. Part of me didn't want to believe it, but why would he make something up like this??!? And why would he be in the bathroom openly discussing it with Jerrell! Now, it all made fucking sense! And if this nigga was telling the truth, I was gonna go crazy! I was gonna run out of here and tell the first adult I ran into what I heard or go and tell the police.

This was beyond fucked up. I was terrified but enraged all at the same time. But my fear overpowered my anger. Scared, I tried my best to stay still so that Tyrone and Jerrell wouldn't hear me.

Some seconds later, I could smell weed smoke pouring into my stall. Then, Tyrone and Jerrell started coughing.

"Damn, this shit is strong as fuck, boy," Jerrell laughed while his nonstop coughing filled the bathroom.

Tyrone smacked his teeth and said, "Boy, you's a bitch nigga. This shit is some regs. Shit ain't strong like that Hydro. Have you ever smoked that shit?"

"Nah... shit, get me some," Jerrell said.

My leg started to get numb from sitting on the toilet seat for a long time. I slowly sat up to give my leg some reprieve But soon as I sat down, the toilet made a weird creak.

My eyes shot open with surprise 'cause I knew they'd hear the sound.

"Yo! You heard that?" Jerrell asked.

"Yeah... I did," Tyrone replied. "YO! WHO'S IN HERE?!?" he suddenly screamed, his angered voice echoing throughout the bathroom. "I'mma fuck you up when I find you!"

CHAPTER TWENTY-ONE

"YOU BETTER COME OUT NOW OR I'MMA SLICE YOU UP IN A MILLION WAYS!" Tyrone continued yelling.

Fear and anxiety overwhelmed me as I heard Tyrone and Jerrell's footsteps rush closer and closer to my stall. Freaking out, I wiped my ass as quick as I could and flushed the toilet.

"Say something now, mothafucka, or else!" Tyrone barked again.

Within seconds, I could see Tyrone and Jerrell's shadows lurking under the stall. One of them tried to open and burst through the stall, but it was locked. Then, I saw someone's eye peeking through the crack in the door. It was Tyrone and he was staring dead at me with his one evil eye.

"It's mothafuckin' black ass oil field!" Tyrone growled once he got a glimpse of me and tried to open the stall again.

"COME OUT, BLACK ASS NIGGA!"

"Leave me the fuck alone, Tyrone!" I screamed back, holding my book bag to my chest.

"Boy, open up this mothafuckin' door or I'm gonna fuck you up for real!"

"Fuck you! Leave me the fuck alone, Tyrone!"

"DAMN! You gon let this punk ass nigga talk to you like that?" Jerrell spat, laughing.

"Nah! I'm giving you to the count of three to come the fuck out!"

Trembling, I hesitated.

"ONE!"

"TWO!"

My heart rate was racing a million miles per hour.

"THREE!"

All of a sudden, Tyrone exploded the stall door open with one mighty kick, busting the lock off its hinge. The door flew back, almost hitting me in the face, but I ducked back, holding tight to my book bag.

"BOY! YOU SMELL LIKE DOOKIE! GET THE FUCK OUT OF HERE!" Jerrell's tall and built ass screamed. Then, both he and Tyrone grabbed me and pulled me out of the stall. I tried to fight them off as best as I could, kicking and punching all over the place, but they overpowered me, throwing me against an adjacent wall near one of the sinks.

"HELP!" I kept screaming to the top of my lungs but Jerrell, who was at least a foot taller than me and played defense for our football team, threw a hard punch to my jaw and muzzled me.

"SHUT THE FUCK UP!" he roared. Funny how Tyrone always called me black as fuck, but Jerrell was my same complexion. Shit, truth be told, he was a tad darker than me.

Tyrone had his hands gripped to my shirt collar as well. He yanked out a knife from his pocket and flashed the blade in front of my eyes. "I should cut that big ass nose off your fucking fat, black ass face, you know that?" he growled as he took the blade and slowly dug the tip into my cheek. "You black ass nigga, I'll kill you."

Tears of rage and fear running down my face, I didn't

know what to do. I was completely motionless. Breathing hard, the piercing of the blade didn't even sting 'cause I had so much adrenaline running through me.

"You were in the bathroom taking a shit and eavesdropping at the same mothafuckin' time. You nosey ass, geeky, no pussy-gettin', Debbie cake-eatin' ass nigga. I oughta cut all this fat off you." Tyrone kept fuming, holding the blade deep in my cheek. Now, I could feel sharp stinging in my face.

"She ain't deserve that. Why did you do that to her?" I shot back.

"SHUT THE FUCK UP!" Tyrone screamed, pinning me harder against the wall. Jerrell just kept snickering as he used his entire body weight to keep me restrained.

"Now listen, you fat mothafucka… if you run your mouth and go snitch on me, I'mma find you and kill you. Don't even think about going to the police 'cause my dad knows some straight goons that'll find you and do you. We'll chop your black, fat ass body up into pieces and throw yo fat ass in the Everglades. Black, fat ass might taste good to them gators, too," Tyrone raged in a voice I never heard from him. His tone meant he was serious as fuck. I could see in his unblinking, red eyes. "You understand me?"

"Yeah," I uttered, tears still falling out of the corners of my eyes.

"Good. Like I said, run your mouth and your life is over, fat nigga," he snarled, releasing me. He slowly pulled the blade from my face and I saw the tip of it was dripping with blood.

Jerrell threw a hard punch into my stomach. All the wind out of my lungs, I fell forward, collapsing onto the dirty bathroom floor. "Fat ass nigga," Jerrell laughed as he and Tyrone began to walk away.

It took me a few moments to gather myself, but I managed to get up and limp over to the sink. Gawking in the spotty mirror, I saw the tiny slash bleeding on my cheekbone. I grabbed a piece of brown paper towel from the dispenser next to me and pressed it against my face to stop the bleeding. I still didn't know what to think. Shit, I could barely move. My torso and mouth were radiating with pain from the hits Jerrell gave me.

Once I managed to stop the bleeding, I rushed out of the bathroom and down the hallway. The school was now virtually empty and not a single teacher or security guard was in sight. My mind blank, all I could concentrate on was getting home as soon as I could. With my nerves shot to shit and fear running through my veins at a thousand miles per second, I ran my ass home as fast as I could, getting back in less than thirty minutes.

"Where were you?" was the first thing rolling out of Shalanda's big ass mouth soon as I stepped through the apartment door. Without bothering to take my shoes off, I stormed down the hallway to my room and slammed the door shut. I locked the door and threw my book bag to the floor. Pacing, I had so many thoughts running through my raging mind.

What can I do? Who can I tell? Is Tyrone lying? Why in the fuck would he do this? The thoughts kept going and going until I felt like I was on the verge of having a complete nervous breakdown.

"AHHHHHH!" I had to scream as loud as I could just to let out the crazy emotions flooding me.

I guess Shalanda heard me scream. I heard her yell, "WHAT THE HELL WAS THAT?!?" Then, some seconds later she came bamming at my door. "DRU! WHAT THE FUCK IS WRONG WITH YOU?!?"

"Leave me alone! Get the fuck away from my door!"

"BOY! WHO THE FUCK DO YOU THINK YOU TALKIN' TO LIKE THAT?!? HAVE YOU LOST YO MOTHAFUCKIN' MIND!"

"LEAVE ME THE FUCK ALONE, SHALANDA!" I screamed as loud as I could, red rage fuming from my body.

"OPEN UP THE DOOR, DRU! What the fuck is wrong with you?!? Did you get into a fight at school?!?" she asked, still pounding on the bedroom door.

Not knowing how to respond or what else to do at this moment, I just started screaming and crying, punching into the air.

"DRU! Please, open up the door, boy! What is wrong with you?!?" Shalanda kept yelling and bamming. Some moments later, she managed to unlock the door.

"LEAVE ME ALONE!"

"DRU! WHAT THE FUCK HAPPENED TO YOUR FACE?!?" Shalanda lunged at me and grabbed my face. "WHO THE FUCK DID THIS TO YOU?!? Did you get into a fight?!?"

"I'mma kill that mothafucka! I swear to GOD! I'mma kill him!"

"DRU! Calm down! Tell me what happened?!?"

"WHY!?!? You not gon help me or do shit for me?!? Why do you suddenly care?!?"

"'Cause you my son! I'm supposed to care!"

"Whatever!" I replied, smacking my teeth and rolling my eyes at this lying ass bitch. *My son*. Bitch, please. Bitch only cared about herself.

"LOOK! Are you gonna tell me what the fuck happened or not?!?"

I stood there in front of her face, breathing hard, my fists clenched tightly. "This nigga at my school. He said he did something to my new friend."

"What did he do?"

"He said he raped her. She was my new friend. I was starting to like her. She liked me too."

Shalanda grew quiet and so did her eyes at my statement. "Wait?!? What?!? How did you even hear this? How do you know this boy did this?!?"

"I heard him in the bathroom. He was bragging about it with this other nigga named Jerrell," I mumbled, tears falling down my cheeks.

Shalanda stood there staring at me with her eyes turning to slits. Rapidly tapping her right foot against the floor, her hands gripped to her waist. "So, this mothafucka took a knife out and cut you and you didn't try to fight him back?!?!"

"No! I couldn't! He said he was gonna kill me! I was scared!" I confessed.

"*Scared?*" Shalanda smacked her teeth. "BOY! His punk ass wasn't gonna do shit! Don't you know niggas be all talk?!? See! I told you! You ain't no mothafuckin' man. A real man wouldn't let some other nigga just come and roll all over him! A real ass man would've fought for his respect and would've even died trying to defend what he loved! But you – a little ass boy – you just stood there and let them punk ass bitches fuck you up all over some lil pissy pussy bitch!"

As Shalanda kept going on and on, my blood boiled even more. My breathing intensified and all the anger I had was now flowing into my hands, ready to once again fuck Shalanda up. I couldn't take her down-talking to me anymore and I thought she would've learned her lesson the last time. But obviously, she didn't.

"BITCH! FUCK YOU!" I screamed, lunging into her face.

Shalanda's eyes widened with surprise. "FUCK ME?!? NO, FUCK YOU AND YOUR WEAK ASS! YOU CAN PUT YOUR HANDS ON ME AND TRY TO BEAT MY ASS,

BUT YOU TOO WEAK TO BEAT UP ANOTHER NIGGA! THAT'S WHY RAHZEL DON'T WANNA HIRE YOUR PUNK, LAME ASS! GO CRY AND READ A BOOK, YOU FAT, WEAK ASS BOY!"

"BITCH! I'M SICK OF YOUR SHIT!" Without hesitation, I threw my hands around Shalanda's throat and slammed her into the wall next to the door.

"LET ME GO!" she yelled, fighting off my grip.

"GET OUT OF MY ROOM! LEAVE ME ALONE!" I cried, releasing my hands from her throat. I thought she would've been scared of me, but she just stood there and smiled, laughing her ass off as if this entire situation was funny.

"Yeah! I'mma leave yo ass alone alright! You ain't no real blood to me! Weak ass! And don't go snitch! Ain't no snitches in my house! You wanna get payback, do what a real man is supposed to do! But knowing you, yo fat ass ain't gonna do shit! And if I hear that you did snitch, I'mma fuck you up! And I mean that!" Shalanda spat, skimming me up and down with her evil bitch eyes. She spun around and stormed out of my room.

"FUCK YOU, BITCH!"

"NO! FUCK YOU, FAT ASS, WEAK ASS LIL BOY!" I heard her scream back as she trekked down the hallway, probably back into the den.

Pacing my floor, I was on the verge of losing my sanity. I was ready to kill. Kill anyone. I'd be damned if I was gonna let someone punk me this way, especially over someone who I was beginning to care about. I was done being everyone's bitch. Now, I was on some "Fuck Everybody" shit. I was ready to fucking kill any and everything around me, even if it meant I was gonna go to jail. Fuck it. Tyrone had to die.

Calm down, Dru. Calm down... you aren't going to kill anyone.

My mind tried to suddenly negotiate a sense of reason

with me. I simmered down and closed my eyes, again wanting to just cry. I couldn't believe Tyrone would do this to Amirah. If he was telling the truth, I had to do something. But the fear of him doing something back to me kept me paralyzed from coming up with a solution. I stopped pacing and tried to get a grip over my crazy fast heart rate and heavy breathing.

I had to do something... something quick.

CHAPTER TWENTY-TWO

Thou shall not kill...
Everyone knew that was like one of the ten commandments. But obviously no one took it seriously. So why should I?

I always wondered from time to time what it would be like to kill someone. To just take a knife and go right at someone's throat. There were times where I wished I had the will in me to go after Shalanda that way – slice her right across her throat and see her blood spill over the place. Doing so was a small, mere fantasy then. A way for me to cope with all the bullshit I had to go through. But today was a different day. This fantasy became a reality.

The next morning when I woke up, all I had on my mind was murder. Nothing but murder. Fuck school. Fuck being a doctor. Fuck God. Fuck life. I was ready to kill this nigga Tyrone.

My mind was still so fucked up from what I heard him say he did to Amirah that I was willing to lose it all. Lose it all for the sake of defending myself and Amirah. And then, I had a point to prove to everyone else. I wasn't no mothafuckin' punk. I was so sick and tired of hearing that shit at this point.

Sitting in my science class, all I could see around me was red. Everything was painted in Tyrone's blood. It was time for this mothafucka to die. The crazy thing was, his bitch ass was sitting right behind me in class. I could feel his eyes drilling a big hole in the back of my neck, too.

When he first walked inside the class this afternoon, he was cocky and confident as usual. He looked right at me, producing the biggest devilish grin. And, as usual, he called me out of my name. Of course, nothing but a flat expression was written on my face. There was nothing to express at this point. No fear. No anger. No rage. No joy. No happiness. When you have murder on your mind, you cannot produce emotion.

"FUCK YOU, FAT ASS, WEAK ASS LIL BOY! YOU AIN'T GONNA DO SHIT!" was all I kept hearing in the back of my mind as Ms. Reid was going over some shit in class. I wasn't even paying attention anymore to this ugly ass bitch. Bet you her ass didn't even ask anyone in the principal's office what happened to Amirah. In fact, no one here had yet to say a word to me about what happened to my girl. Yeah, *my girl*.

There were about fifteen minutes left on the clock before the bell was about to ring. This was my first and last opportunity I had to drive this knife I had in my book bag right into Tyrone's chest. Yeah, I was gonna stab this nigga to death in front of everyone. I wanted everyone to see that I wasn't some quiet, docile, punk ass nigga. I had the will to kill in me. The will to even die at this point... so long as I brought somebody to death with me.

With no more time to spare and time winding down before the bell would provide Tyrone an escape, I grabbed my book bag off the ground, slowly opened it, and crept my hand inside where I took hold of the huge steak knife's handle.

Gripping it hard, I strategized just exactly how I was gonna do this. Once he stood up and walked past me, I was gonna stand up, pull the knife out and stab him right in his back. Then, I'd pull the knife out. He'd spin around in shock. He wouldn't even know it was me. And before he could gain the strength to defend himself, that knife was gonna go right into the middle of his chest, straight into his heart.

"So, as I was saying, Vitamin D is not technically a vitamin. It is considered a hormone. It is produced by your skin when sunlight hits your skin. This is why it's important to get good amounts of sunlight every day to make sure your Vitamin D levels are stable," Ms. Reid rambled as she went over some bullshit about Vitamin D in our science textbook.

Not a damn thing this bitch was saying was even sticking with me. Every second that tick-tocked on the classroom clock was a countdown to Tyrone's grizzly death. I just knew this shit was gonna be all over the news, too. I hope his folks had life insurance to pay for this funeral.

"So, Ms. Reid, I have a really serious interesting question?" Tyrone asked in a semi-goofy voice, sounding all sarcastic and shit.

Ms. Reid, standing at the chalkboard, raised an eyebrow. "Yes, Tyrone?"

"So, like, you said sunlight is produced by your skin, right?"

"Yes."

"So, like, the darker you are, you are essentially not gonna get as much Vitamin D, right?"

"Yes... like in Africa, Africans have very dark skin, so they would need more sun exposure. Luckily for all Africans, sunlight isn't as much an issue... unless you spend most of your time indoors. But a lot of Africans still live in villages and farms where they get plenty of sunshine."

"So, like, black ass oil field over here, Andrew, he can't live in the United States. His black ass would need to go back to Africa, right?"

"AHAHAHAHAHAHAHAHA!" the entire classroom exploded into a huge roar.

"HEYYY! SHUT THE HELL UP! TYRONE! That's IT! Get out! I've had enough of you! Go straight to the principal's office and stay put until I come down there. I'm done with you!"

"MAN, WHATEVER! I was just trying to help my nigga out over here!" Tyrone laughed as he stood up from his seat, quickly packed his book bag, and proceeded to make his way out of the classroom. As he passed by me, he looked at me with this gawk as if he knew what I was gonna do to him. It was almost as if this nigga read my mind and knew he was seconds away from death.

See, Tyrone thought he was invincible. Fuck nigga thought just 'cause he was the top football player in the school and none of the teachers nor the principal fucked with him, he could get away with everything. Nigga thought he was God. But I was gonna show this nigga today that I was God. I was gonna decide his fucking fate.

Damn, Dru, you starting to sound crazy, I thought to myself as I somewhat loosened my grip off the knife's handle. *Just tell someone what happened. Stop being stupid and tell someone what happened. The police will handle it and arrest him. Stop being so irrational.*

Once again, a voice of reason tried to impart some sense in me But soon as Tyrone angrily slammed the classroom door and saw Ms. Reid jump out of anxiety, I snapped right back into a mindset of murder. This nigga was obviously a nuisance to everyone.

He was lucky he got away, but his time was coming. Maybe I could figure out a way to catch up with his ass after school. I knew he'd be lurking in the bathrooms to smoke weed or to do some other stupid shit.

Truth be told, I couldn't even believe I had snapped like this, when I didn't even know the full story or the truth about what happened to Amirah. But once again, she wasn't in school today and, because of that, I knew Tyrone had to have been telling the truth. Besides, why would he lie and make something up like this? Like, what nigga goes around and brags about raping a girl? Nah, that nigga wasn't lying. He was telling the truth. And a nigga he was so bold to tell that type of truth didn't deserve to live. Even if it meant that I had to go to jail for the rest of my life, I knew a nigga like that didn't belong on the streets.

Disarming myself, I slipped my hand back out of my book bag and zipped it up. Crazy how I was even able to get a knife inside the school. My school didn't even have metal detectors and the security guards barely cared about shit, although there was a fight damn near every day.

The class free of Tyrone's ignorant presence, Ms. Reid carried on with her Vitamin D lecture until the school bell rang. I stood up, quickly trying to rush out of the classroom, but Ms. Reid started calling my name. "Andrew! Don't leave yet. I need to talk to you for a second," she said, approaching me.

"Okay," I responded, my voice low and cracking from crying so much last night.

Skimming the classroom, she threw her arm around me and escorted me back to her desk. "Have a seat. I'mma wait until everyone is out to talk," she said.

"Okay," I responded once again. *Damn, did she know I had a knife? Could she tell I was about to pop off?*

Once the classroom was clear, she rushed over to the classroom door and closed it. I forgot Ms. Reid spent the next two periods as her planning block, so no students were gonna come in anyway. She rushed back over to her desk and sat down. Taking a deep breath, she looked at me with her lips tight and her eyes wide with this grimness. This grimness I knew meant she knew something.

"Andrew... what happened to your face?"

"I got into a fight with my brother," I lied.

"Oh... damn." She took another breath. "Listen, I called Ms. Amirah's folks last night. I was worried too that she hadn't shown up to class since she's new. What I'm about to tell you is something you CANNOT, I mean, CANNOT at all share with anyone at school and at home. What I am telling you is absolutely confidential and can get you and me in trouble. The only reason why I am telling you is because I trust you and I know that you and Amirah seemed like you two were beginning to become best friends. Do I have your word you won't say anything?" she asked, looking dead at me again with the most serious eyes I'd ever seen her have in her possession.

"Yes, ma'am," I replied, gulping, my hands trembling. I kind of had an idea of what she was going to tell me, but I still wasn't ready to let someone else tell me. I could almost feel my eyes begin to get watery.

Ms. Reid pulled out a box of tissue from her desk drawer and sat it on her desk close to me. "Well, Amirah isn't doing too well, Andrew. She's in the hospital in a coma... she's on life support. Her grandparents don't know if she's gonna make it."

"Huh? What do you mean?"

"Andrew... she... she was..." Ms. Reid closed her eyes and shook her head. She was trying to fight back tears. And so was I. "She was badly beaten and raped by someone and found in an abandoned house not too far away from where she lived. She's currently over in the ICU at Jackson North. The police are doing an investigation. They don't know who it did," she muttered as a tear escaped the corner of her right eye, trailing down her round cheek.

Hearing those words roll into my ears made me clutch my mouth, and I used all the strength and rage I had brewing in me to fight back tears. My chest burning and squeezed tight, it seemed like someone wrapped tons of dynamite around my heart and exploded it. My soul and mind were torn to pieces.

All of a sudden, I started to gasp and sniffle and I couldn't help but cry. "She gon die?" I asked.

"I don't know, Andrew. I'm sorry to tell you this. I really am. She seemed like such a nice girl, too. I really hate that this happened. We have to pray for her and hope God brings her out of it," Ms. Reid explained, massaging my shoulder while trying to console me the best way she could. She yanked some tissue out of the tissue box and wiped my face. "It's gonna be alright," she mumbled as she began to cry herself, too.

"No, it's not... it's messed up. I wanna—" Just before I was about to drop Tyrone's name and tell Ms. Reid what happened, Shalanda's voice echoed off in my head. *"Don't snitch, Andrew. Or else..."*

"You wanna what?"

My eyes water and pained, I stared at Ms. Reid, trying to fix my last statement. "I wanna... I wanna visit her. Is that possible?"

"I don't know, Andrew. I don't know about that."

"Please? I won't tell anybody," I said as I wiped my face.

Ms. Reid closed her eyes and, once again, took a huge, deep breath. "Fine," she exhaled. "I think we can swing by and see her. Let me just call the hospital right quick and see."

"Okay," I softly replied, tears kept strolling down my face.

Ms. Reid was one of the few teachers who had a phone in her classroom. She dialed 4-1-1 and got the number to Jackson North, which was a hospital about a good twenty or thirty minutes away from the school. Once she was connected, she asked the receptionist at the hospital to connect to the ICU. And, from there, she was given permission to come by and visit.

Once Ms. Reid hung up the phone, she said, "I'm gonna write you a late slip for your sixth period. When the final school bell rings, come right back to my class and then we'll head to the hospital together. You think your mother will be okay with you going with me?" she asked.

"Yeah... she will," I lied. Shit, at this point, I didn't have a mother, so fuck what Shalanda thought. Trifling ass bitch could kiss my fat, black ass.

"Okay, cool." Ms. Reid pulled out some more tissue paper and patted my face down. "Don't tell anyone, Andrew."

"I understand, Ms. Reid. I promise I won't tell anyone. You can trust me," I said, standing up from her desk. She wrote me a late slip and I took off to class.

After seventh period ended, as Ms. Reid instructed, I zipped right back to her classroom. She and I then headed to the hospital.

Some thirty minutes later, Ms. Reid and I walked into the entrance of the hospital and made our way to the guest desk. A short, older Latina woman with curly hair and the reddest lipstick was sitting at the desk when she glanced up at Ms. Reid and asked, "How can I help you?"

"Yes, I'm here to visit one of my students who's in the pediatric ICU. Her name is Amirah Paschal," Ms. Reid said.

"The pediatric ICU is on the fifteenth floor. Just take those elevators over to the right and then go to the fifteenth floor. The nurses will direct you to the patient's room," the guest desk receptionist said and then threw her attention back to a Miami Herald newspaper crossword puzzle.

"Thank you." Ms. Reid smiled, then the two of us began trekking over to the elevator section. Once we made our way up to the fifteenth floor, out of nowhere, an atomic bomb of butterflies exploded inside of me. Intense anxiety and dread cloaked me as we got off the elevator and started walking through the brightly lit, chilly hallway of the quiet ICU unit. Nothing but the sound of ventilators swishing air into the lungs of comatose kids could be heard on the floor.

We approached the nurse's station. An older, dark-skinned woman with long braids who looked thirtyish sat behind the desk, sipping coffee. She glanced up at Ms. Reid. "How can I help you?"

"Yes, I'm here to see one of my students. Amirah Paschal is her name," Ms. Reid uttered in a low and respectful tone.

The nurse's eyes widened and then she looked at me, then back at Ms. Reid. "She's in room 1567. Her grandmother is currently in the room with her," the nurse explained.

Ms. Reid smiled and replied, "Thank you, ma'am." The two of us slowly walked down the hallway, making our way to room 1567. And with every step I took, my heart pounded faster and faster. Each room we passed, I took a quick glimpse in, seeing babies, kids, and teens of all ages hooked up to ventilators. Their bodies motionless, damn near looking lifeless, so many pipes ran in their noses and mouths. My mind couldn't even fathom what it would be like to be thrown into that state of damn near death.

"This is it," Ms. Reid said as we approached Amirah's room. Ms. Reid, standing to my left, blocked my view of the room But as soon as I turned my attention to the inside of the room, I saw Amirah in the bed. And just like every other kid in the ICU, she had pipes running in and out of her nose and mouth. Dressed in a gown, her frail body was completely motionless. Thick white gauze was wrapped tightly around her head. A blot of blood, the size of a CD, was visible from a mile away on the bandage. The ventilator breathing life into Amirah's lungs, along with the beeping sound of a heart rate monitor, sung a sad melody to Amirah's current state.

Her grandmother, a skinny brown-skinned woman with silver hair who looked to be in her late-sixties, sat off in the far right corner. Her sunken-in, dark-circled eyes were latched onto Amirah. Ms. Reid and I stood at the entrance of the door and, before Ms. Reid could announce her presence, Amirah's grandmother turned her head at us and produced a nervous smile. "Yes?" was all she said in response to our silence as we stood there.

"Hi... I'm Ms. Reid. I'm Amirah's science teacher. I was the one who called last night," Ms. Reid explained.

"Oh yes, dear. Come in. And who is he? Your son?"

"No, ma'am," Ms. Reid then looked at me and said, "this is Amirah's new friend. Andrew. He was actually the one who told me he hadn't seen her in a few days and he felt like something was wrong."

"Oh... oh, okay," Amirah's grandmother mumbled.

"Do you mind if we see her?" Ms. Reid asked.

"No. Not at all. Come on in. I was just here by myself. My husband is down at the police station doing another interview."

My eyes watery, I couldn't help but sniffle and gasp seeing Amirah laid out in the bed. Ms. Reid heard me and quickly threw her arm around my shoulder, hugging me as tight as she could.

"He's very upset about all of this," Ms. Reid explained. "He's one of my top students and they sat together in class."

Amirah's grandmother shook her head and said, "I can't believe someone would do this to my grandbaby. Whoever it is needs to be brought to justice. Immediately. I just kept telling my husband we needed to move. I kept telling him that those boys in the neighborhood were dangerous. But he didn't want to leave because Opa-Locka is all we know. All we care about. We love our neighborhood."

"I'm so sorry to hear that, ma'am," Ms. Reid responded as the two of us moved deeper into the room and, now, we stood inches away from Amirah. Taking a closer look at her, I noticed her eyes were blacked out, her lips were busted up and her entire face was swollen. She was damn near unrecognizable. I looked at her arms and noticed those were completely swollen, too. My mind still couldn't wrap around the fact that Tyrone did this. But something told me Tyrone alone didn't do this. With the way Amirah looked, it just seemed like someone else did this. Jerrell? Another football player? Tyrone's dad? Someone else did this... but Tyrone proudly confessed he did this.

I reached my hand out and touched Amirah's, gently rubbing it. "I'm so sorry, Amirah. Please wake up," I muttered, millions of tears running down my face. "Please. Don't die."

"My baby... my poor grandbaby," Amirah's grandmother wept along with me.

Ms. Reid grabbed me and held me tight, gently rubbing my back. I cried and wailed. I'd never cried so hard in my life. Truth be told, I didn't even know if I could even cry this hard for my own damn mama.

But these tears – while they were tears of utter sadness, they were also tears of downright rage. Once again, I found myself ready to kill any and everyone responsible for this... even if it cost me my own freedom.

And why was I willing to go that far?

Deep down, I felt like Amirah was the only person who was beginning to show me what true love was going to be. And now with her life almost gone, it seemed like I'd never get a chance to experience such *love*. So, what was the point of even being *free* if my heart was bound to love someone who I'd never see again.

After we left the hospital, Ms. Reid and I spent the entire car ride in silence. A good hour later, she pulled her Honda into my apartment complex's parking lot, passing all of the dope boys hanging out as usual near their box Chevys. With their eyes glued on us, they puffed on their blunts, not flinching. Once we pulled up near my unit, my eyes landed on Rahzel's coupe parked in front.

"Everything alright?" Ms. Reid asked.

Guess she noticed my gaze was attached to the car. "Yeah," I responded. "Just thinking about everything..."

"Okay, well, don't think too hard. Just pray and hope Amirah pulls through."

"Do you think she'll ever wake up again, Ms. Reid? I mean, it can happen, right? Doctors can pretty much fix anything if they get to someone in time, right?"

"Yeah... they *can*... sometimes. It just depends." Ms. Reid exhaled and said, "But sometimes, doctors can't fix everything. Just pray for Amirah, Dru. That's all anyone can do at the moment."

"Yes, ma'am," I responded as I grabbed my book bag from the back and hopped out of the car.

"I'll see you tomorrow in class, Dru."

"Yes, ma'am," I replied and closed her door.

Ms. Reid took off, and I slowly made my way up the staircase. Although it was now nearly six pm, the sun was still out, its warmth beating down my neck. Once I made it to the front door, I pounded twice and waited for Shalanda to answer. I saw her look out the blinds and then she creaked the door open, skimming me up and down with her nasty eyes. "Where the fuck were you? Boy, it's almost seven!"

"I stayed after school late to help my teacher with a project," I lied.

Shalanda stared at me for a few more seconds before she fully opened the door. "Take your shoes off, too," she instructed as I stepped in. My eyes landed on Rahzel. His arms spread out on the couch, he stared at me and then cracked a smile, his teeth glistening from light inside the den.

"Young God...As-Salaamu 'Alaikum."

Slowly taking my shoes off, I stared back at him and mumbled, "Wa 'Alaikum As-Salaam."

"I see you still got the knowledge I gave you... that's good."

"Yeah," I replied with Shalanda still off to my side. She closed the door and locked it, then trekked back into the den and sat next to Rahzel.

"Your mother told me you're dealing with a little situation at school."

"Yeah."

"She didn't go into much details, but she told me some nigga was messing with this girl you into?"

"Yeah."

"So, what you gon do about it?"

"I don't know," I lied, although I was still so unsure if I could even kill at this point. Seeing Amirah in that state zapped so much energy out of me.

"There you go again."

"Fuck you," I replied, my face now screwed up with anger.

Rahzel chuckled. "Damn, what I do, young god? I'm just here to see what you gon' do. Your mother told me you might be ready to put in some work. But I don't believe her. 'Cause I still see the little ass boy in your eyes."

"Fuck the both of you," I said, strolling down the hallway.

"Oh, this lil nigga got some balls now. But not balls enough to deal with that other nigga. Anyways... I'm out.

Stop calling me over here to raise little ass boys. Too bad your other son had to go live with his grandparents."

I paused in the hallway for a moment and then turned around. Rahzel was now standing near the door pulling lint off his Versace shirt. He looked at me and smiled once again. "Why you lookin' at me like that? I'm not your enemy. Your own pussy ass attitude is. Be a man and handle your shit, young god."

"Rahzel."

"Wassup?"

I slowly walked up to him, unzipped my book bag, and pulled the knife out. "I was gonna kill that nigga today, but he left class early."

Rahzel fell silent and gawked at me with his mouth flung open. This time, he wasn't smiling. "So, you are ready to put in work then," he said. "That's some cold shit though... I'm not gonna lie. But some dumb shit, too. Go put your book bag down and come with me. I'mma show you how a man is supposed to handle his business. But if I help you, you need to help me. Are you ready to work for me?"

"Yeah. Yeah, I'm ready now."

"Not unsure, right? You're ready *ready*?"

"I'm ready."

EPILOGUE

Quiet and nervous, I stared out of the tinted passenger window. My restless mind was blank, yet hazy like the purple dusky sky outside. Without a cloud in sight and night on its way, I felt myself morphing into a new person.

As the sun began to fade away, so did my conscience. At this point, I didn't give a damn about anything anymore. I just wanted to see Tyrone dead. Whatever Rahzel was going to teach me, I was now willing to be his top student.

We'd been in the car now for about fifteen minutes and Rahzel hadn't said a word. He just sat back and bobbed his head to the music blasting from his car's speakers. Some moments later, he reached over and turned down the volume. "First thing you're gonna learn about working for me, young god, is that I need absolute loyalty," he said. "All of my niggas that rock with me take a pledge not to cross me or the organization the wrong way. You feel me?"

"Yeah, I understand. But you loyal, too, right?"

"Good answer, young god. Good answer." Rahzel looked at me and smiled, saying, "Yes, I am. Don't fuck with me, I won't fuck with you. Fuck with me, I'll fuck with you. It's a simple golden rule. And I mean that, too, 'cause the last thing I want is to have to kill another youngin'. So, I'm gonna ask you one last time. Are you ready to put in work?"

"Yeah," I replied. "So, what I gotta do?"

"Prove to me you really a killer. That's what the fuck you about to do."

My eyebrow raised out of curiosity. "So, you want me to kill someone first?"

"Yeah... you wanna kill another nigga, why not practice first?"

Staring ahead at the heavy traffic on the road, I didn't know what to think anymore. Part of me wanted to proceed and do whatever Rahzel wanted me to do, but then there was a part of me still trying to convince myself I was going down the wrong path. This voice kept trying to convince me to just hop out of the car and run to the closest pay phone I could find, call 9-1-1 and tell them everything that happened. But then again, I knew if I did that, my life would be over. Rahzel would probably kill me. And if he didn't get to me, Shalanda or someone else would. I was paranoid now. But fuck it. I had to do what I had to do. I was tired of everyone thinking I was some little boy or a punk ass nigga.

"So, who you want me to kill?" I asked, now nervous as fuck.

"Some lil nigga that's been stealing from me and disrespecting my shit."

"Okay," I replied as I sat back and tried to simmer down my burning nerves. "Rahzel... some days ago, I asked you about my dad and you told me he killed someone. You said you never killed someone. Did you lie?" I had to ask.

"No, I didn't lie. But just because I had niggas dealt with doesn't mean I did the dealing. Now, just sit back and stop asking so many mothafuckin' questions," Rahzel said.

"Okay," I replied and kept my lips sealed until we arrived wherever he was taking me.

Some twenty minutes later, we arrived at what looked like another warehouse that sat by itself off the road. It was a big beige building with a single door leading inside. Across the street were a bunch of stores and shops that had signs written in Spanish. I figured were in the middle of Hialeah. This area was filled with nothing but Cubans. Maybe this was another spot that Rahzel owned.

Rahzel slowly pulled into the parking lot. To my right, I saw two black Suburbans were parking in front. Some of Rahzel's crew was already here. We got out of the car and walked inside the warehouse. Looking around, it was the same set up as the warehouse Rahzel owned in Downtown. The difference was it seemed smaller and cleaner. We walked down to an office near another entrance and there I saw some of Rahzel's guys hanging out.

"Wassup, soldiers, I got us a new member to add to the team," Rahzel announced. Looking at the men, I recognized a few of them, including Gino.

"Oh, it's lil man from last Saturday. This dude ready to put in the work?" Gino asked with a smile.

"Yeah, he says he ready, but we finne see. Gino, is that nigga Tay still on the corner slinging in the high rises?" he asked.

"Yeah... and he still claiming he didn't steal from the stash?"

"You already know... young nigga think he slick, too."

"Cool. Well, I'mma have my young god, Dru, handle that then. Since he said he's *ready* to show me he's a man," Rahzel laughed.

"Hahaha, you gon have this dude clap that clown down?"

"Yeah... why not? Shit. They about the same age," Rahzel

said. "He got a beef to settle anyways, so I guess we just finne see how good young god can shoot."

My heart racing with anxiety, I now realized what the fuck I was stepping into. This was an underworld I wasn't yet prepared to experience. Doubts began to swim in my head again and a part of me just wanted to run out of the warehouse. Listening to Gino and Rahzel go back and forth about the plan for me to kill whoever this nigga was had me on pins and needles.

Just run, Dru. Run. This ain't you. You were never gonna kill someone in the first place. My mind kept racing, sowing so much doubt inside of me. What in the fuck was I getting myself into? Truth be told, I said I wanted to kill Tyrone, but did I really have that in me? Was I really that stupid to wanna just take someone's life? The more my mind kept planting seeds of doubt, the more pulsing energy I had to just run away.

But I couldn't.

I was in too deep now. And, besides, as I kept doubting myself, all I kept seeing were flashes of Amirah in that hospital bed. And the more I saw her, the angrier I got all over again.

"Young God... wake the fuck up?!?!?" I suddenly heard Rahzel shouting.

Damn, was I in a daze or something?

"Sorry," I apologized and gulped.

"We 'bout to head out over to Pork-N-Beans. You ready to do that thang?"

"Yeah," I lied. "I've been ready."

By now, complete darkness had overtaken the skies. A full yellow moon was glowing. The bustling traffic that crowded the early evening streets was now beginning to die down. I was sitting in the back seat of one of the Suburbans, quiet and more nervous than ever. Rahzel sat next to me staring out of his passenger window. He hadn't said a word the entire car ride. Kareem, one of Rahzel's guys, was at the wheel, commanding the Suburban toward Pork-N-Beans.

I rarely often visited Liberty City. Once in a while, just to visit Grandma, Shalanda's mother. But Shalanda and Grandma didn't really get along that much, so we came by maybe once or twice year, if that. Truth be told, I never fully understood why Grandma and Shalanda never got along. But when we did drive through Liberty City once in a while, I always wondered about how niggas lived in Pork-N-Beans. Everyone in fucking Miami knew it was one of the worst housing projects in the county. Pork-N-Beans was like a fortress right in the heart of the city and every fucked up problem you could think of lived here.

We cut a few street corners, then made our way closer to the projects. Then, I saw nothing but niggas, hoes, crackheads and other types of people aimlessly roaming the streets. Everyone out here looked like they were on straight up bullshit. A few of the guys hanging out by cars looked dangerous as fuck, probably strapped up. I hoped Rahzel didn't want me to shoot any of these guys 'cause I just knew they were gonna shoot back.

We cut another corner and it seemed like all the people outside disappeared. Kareem brought the truck to a halt and parked on the side street right across from one of the project buildings.

I was sitting on the right hand side close to the curb of

the street. I looked out the window and got more terrified thinking about what I was about to potentially do. Damn, I was really about to kill someone. I couldn't though. This just wasn't me. *Dru, what the fuck are you doing?* An ocean of doubt was began to flood my mind again. Earlier, my conscience faded away, but now it was choking me with guilt.

"Dru, you see that nigga standing about four doors down next to that light blue building? The one with the red hoodie on?" Rahzel asked as he looked over my shoulder.

Trying to see what he saw, I peered out the window, looking straight ahead pass the iron gate that wrapped around the entire complex. Then, I saw some dude standing guard in front of a building with this red hoodie on. It was hot as fuck, so I wondered why this dude was wearing a hoodie this time of the year.

"Yeah, I see him," I said. "That's the dude you want me to kill?"

"Yeah," Rahzel said. "Kareem, pass me that nine."

Kareem leaned over and opened up the glove compartment. He whipped out a nine from it, then handed it to Rahzel. "Full clip?" Rahzel asked as he examined the gun.

"Yeah, boss," Kareem responded.

Gawking at the gun, all I could do was remain quiet and gulp. Rahzel held the gun up to my face. "This is a semi-auto. You ever held one of these before?"

"Nah," I responded, scared more than ever.

"It's not that heavy, but it got some serious action to it," Rahzel explained. He unloaded the clip from the gun, examined the clip and loaded it back in, then cocked the gun back. "It ain't that hard to shoot. Just hold that mothafucka tight in one hand. Tight as you can and squeeze the trigger. Empty the clip out on that mothafucka," Rahzel said.

Breathing hard, damn near gasping, my conscience was sounding the alarm. But I knew if I backed out now, Rahzel would probably just kill me. Rahzel scanned me up down and asked, "You scared or something? Why you breathing all hard?"

"Cause… I'm about to kill someone. It just seems kind of fucked up."

"Ain't nothin' fucked up. It's a part of the game. This is Chess. This nigga out there was a trusted soldier and he crossed me the wrong way. In other countries, a nigga like that would've been beheaded. Don't you know here in the US if a soldier commits treason, they get the death penalty?" Rahzel explained. "But you know what… you on that little boy shit again. Kareem, let's bounce—"

"Give me the gun," I said. Just like that, I first killed the conscience and soul inside of me.

Rahzel paused for a moment and his eyes turned to slits. He handed me the gun then said, "Before you go and do your thing, put these gloves on and this hoodie."

Rahzel reached down and pulled out a black hoodie and a pair of leather gloves.

With the gun resting in my lap, I threw the hoodie on, then put the gloves over my hands. Crazy thing was both the hoodie and gloves were a perfect fit. I threw the hood over my head, then grabbed the gun out of my lap. I looked at Rahzel. "Just squeeze the trigger and empty the clip, right?"

"Yeah," Rahzel said. "Just like that. Get up and close. Then shoot. And run your ass back."

Looking straight ahead at the nigga in the red hoodie, I closed my quaking, strained eyes and killed my conscience that seemingly kept coming back from the dead to haunt me. Once I killed my fear for a second time, I took a huge deep breath and murdered the growing tension in my stomach. *Stop being a punk ass nigga, Dru*, I thought to myself as I slowly opened the door.

Just before I could step out, Rahzel threw his hand on my

shoulder and leaned into my ear whispering, "Body, body, head. Make sure you blow that nigga's wig back."

I gulped, "Got it." I hid the gun in the hoodie's pockets and stepped out of the truck and onto the cracking sidewalk. Quickly looking around, I saw nothing but broken crack pipes, broken syringes and empty red-top vials splattered all over the place. Damn, Pork-N-Beans was truly hell on Earth. I even felt that shit, too, now that nighttime humidity began cooking me with this heavy ass black hoodie on. Beads of sweat began dripping down my brown and onto my cheeks.

Once again taking a deep breath, I proceeded to walk and entered through the complex's gate. Slowly and carefully walking the polluted sidewalk inside the complex, I made my way toward the fourth unit. My eyes were fastened to the young nigga wearing the red hoodie. It was weird how he was just standing there with his hands in his pockets, not making a single move. It was if he was expecting someone.

As I got twenty feet away from him, my grip on the gun got tighter and billions of butterflies filled my stomach. *Just run away, Dru. Just run. This is your last chance. You ain't about this life. Stop doing this, nigga. You will get killed yourself. Shut the fuck up, Dru. Stop being a bitch. Fuck this nigga. He knows what the fuck comes with this life he got himself into. And if Rahzel said he was stealing, he should've never been stealing in the first place. Clown ass nigga deserve to die.*

My mind conflicted, I settled on my last decision. Fuck it. I couldn't back out now. It was too late. Ten feet away, I had to do this, otherwise this dude might pull a gun out on me and try to kill me. It was now the time to kill to survive.

My hands wrapped around the trigger of the gun. I was now ready to pull it out and get to blasting. But once I took another step, suddenly, the dude spun toward me and threw his full attention toward me. I suddenly gasped and my eyes shot wide open with surprise.

It was Tyrone.

"TAR BABY! What the fuck is your ugly, black ass doing out here?!? Nigga, I should fuck you up right now!" he growled, looking me up and down.

Not saying a word, I just stared at him with my mouth flung wide out open out of surprise. Trembling, yet frozen with fear, I didn't know what to do next.

"How the fuck you even knew I hung out around here?!? What?!? You was gonna come out here and try to fight me or some shit?!? Your black, fat ass finally got some heart, huh?!? I should've known your stupid ass was gonna try to—"

"SHUT THE FUCK UP!" I interrupted with a yell, quickly yanking the gun out and aiming it right at Tyrone.

All of a sudden, Tyrone threw his shaking hands up in surprise. "What the fuck?!? You gon kill me?!? Nigga, is that even a real gun?!?" he asked, laughing.

"Yeah, it's real, nigga!"

POW!

TO BE CONTINUED...

ABOUT THE AUTHOR

QUAN MILLZ is a prolific and profound urban fiction writer known for writing some of the most mind-captivating urban fiction thrillers in the contemporary urban fiction space.

Follow Quan Millz on Facebook Instagram for the latest updates on book releases and upcoming film projects!

Printed in Dunstable, United Kingdom